Take Me There

Acclaim for Julie Cannon's Fiction

In *Smoke and Fire* "Cannon skillfully draws out the honest emotion and growing chemistry between her heroines, a slow burn that feels like constant foreplay leading to a spectacular climax. Though Brady is almost too good to be true, she's the perfect match for Nicole. Every scene they share leaps off the page, making this a sweet, hot, memorable read."—*Publishers Weekly*

Breaker's Passion is "an exceptionally hot romance in an exceptionally romantic setting…Cannon has become known for her well-drawn characters and well-written love scenes."—*Just About Write*

In *Power Play* "Cannon gives her readers a high stakes game full of passion, humor, and incredible sex."—*Just About Write*

About *Heartland*…"There's nothing coy about the passion of these unalike dykes—it ignites at first encounter and never abates… Cannon's well-constructed novel conveys more complexity of character and less overwrought melodrama than most stories in the crowded genre of lesbian-love-against-all-odds—a definite plus." — Richard Labonte, *Book Marks*

"Cannon has given her readers a novel rich in plot and rich in character development. Her vivid scenes touch our imaginations as her hot sex scenes touch us in many other areas. *Uncharted Passage* is a great read."—*Just About Write*

About *Just Business*…"Julie Cannon's novels just keep getting better and better! This is a delightful tale that completely engages the reader. It's a must read romance!"—*Just About Write*

"Great plot, unusual twist and wonderful women…[*I Remember*] is an inspired romance with extremely hot sex scenes and delightful passion."—*Lesbian Reading Room*

By the Author

Come and Get Me

Heart 2 Heart

Heartland

Uncharted Passage

Just Business

Power Play

Descent

Breakers Passion

Rescue Me

I Remember

Smoke and Fire

Because of You

Countdown

Capsized

Wishing on a Dream

Take Me There

Visit us at www.boldstrokesbooks.com

Take Me There

by

Julie Cannon

2017

TAKE ME THERE

ISBN 13: 978-1-62639-917-4

This Trade Paperback Original Is Published By
Bold Strokes Books, Inc.
P.O. Box 249
Valley Falls, NY 12185

First Edition: September 2017

Credits
Editor: Shelley Thrasher
Production Design: Stacia Seaman
Cover Design by Sheri (graphicartist2020@hotmail.com)

Acknowledgments

It takes a village, and sometimes it takes an army. I'm grateful for everyone who has touched this manuscript and made it the fabulous end product you hold in your hands today.

For Laura and all the times you continue to take me there.

Chapter One

"Oh my God!" Lauren cried, dropping back onto the bed.

Elliott raised her eyes, careful not to move her mouth from her wife's favorite place. Actually, it was her favorite place as well. Lauren's breasts rose with each inhale as she tried to regain her breath. The taut pink peaks sent tingles down Elliott's back to settle between her legs—again. When Lauren relaxed her death grip on the sheet, Elliott started to move her tongue once more.

"Oh, God, Elliott. I can't," Lauren said, her voice barely a whisper. Elliott didn't mind if her wife was lying. She knew otherwise. The tightening of Lauren's thigh muscles wrapped around her neck, the quickening of Lauren's breathing, the wetness on her mouth told Elliott a completely different story. Lauren wasn't a one-and-done girl. Rarely was she a two- or three-timer either. Never was and never would be, as long as Elliott had any say in the matter.

Lauren could come as many times as Elliott would make her, and nothing gave Elliott more pleasure than to give it to her, the woman she planned to spend the rest of her life with. This was the way she wanted to start and end each and every day. And for the most part they had. For the last four years, she'd had Lauren like this. Some days it was in her dreams, but most were like this. In their house, in their bed, sharing their love. Elliott quickened her pace as Lauren rotated her hips. It had taken a long time for Elliott to gain Lauren's trust in bed, but when she did, she took control of what she wanted and learned to ask for more, to demand satisfaction or to simply let go.

"God, just like that." Elliott loved it when Lauren told her exactly what she wanted. All too soon Elliott felt Lauren's clit harden into a tight button, and she knew, from the hundreds of times before, Lauren was about to come. Elliott slipped one finger deep into Lauren's center, then another. Lauren tightened around her and grew hard again against her tongue, and she exploded.

Stars danced before Lauren's eyes, and the roar of her orgasm rocketing through her was the only thing she was capable of focusing on. Elliott had the most magical tongue and hands, and they always aroused her. Drove her out of her mind was a more accurate description.

She hadn't known what to expect from a long-term relationship with a woman. Especially if that woman was Elliott Foster. She'd heard stories about lesbian bed death after the initial thrill and hot-for-you phase wore off. But at what point did that happen? Four years? Seven? Twelve? She thought that work or stress or exhaustion or even boredom might temper their sex life, but so far none of that had materialized. As a matter of fact, their sex life had grown more adventurous and frequent. She still entertained butterflies whenever she thought of Elliott. Tingles ran up and down her spine when she heard her voice. Other parts, farther south, grew warm and wet and pulsed with need when Elliott looked at her that way. And lately, that way was any way.

Lauren was an avid reader, and as an attorney she'd been trained to use research to her advantage. She devoured volumes of material and information on the joys and sorrows of relationships, but so far none of it was true for her and Elliott. They still wanted to spend every minute they could with each other. Their urge wasn't smothering and didn't indicate any kind of codependency. They simply enjoyed each other's company, whether they were sharing a pot of coffee, going to the movies, binge-watching a Netflix original series, or, like now, making love on an early Tuesday morning.

They each had their own life. Elliott was very involved in her philanthropic causes, and Lauren was in her sixth year of mentoring Tonya, an inner-city teenager who'd grown into a wonderful, responsible college sophomore. They weren't attached at the hip unless some bumping and grinding was going on, but they spent as much time together as they could.

Lauren had never expected to find her soul mate, significant other, other half, or whatever other corny phrase was used to describe the woman she would give her life for. But when she saw Elliott in her tuxedo looking so hot and all that at a charity event, she knew it.

"Enough," Lauren said, reluctantly pushing Elliott's head from between her legs. "I have a meeting with a new client this morning. I can't meet her with that thoroughly fucked look." She shuddered as Elliott kissed her one last time on that very special spot, and for a moment she almost said to hell with it.

"Thoroughly, huh?" Elliott crawled up her body like a jungle cat with a very satisfied grin. Lauren waited until Elliott kissed her on the mouth before she pushed her onto her back and gave new definition to the phrase *thoroughly fucked.*

CHAPTER TWO

Sloan Merchant parked her BMW in her customary spot on the fourth floor. The parking garage didn't have any reserved places, but she usually had the top floor to herself. Everyone seemed to jockey for the closest parking spot, but she preferred to use the distance and the stairs for exercise as well as to lower the risk of having a carelessly opened car door ding her blue beauty. She'd spent a fortune on her car, and it was still as perfect as it had been when she drove it off the lot a year ago.

Sloan let the song on the radio end as she waited for the top of the convertible to close and latch. It was a beautiful spring morning in San Diego, and she'd enjoyed the sun on her shoulders and the wind blowing through her short hair during her twenty-minute commute. Most days she took the train from her apartment to the offices at Foster McKenzie, but today she had a dinner date after work. She wouldn't have time to go home, change, and meet her date, Joanna, at the ballet by curtain.

Traffic in San Diego, like in most other metropolitan cities, absolutely sucked. No way would she risk being late tonight. Joanna was charming, attractive, and looking for exactly what Sloan was—absolutely nothing more than an enjoyable time. No strings, no commitment, no drama. Sloan was married to her career, but a mistress now and then suited her just fine.

"Good morning, Ms. Sloan." The security guard always greeted her when she stopped by the large lobby desk.

"Good morning, Stuart." She signed her name with little more than a scrawl on the after-hours log. The building required occupants to sign in if they entered before seven a.m. and exited after seven p.m. She considered that an unnecessary step, since the swipe of her badge recorded the same. But the sixty-eight-year-old security officer was just doing his job. Occasionally she would stop and chat with him about the Padres, the win/loss record of the Chargers, or the price of a barrel of crude oil. His voice was gravelly, like that of a long-time smoker, but she never caught a whiff of tobacco. This morning, however, she needed to get to her office and review the notes in her briefcase one more time before her nine-thirty meeting.

Sloan bypassed the elevators and hustled up the twelve flights of stairs. She hated elevators, after getting stuck in one for several hours nine years ago. Ever since then, she'd suffered from a severe case of claustrophobia. When she had to ride an elevator, if the doors didn't immediately open when the car stopped, she broke out in a sweat. If the car didn't immediately move when the doors closed, she began to panic. She'd tried everything from immersion therapy to meditation, medication, and a rubber band on her wrist, none of which worked. So she avoided the elevators when possible and gritted her teeth when she couldn't.

The twelfth floor of Foster McKenzie was quiet. The eco-friendly lights clicked on as Sloan passed each sensor, the final one when she entered her office. She slid her laptop out of her briefcase and into the docking station and jiggled the mouse to wake it up. She loved this time of the day. The office was quiet, and she had a beautiful view as the morning sun lit up Mission Bay.

Three hours later her phone rang, and she glanced at the display before she picked it up. "Hello, Mother."

Julia Merchant called only during office hours, saying it was far too difficult to reach Sloan on her cell phone. That was partially true. She was rarely in a position to answer it, either driving or on the train or doing something she really enjoyed with a woman who wouldn't appreciate the interruption, especially from her mother.

Her family wasn't close. Sloan couldn't remember the last time she'd talked to her brother, and she hadn't seen her sister in more than a year. Everyone lived within easy driving distance of each other, but they had their own lives, which rarely interconnected. Sometimes it felt like her parents were the only thing holding them all together, in a rather tenuous knot at that.

They chatted for a few minutes about her siblings and their offspring and her father's latest obsession—flying. He had recently retired from the area's largest hospital as chief of surgery and taken up the hobby. He'd bought a plane the day he received his pilot's license, and Sloan had yet to be a passenger. Of course, she hadn't asked either, and her father never invited her.

While growing up she'd wondered if her parents had really wanted children. She didn't remember ever playing a game of hide-and-seek or hearing a bedtime story from either of them. She did, however, remember how their housekeeper Robin had bandaged her skinned knee, packed her lunch, taught her how to ride a bike and use a tampon.

This was her mother's obligatory call to her youngest child. Sloan was certain it was on her calendar as a reoccurring appointment. She hung up the phone knowing both of them had checked that duty off their bi-weekly list.

❖

"Callie," Adrienne called for the third time in the last five minutes. "Come on, sweetie. Mama's gotta go." The terrible twos had turned into the trying threes, and according to Mandy, her brother John's wife, the fucking fours were worse. Mandy would know. She was on her third four-year-old, and in addition to handing down clothes and toys to Callie, Mandy was Adrienne's go-to for parental advice and support.

The towheaded toddler with sparkling, mischievous blue eyes and pigtails ran out of her bedroom carrying her bunny, one of the many stuffed animals that accompanied her in the car every day. Adrienne's heart skipped at the mirror resemblance of her daughter to her mother. Every day Adrienne missed Brenna as much as the day before, and every day was one day less that Callie would know her mother.

"Go, Mommy, go," Callie demanded, as if she'd been waiting on Adrienne. Five minutes later they were in the car, Callie singing to her bunny in the backseat.

Adrienne reviewed the schedule for the day in her mind. She and Robert Douglas, CEO of Auburn Pharmaceuticals, were meeting with Elliott Foster and the attorney from Foster McKenzie today, hoping to secure $400 million in venture capital. Auburn was a family-owned small pharmaceutical with a blockbuster drug in development. All indications were that SV 90 would be a major player in the treatment of Alzheimer's. Auburn needed the money to continue with this research and take the drug to trial. Foster McKenzie was their first and hopefully only stop for the cash they desperately needed.

Adrienne had taken care with her appearance this morning, choosing her best don't-fuck-with-me suit and pulling out the serious jewelry. She didn't spend money on clothes, preferring the casual, comfortable look, but she had invested in a classic Vera Wang dress, two Ralph Lauren suits, and a pair of ghastly expensive black pumps. Her diamond hoops were in her ears, her three-carat-diamond pendant securely around her neck, and her wedding ring where it had been for the past five years.

This wasn't any ordinary meeting, even if it was with Foster McKenzie, one of the largest venture-capitalist firms in the country. This was more than Adrienne doing her job representing one of her clients. This was more than a major milestone in a company's progression to the next level. This was personal, and Adrienne had never been more nervous.

She pulled into her mother's driveway, turned off the key, and grabbed what she called Callie's toddler-crap bag from the floor of the front seat. She unbuckled Callie, who scampered out of her car seat and ran around the front of the car and up to her parents' front door. Adrienne's heels clicked on the driveway, and she could barely remember the last time she'd worn them. This meeting was more than a financial courtship, and she needed every advantage to get through it.

"Adrienne, you look lovely today," her mother said, scooping her granddaughter up and planting a sloppy, wet kiss on the toddler's cheek. "Today's the big day?"

"Yes, Mom. Gotta run." She handed the bag to her mother and kissed Callie on the cheek. "You be good for Grandma today. I'll see you later, okay?"

"Okay, Mommy. Bye." Callie was squirming out of her grandmother's arms, eager to get inside and play with her cousins.

Adrienne didn't know what she would do without her parents, and other family members, for that matter. They had pitched in and helped in more ways than she could say or that she could thank them for. She was the fourth of six children, the older of two girls. That in and of itself had made her childhood challenging and her dating next to impossible. Four brothers were a gauntlet for anyone to get through in order to take her out on a date.

But that didn't deter Brenna, who had won over her family the first time Adrienne had brought her to dinner. Adrienne shut those thoughts out of her mind as she got back in her car and traversed the surface streets to get to her office. She needed a clear head today, and thinking of Brenna wouldn't help in any way.

❖

When Adrienne walked into her office, her paralegal Michelle was typing furiously, fingers flying over the keyboard, earbuds stuffed in her ears, bright-pink bubblegum popping bubbles. Adrienne had hired Michelle fresh out of paralegal school and hadn't regretted giving the woman a chance. Admittedly, Michelle's spiked hair, which this week was purple, and the tattoos on her forearms, especially the one of a spaceship on the left side of her neck, had concerned Adrienne at first. She had no idea how Michelle typed so fast and accurately with her long nails, today painted neon green. However, when she'd started talking with her, she realized Michelle was very, very smart and would be a significant asset to Adrienne's growing firm. That had been six years ago and three times as many boyfriends later, none of which had affected Michelle's work product in the slightest.

"Hey, Boss." Michelle disconnected the earbuds from her ears. "Mr. Douglas called to remind you that he'll meet you in the lobby of Foster McKenzie. You ready?"

"As ready as I'll ever be. Thanks." She dropped her briefcase onto her desk and pulled out a thick stack of papers bound together by a bright-green binder clip. Michelle, who ordered the office supplies, would never order the traditional basic black.

While Adrienne waited for her computer to fire up, she filled her coffee cup from the pot in the corner and opened the file for one last look. Her hands were shaking as she held the summary sheet in her hands. She was more nervous than she'd ever been, except for the day she'd asked Brenna to marry her.

They'd been twenty-six years old, in love, and thought they were invincible. They had planned a life together, things they would do, places they would see, and children they would have. But that dream died twelve weeks and three days after Callie was born.

"For God's sake, Adrienne," she said, shaking her hands as if trying to shake off her shredded nerves. "Focus, concentrate, buckle down, and get your shit together. Auburn needs this and you need this. You can do it. It's just another meeting." Forty-five minutes later she repeated those same words as she stepped into the lobby of Foster McKenzie.

CHAPTER THREE

"Mr. Douglas and Ms. Stewart are in the conference room," Sloan's administrative assistant, Beth, informed her. Sloan glanced at the Tiffany clock on her desk. Ten minutes until the meeting. Her paralegal Jeff was right behind Beth. Sloan thanked her, then motioned Jeff to the chair across from her. He looked at his watch.

"Elliott will be here in a few minutes. Tell me again what you found out about Ms. Stewart." Jeff searched through his stack of folders and pulled out a red one. He opened it and started to read.

"Adrienne Stewart, age thirty-four, is the sole proprietor of Stewart Law. She graduated from San Diego State Law School and spent the next five years in the public defender's office, then opened her own practice. No complaints to the bar, exemplary record. Small business is her primary focus, with some pro bono for wills and estates. Auburn Pharmaceuticals has been her client for seven years." Jeff rattled off a few more details that were of no consequence to Sloan, and he stopped when Elliott walked in.

"Ready?"

Sloan noticed a faint glow on her boss's face and knew her wife Lauren had more than likely put it there. Probably just a few hours ago, she thought jealously. Sloan never had morning sex because her evening sex rarely turned into overnight sex, and she was always home in her own bed by the time the sun rose.

"All set," she said. She followed Elliott to the conference room, again thrilled to have this opportunity. She had met Elliott several years earlier at a conference in Phoenix. Elliott was the keynote speaker, and when she had opened the floor for questions, Sloan had been the first to the microphone. After the session, Elliott had sought her out and asked her to lunch. Five weeks, seven interviews, and one big signing bonus later, she was chief counsel for Foster McKenzie.

Elliott entered the conference room first, followed by Sloan. She extended her hand. "Mr. Douglas, Elliott Foster. Pleased to meet you."

"Yes, Ms. Foster, thank you for seeing us. Please call me Robert."

Robert Douglas was no more than five feet tall and reminded her of a younger Mick Jagger without all the wrinkles. He turned to the woman beside him.

"This is my attorney, Adrienne Stewart."

The attorney's back was to Sloan during the introduction, but she noticed something familiar about her. Sloan wracked her brain trying to place her. Elliott turned her way.

"This is Sloan Merchant, our corporate counsel."

Sloan greeted Robert, but her heart stopped when she shifted her attention and looked into familiar deep-green eyes. Very familiar, very knowing eyes.

Sound refused to penetrate her brain, and their voices sounded as if her hands were over her ears. The world was spinning, and she leaned against the table to steady herself. She was having a hard time breathing, and the last thing she wanted was to faint in front of Elliott. Elliott, hell. The last thing she wanted to do was faint in front of Adrienne Stewart.

"Ms. Merchant," Adrienne said, extending her hand.

Sloan knew it would be impolite to rebuff the greeting but wasn't sure if she wanted to touch Adrienne again. Years ago, a simple touch could instantly ignite her, which often led to other heated things. The recognition in Adrienne's eyes said she remembered the same thing. Sloan looked at the hand outstretched in front of her. Adrienne's nails were polished and her pinkie was still crooked, the result of a pickup game of basketball in college. She remembered those fingers floating over her skin like a soft breeze one minute, demanding a response in another.

"Ms. Stewart?" Sloan said, a question in her voice when she said her last name. *When did that change? Jeff is definitely going to have a new asshole by the end of the day.*

"Yes," Adrienne replied.

Their hands touched, and a jolt of electricity shot up her hand and landed right between her legs. The expression on Adrienne's face gave no indication she felt the same, or anything else for that matter. When Elliott cleared her throat, Sloan realized she was still holding Adrienne's hand.

"Shall we sit?" Elliott asked.

Yes, please, before I fall down. What in the hell is Adrienne doing here? It had been twelve years and four months since she'd last seen her, and Sloan hadn't realized she'd been counting.

Sloan concentrated on her breathing—in, out, in, out—and tried to focus on something other than her former lover. But it was next to impossible. Adrienne took her breath away today, as she had all those years ago.

The years had been good to her. She had gone from a twenty-two-year-old college girl to a mature, beautiful woman. Her hair was a little lighter than the fiery red it had been and at least ten inches shorter. It still looked as thick and luxurious as she remembered, and her fingers involuntarily twitched to touch it again. Her eyes were crystal clear and still as green as freshly cut bluegrass. She had a smattering of freckles across her nose that Sloan always found endearing. The beautiful suit she wore was stylish and fashionable, her silk blouse a lighter shade of green with a thin pinstripe pattern. Sloan had glimpsed a pair of legs and killer high heels when she first came into the room. Adrienne was thinner, almost too thin, with a sadness about her that Sloan had never seen before.

"Sloan?"

Elliott's voice got her attention, and she blinked a few times to settle herself. "I'm sorry. What did you say?" Sloan hated to ask, but she had no idea what the subject was or who had said what to whom.

Elliott frowned. Such a lapse was so unlike her. She was always entirely focused on her work.

"I asked if you'd like some coffee."

"No, thanks." The last thing she needed was to be even more jittery than she already was.

"Ms. Stewart…" Elliott said.

"Please call me Adrienne."

Sloan watched Adrienne's mouth move as she talked. She remembered when that mouth—

"Sloan, do you have the report from the advisory bank?"

Sloan jerked. "What? Oh, yes." She handed the one-inch-thick spiral-bound report to Elliott. She rubbed the pads of her fingers with her thumb, then just as suddenly stopped. Her nervous gesture was a dead giveaway when she was stressed.

Far from over her shock at seeing Adrienne again, Sloan forced herself to pay attention during the rest of the meeting. Elliott, Robert, and Adrienne discussed various aspects of the preliminary report. Adrienne's voice was strong and confident as she provided a brief overview of Auburn Pharma. She had a rhythmic way of talking that wasn't so fast you couldn't keep up nor so slow that it lulled you to sleep. She definitely knew what she was talking about.

Adrienne waved her hand to make a point, and the diamond ring on the third finger of her left hand caught the light. That was why she didn't know Auburn's attorney was Adrienne, Sloan thought. That, and Jeff pronounced her name Adrian, not Adri*enne*. He also failed to mention she had graduated from Howard College but simply identified the pertinent law school. Even if he had, she wasn't sure she would have put two and two together.

The last she knew, Adrienne had been on her way to art school in Italy after graduation. Sloan had no idea Adrienne was even interested in law. How did she end up as a public defender and sitting across from her now? And she was married? Adrienne never gave any indication she was anything other than pure, one hundred percent lesbian. Sloan never thought Adrienne would take the conventional route in anything she did. Obviously, Sloan didn't know her as well as she thought she had, except in the biblical sense.

"Sloan, do you have any questions?" Elliott asked.

Sloan looked from Elliott to Adrienne and saw apprehension in her eyes for just a moment before she blinked and it disappeared. Maybe she'd imagined it. Maybe Adrienne was just as affected by their meeting as she was. No. That couldn't be right. She hadn't changed her name or her career choice. Adrienne had to have Googled her before this meeting. She knew exactly who she was meeting with this morning, and that advantage angered Sloan.

"Not right now, no," Sloan replied, some of her anger slipping out. Elliott saw it and frowned at her, again. Knowing Elliott, she'd ask her about it later.

"Thank you for coming in, Robert, Adrienne," Elliott said, shaking their hand. "You'll hear from us within the week. Jeff." Elliott turned to the young paralegal. "Would you walk our guests out?"

"Yes, ma'am," Jeff said, jumping to his feet.

Adrienne hesitated in front of Sloan on her way out. Sloan wondered if she would say anything else to her. Should she? But what the hell would it be? "Quite a change in twelve years?" Sloan simply extended her hand. "We'll talk soon." She watched Adrienne walk out of the room, her hand tingling.

"You want to tell me what that was all about?" Elliott asked, her eyes piercing. Her words were firm, but her tone was light. Sloan had learned much about her boss in the last four years. Elliott was tough but fair. She was always prepared and expected everyone around her to be as well. And she did not tolerate fuck-ups.

Elliott was not a typical CEO. She didn't play golf or hobnob with other bigwigs. She worked hard, knew every aspect of her business, and was involved in every deal. She knew the companies Foster McKenzie invested in and could recite their profit and loss at any meeting. She was completely dedicated to two things: Foster McKenzie and her wife Lauren Collier.

Sloan realized Elliott was waiting for an answer. She could lie and say nothing, or come clean and tell Elliott that she knew Adrienne Stewart when she was Adrienne Phillips, a nineteen-year-old with an infectious laugh, a kind word for everybody, a brilliant mind, and an insatiable appetite for her.

"What do you mean?" Sloan asked, to give herself some time to determine how to answer the question.

"You looked like you'd seen a ghost, and you hardly said anything. That isn't like you, Sloan," Elliott said sternly.

"It's nothing. Just a little under the weather this morning. I didn't need to ask anything. You were doing it all. I knew you were paying attention when we talked about this the last few weeks," she added jokingly to get Elliott's mind off her. "Besides, she'll be back next week, and I'll have plenty of time to talk with her and Robert."

Sloan looked at her watch. "I have to run down the hall. Then I'll be right in for our other meeting." Sloan was lying for the second time in less than five minutes. She also realized she'd lied to herself all those years when she'd thought she was over Adrienne.

CHAPTER FOUR

Sloan was everything Adrienne had thought she would be. She was stunning in a dark-blue suit with a plum-colored blouse. Her brown hair was longer than when they were in college but still shorter than most men's. It must be a concession to a corporate job. She owned her space and oozed confidence and sensuality. Her skin was tanned, her eyes sharp and didn't miss a thing, including what had passed between them when they shook hands.

Adrienne didn't even try to hide her reaction; it wouldn't have been possible. She knew she would react to Sloan and had made it a point to accept that fact and move on. Sloan, on the other hand, obviously had no idea she would be there. Her reaction had lasted several seconds, and then it was gone.

Adrienne had to force herself to concentrate and not look at Sloan unless she was speaking. Fortunately, that hadn't been very often. Sloan kept rubbing her fingers with her thumb, and Adrienne remembered she did that when she was nervous. She'd felt Sloan's eyes on her more than once, and it was all she could do to not return the attention. She had to keep this professional. Hell, it was professional. It couldn't be anything else. What they'd had was a lifetime ago.

"Their attorney was pretty quiet," Robert commented. "I expected her to grill us. She has a reputation as a tough negotiator."

They were in the elevator headed down toward the lobby, and Adrienne didn't know if her stomach was quivering due to the quick descent or the aftereffects of seeing Sloan.

"Adrienne, are you all right?" he asked. He had given her a chance early on in her professional career and stayed with her faithfully.

"Yes, of course, Robert. Just unwinding from the meeting." And trying not to remember every minute she'd been with Sloan. Every laugh, every touch, every quiver of desire, every whisper in the dark.

They exited the building, the bright spring morning air crisp and cool. Adrienne had ltaken an Uber to the meeting, and while she waited for a new driver to take her back to her office, she raised her head and counted the floors of the building they had just left. No way could she know which window was the conference room, but she tried anyway. A movement on the floor above where she was looking caught her eye. Her heart raced. Was it Sloan? Was she trying to catch a glimpse of her one more time?

The Uber driver pulled up, and Adrienne scoffed at her ridiculous thoughts. She got in, buckled her seat belt, and looked up one more time.

❖

"Sloan, are you coming?" Elliott asked from behind her. Sloan watched the gray car pull away from the curb and around the corner before answering. "Yes. I'll be right there," she replied, dragging her eyes from where she'd seen Adrienne getting into the car.

She was still reeling from the shock of seeing Adrienne again. She was the last person Sloan expected to meet with today, or any day, for that matter. Adrienne had caught her off guard, and she was pissed. She was pissed that Auburn Pharmaceuticals had the advantage because of it. Well, now that she knew who she was dealing with, it would not happen again.

"Do you know Adrienne?" Elliott asked a few minutes later in her office. Her tone signaled to Sloan that she might already know the answer.

"Why do you ask?" Sloan asked guiltily. Responding to an uncomfortable question with a question like that was a clear indication of evasion.

"I don't know. You just seemed a little surprised when we walked in."

"I guess I was," Sloan said, grabbing the opening. "I expected some stodgy old attorney."

"Ms. Stewart is very sharp," Elliott commented.

Sloan's chest filled with pride at the compliment, but she quickly realized she had nothing to do with Adrienne's competence.

"She's also quite attractive," Elliott added.

Sloan felt a tinge of jealousy, then chided herself. Adrienne was not hers to be jealous of, and Elliott was totally devoted to Lauren. Her comment was only an observation.

"Yes, on both counts," Sloan replied. She had to say something. She couldn't very well say, *Well, considering she wanted to be an artist and now she's in front of us negotiating a multimillion-dollar deal, and yes, she's more than attractive. She's breathtaking*.

Teresa brought in lunch, and she, Elliott, and several others worked through the numbers for the rest of the afternoon. Images of Adrienne danced in her mind, and several times she lost track of the conversation. Mercifully the meeting was finally over and Sloan could escape to her office.

"Thank God for Google," Sloan said to her screen as she typed in a few key words to narrow her search. "There you are." The image and bio of Adrienne popped up on the screen. Sloan read the information, and it said exactly what Jeff had told her earlier, with no mention of why her name was Stewart. It didn't matter. That, and the three carats on her ring finger, told her everything she needed to know.

Sloan jumped when her phone rang. She didn't recognize the number. Adrienne? She cleared her throat and picked up the handset. "Sloan Merchant."

Her heart dropped when a male voice started talking. Twenty minutes later she was finally able to hang up, not exactly sure what the conversation had been about. Her mind kept drifting to Adrienne, and she laughed at herself. Did she really think she could get any work done today? Of course she would. She had buried herself in her job before to get over Adrienne. She could do it again.

CHAPTER FIVE

"Mama," Callie screamed, scampering off the couch and stumbling across the room. No matter what kind of day Adrienne had, how tired she was, or how much her heart was hurting, one look at her little girl and everything was right in the world. Adrienne scooped up Callie and was rewarded with a tight hug around her neck. She smelled like cookies and little girl, and Adrienne kissed the top of her head. She sat down on the couch, Callie scampering off her lap. Callie was babbling about something when Adrienne's mother came into the room.

Maria Phillips had gone back to school and earned her teaching certificate after her youngest child started first grade. She'd taught for seventeen years before she'd had an important conversation with Adrienne one day.

"It's time Callie stays with me."

"What?" Adrienne asked, more focused on wiping baby barf off her pants than what her mother was saying.

"Callie. She needs to be here with me. You have more important things to do than chase a baby around all day. I was going to watch her anyway when Brenna went back to work. I understand why you want her with you, but it's time."

"Mom, there's nothing more important than my child," Adrienne said defensively.

Maria sat down beside her and pulled her into a hug the way only a mother could. She smelled like lilac. The scent had always reminded her of her mother. "That's not what I mean, and you know it. You need to focus on your practice in order to provide for her. She's old enough to stay with me during the day."

"But you have your job, your students."

"I'm ready to do this, Adrienne. I want to do this. Your father and I talked about it. It's more important for Callie to be in a loving home when she's not with you. Besides, I want to spoil my granddaughter, not try to teach a bunch of spoiled teenagers the mysteries of English literature."

Adrienne thought about her mother's offer for several days. After Adrienne had been left alone to care for Callie, she'd remodeled her office, transforming a small file room into a nursery. Between Michelle and her admin assistant Ruth, it was tag-team childcare. They even taught their summer intern Josiah how to change a poopie diaper without gagging. Callie came to work with Adrienne every day until it was more than they could handle and still get their work done. Maria stepped in after that, which was a godsend. The last thing Adrienne needed was to worry about the care her child was receiving at some mega-chain day-care center.

"How'd it go today?" Maria had helped Adrienne strategize on how to approach Foster McKenzie for the money Auburn Pharmaceuticals desperately needed. Adrienne hadn't told her mother about her history with Sloan. That was old news better to not be remembered.

"Better than expected. Elliott Foster was, hmmm, how can I describe her?" Adrienne searched for the right words. "I guess I'd say she was sharp, quick, with kind, dark eyes, and very, very smart. She's a runner, so she has that lean, graceful body I wish I had."

"Nonsense," her mother said. But Adrienne knew her mother thought she was too thin. She'd lost almost thirty pounds after Brenna died, and her appetite had never really returned. Some days she had to remind herself to eat.

They chatted for a few more minutes while Callie played with Max, her mother's new beagle puppy.

Adrienne looked at her watch. "Time to get ready to leave,

Callie. We're going home in five minutes." Adrienne had learned it was less disruptive if she gave her daughter a few minutes' notice about what was going to happen next. Especially if she was happily playing with something. With her frazzled nerves, the last thing she needed was a temper tantrum to try her patience.

Adrienne stood and put both hands behind her, just above her waist. She arched her back, the tense muscles protesting. The combined stress of the meeting and her nervousness over seeing Sloan again had taken its toll. She hadn't slept much. A bedtime story for Callie, a soak in a hot bath, and a glass of wine would right her world. It had always worked before.

Callie must have sensed Adrienne's anxious mood because it took longer than normal for her to go down. Adrienne wandered through the house looking at and touching all the photos of Brenna. She smiled, and a familiar warmth coursed through her as she gazed at the two crumpled tickets in the frame on the side table and the memory they evoked.

On a balmy evening in May eight years earlier, Adrienne rounded a corner and ran right into another passenger. She and her BFF Char had boarded a dinner cruise an hour earlier, and she was hurrying to get back from the bar to their table before dinner was served.

"Oh, my gosh. I'm so sorry," Adrienne said, her heart racing from the shock.

"Shit," the woman replied, looking down at Adrienne's margarita soaking the front of her tank top.

Adrienne followed her gaze, and more than the drink was showing. The liquid was quickly penetrating the thin material, clearly outlining a perfect pair of breasts. She felt her mouth gaping open and closed like a fish trying to breathe as she struggled to do the same. Somehow remembering her manners, she finally dragged her eyes away from the breasts and up into the face of the most beautiful woman she'd ever seen.

Between finals and studying for the bar exam, Adrienne hadn't been out of her apartment much in the past few months. Without the real threat that Char would drag her out by her hair, she wouldn't even be here. And she wouldn't have run into this woman.

Adrienne hadn't dated much in law school, preferring to concentrate on her studies, and she couldn't remember the last time she'd had a date. She even had trouble remembering the last time she had sex. It had to have been since Sloan left, but it didn't matter.

"I'm so sorry," she said again. "I...I..." She stammered. She didn't know what to do. Suddenly she realized she could do something. She tugged off her just-in-case-I-get-cold sweater from around her neck. "Here. You can have this." She offered it to the woman, who looked at her like she'd lost her mind. "Really, it's the least I can do. It'll be at least two hours before we get back to shore, and you can't wear that the rest of the evening." With her outstretched hand and the sweater, she indicated the woman's now-almost see-through top.

"Shit," the woman said, pulling her top away from her body.

Adrienne had no idea if she would put the sweater on or take it and throw it back at her. Finally, the woman looked at her, and Adrienne's world tilted more than a little.

Her hair was jet black, but her eyes were an unusual shade of blue, the combination striking. She was a few inches shorter than Adrienne and solidly built. She looked at Adrienne, sizing her up. She reached for the sweater.

"Thank you. I appreciate it."

She had a slight accent, and Adrienne suspected she was British. "I'm Adrienne Phillips," she said for lack of anything wittier to say. She didn't want the woman to just walk away.

The woman paused again before saying, "I'd say nice to meet you but..." The woman looked at her shirt and scowled. "Brenna Stewart." Brenna extended her hand in greeting.

The following week was their first date, four dates later the first time they made love, eight months after that their first apartment, another five months before they were married, and four years later on a warm Friday evening sitting by the pool enjoying the beautiful sunset, Brenna said, "I think we should have a baby."

Adrienne choked on her swallow of beer, half of it spewing out of her mouth and the other down her windpipe. A minute or two later she was finally able to speak, but her throat was sore from coughing. "A baby?"

"Yes, a baby."

"You think we should have a baby?" Adrienne knew she sounded ridiculous, and for an attorney who could argue whether it was Tuesday or the day after Monday, she was having a hard time finding any words.

Brenna, on the other hand, was perfectly calm. "Yes, a baby."

"And how exactly would we do that?"

Brenna looked at her like she'd lost her mind.

"Okay. I have a good idea how we would do it," Adrienne said. She took a breath, not knowing if she wanted to know the answer to the next question. "Why do you think we should have a baby?" Adrienne guessed that if she repeated it enough times it would sink in.

"Because I think it would enhance our life together."

"Do you feel we're missing something?" Adrienne asked cautiously.

"No. I love you and want to spend the rest of my life with you."

Adrienne knew she wanted to say more. She prompted Brenna. "But?"

"But I want us to raise children together. You would be a fabulous mother. You're kind and smart, and she might look just like you."

Adrienne sat up in her chair. "You want me to be pregnant?" That idea was scarier than the idea of being responsible for another human being.

Brenna laughed and came over and sat beside her. She put her arm around Adrienne's shoulders and kissed her cheek. "No, silly. I'll carry our baby."

"Then how will it look like me?" Adrienne didn't know why she asked the question. She knew they could pick a donor from the sperm bank that had her characteristics.

"We'd use your egg."

"You've obviously spent a lot of time thinking about this." Adrienne didn't know if she should be angry or upset.

"Yes, I have."

"Why didn't you discuss it with me?"

"I am discussing it with you.

The idea of having a baby was not abhorrent to Adrienne. It was just something she'd never thought about. She didn't have a ticking clock on her eggs, and she'd been so busy getting through school, then working, then starting her own practice that she just never considered something so domestic.

"Is it that bad an idea?" Brenna asked softly.

"No," Adrienne said quickly, surprised the word came out of her mouth. She must be warming to the idea. "You just surprised me. It kind of came out of nowhere."

"I know, but I had to bring it up sometime. Obviously, you need to think about it. Take your time. This isn't something we should jump into."

"So, if we were to have a baby, what would happen? I mean, who would watch it, Catholic or Lutheran, public or private school, that sort of thing?" Adrienne liked to consider all the facts before she decided anything. Brenna laughed, and Adrienne felt herself relax.

"It's a bit soon to worry about schools, honey, but as for the other, I would take off the twelve weeks I get from work, and I thought your mom could watch her during the day."

"She?" The idea of a little girl that looked just like Brenna was suddenly appealing.

"Figure of speech," Brenna said, this time kissing the top of her head.

"My mom would love that," Adrienne replied, knowing that was an understatement.

"Just think about it. We can talk more, but I know how you need a lot of information. My thoughts are daycare for socialization when she's three or four, private school, we start going to church, I like

Callie Elizabeth or Spencer Albert—but I'm flexible on that, and maybe a brother or sister later on."

"Brother or sister?" Adrienne managed to squeal out. She was just getting used to the idea of one, and now Brenna was talking about more than that? She'd been around a lot of children and nieces and nephews, so kids didn't scare her, but it was something different when it was your own.

Setting the frame back on the table, Adrienne double-checked the locks on the front and back doors before heading upstairs. After peeking in at Callie, she set the baby monitor on the nightstand, sat on the bed, and picked up her favorite picture frame.

The photo had been taken the minute Brenna realized Adrienne was proposing. Adrienne had enlisted the help of her BFF, and she and Char had worked out a plan. Having Adrienne down on one knee provided the perfect angle for Char to take the picture. Adrienne remembered the day, and she fought back the tears. Some days they were just behind the surface.

"I loved you so much, Brenna. I really did." Adrienne ran her fingers over the image of her wife, her voice soft and full of emotion. "You were everything to me. We had such plans. I never loved anyone the way I loved you, and I never will. You will always be in my heart." Adrienne stopped fighting the emotion she felt when thinking about Brenna. Time does not heal wounds, she thought. It just lessens the impact a bit.

Adrienne locked her bedroom door and lay back down on the bed. One time she hadn't locked her door, and she didn't hear Callie get out of bed and come into her room. It wasn't until Callie was standing beside her bed, looking at her peculiarly that Adrienne realized she'd caught her in the act. Callie was only two and had no idea what her mother was doing to herself under the covers, but Adrienne had been mortified nonetheless.

Adrienne propped the picture of Brenna on the empty pillow beside her. She'd gotten pretty good at masturbating while looking at the picture. When she closed her eyes, she imagined Brenna's hands on her, tweaking a nipple, rubbing her stomach, her hand drifting lower with each stroke. She imagined Brenna's voice telling her how much she loved her and how good she felt. She imagined Brenna's fingers between her legs, stroking and teasing until she was ready to explode. Brenna was thrusting inside and then slowly drawing out in a perfect rhythm. Brenna was there when Adrienne begged her to go faster, to fuck her harder, and she imagined Brenna's eyes when she climaxed.

But this time when she closed her eyes, she saw Sloan, who took her to the place where she had taken her hundreds of times before.

Guilt overcame Adrienne. It had been three years since Brenna's death, and she hadn't once looked at or even thought about another woman. She had accepted that no one would ever take Brenna's place in her life. She would never love anyone like she loved Brenna. No one would be Callie's mother like Brenna would have been. She would raise Callie alone. She had the help of her friends and family to protect both her and Callie from the painful reminder that Brenna was gone. She rolled away from Brenna's picture and sobbed. Brenna was slipping away.

CHAPTER SIX

The last thing Sloan wanted to do was sit in a dark theater watching a ballet she knew nothing about and had no interest in. Joanne had suggested it, and in a weak moment, Sloan had agreed. They'd been seeing each other off and on for several months. It wasn't by any means serious for either of them, simply someone to enjoy a nice dinner, attend an event or, in this case, the ballet with. And have sex. They weren't really friends with benefits because they weren't really friends. They went out, did something, then went back to Joanne's apartment and had sex. That was just how Sloan wanted it—great sex with no strings and nothing messy when it was over.

Adrienne dominated her thoughts the entire evening. She had no idea what was going on onstage, and thankfully she hadn't had to try to follow a conversation with Joanne. However great the sex would be, it wouldn't be fair to Joanne to be thinking about Adrienne while she was in bed with her. She might not want monogamy or commitment, but she wasn't an ass. She did feel a little guilty when, as they were walking to their cars, she told Joanne she had a ton of work to do and needed to go home.

Sloan pulled into the garage, turned off her car, and sat motionless. She had a reserved space in her building, the cars on either side parked in their assigned spots. The familiar Volvo was to her left and the shiny new Audi next to that. Even though she owned the building, she didn't know the owners of any of the cars parked below the four-level structure. She left the day-to-day running of the building to the management company. They didn't even know she was the owner. Sloan preferred it that way.

Six years ago she'd bought the dilapidated building with the money her grandmother had left her. She had wisely put the entire amount into a trust, with herself as the sole trustee.

The complete silence in her car was peaceful yet unnerving. Was this what it felt like to be deaf? She couldn't even hear her own breathing. She was still rattled by Adrienne being in the office today, and she let her head fall back, closed her eyes, and remembered the first time she saw her.

"Are you here for the bride or the bride?" Adrienne's voice was as clear now as it was that first day all those years ago.

Sloan turned toward the voice and looked into the greenest eyes she'd ever seen. The woman was a few inches shorter than her, and her hair was a shade of red Sloan found impossible to describe. She wore just enough makeup to make Sloan question if she even had on any. If she was a fellow student, how had she missed her?

"The bride, of course. How about you?"

The woman smiled sweetly, catching the pun before she answered. "Same. Nice wedding."

"Better food," Sloan replied.

"And drink," she said, lifting her beer bottle in a mock salute.

"So enough with the small talk," Sloan said. "I'm Sloan Merchant." She extended her hand. The beautiful stranger switched her beer to her other hand and took hers.

Sloan wasn't a hearts, flowers, and birds-singing kind of person, but at that moment she would've sworn she was in a Disney movie where hearts were floating around her, flowers popping open, and birds chirping nearby. She had been with many women, experienced severe lust and desire, but none had affected her like this one had in just a few minutes.

"Adrienne Phillips."

They spent the remainder of the reception together talking smack about the other guests and getting drunk. They were both on the guest list solely because each of them lived in the dorm of their respective bride.

After dinner and dancing, Adrienne had been anything but shy when she suggested that they go to Sloan's room, and when they stepped inside and Sloan asked her if she would like something to drink, Adrienne had replied, "Maybe later. The only thing I want to taste right now is you."

The screech of an alarm as someone locked their car jolted Sloan out of her daydream. She exhaled, grabbed her briefcase from the front seat, and locked her own car door behind her.

Sloan counted the steps to the top floor like she did every time she used them, which was at least twice a day and several times on the weekends. The plush carpet muffled the sound of her shoes as she walked down the hall toward her front door. She entered a set of numbers into the keypad, and the lock clicked open. When she'd remodeled the apartments, she'd had the pad installed on her unit. She was forever forgetting her keys, and the one to her front door was one less she had to worry about.

"Lights." Sloan spoke to the voice-command unit. Her place had top-of-the-line electronic gadgets, and voice command was her favorite. No more fumbling for light switches or forgetting to turn them off when she left the room. The command was her primary setting, powering on the lamps on either side of the sofa in the room as well as the overhead light in the foyer. She had a similar setting for each room, but she typically didn't venture much outside this one, the kitchen, her bedroom, and her office. Sylvia, her housekeeper, changed the sheets in the two guest rooms weekly just in case Sloan ever had guests. But she rarely did, and during the years she'd lived here, no one had seen her bedroom. She preferred keeping the location of that activity in places where she could determine when it was time to leave.

She toed off her shoes, dropped her jacket on the back of the oversized chair, and fixed herself a cocktail. She was trying to cut down, but if there was ever a night when she needed one, it was this one.

❖

"Something was off with Sloan today," Elliott commented as she set the table. She hadn't expected Lauren to be home and was pleasantly surprised when the scent of dinner greeted her as she walked in from the garage.

"What do you mean?" Lauren asked, pulling the lasagna out of the oven and then closing it with her hip.

"I can't quite put my finger on it. She didn't seem to be one hundred percent there. Like her mind was somewhere else." Elliott shook her head. "I don't know. I can't explain it. She just wasn't herself."

"Did you talk to her about it?"

"She said it was nothing. But I swear it was as if…" Elliott filled their wineglasses. "It was as if something had spooked her."

"Doesn't sound like Sloan at all." A few minutes later, Lauren asked, "Is she seeing anyone?"

"Not that I know of. You'd probably know better than I."

Elliott and Lauren often socialized with Sloan. When Sloan had moved to San Diego to take the job, Lauren had appointed herself as Sloan's tour guide, shown her around and helped her find a place to live. They had often been a foursome with Sloan and a date at a charity or sporting event. They'd even run the San Diego Marathon together last year. Lauren enjoyed Sloan's company and genuinely liked her. Sloan had a different woman every time they went out, and Elliott remembered Lauren commenting about Sloan's revolving bedroom door.

"Jealous?" Elliott had asked her teasingly.

"Absolutely not."

"But…"

"But nothing," Lauren replied, but Elliott knew better.

"Do you wish you'd sown some wild oats before you married me?" Elliott asked carefully. Lauren wasn't sensitive about her lack of sexual experience prior to meeting her, but Elliott still trod lightly.

"In the beginning, I wished I knew more…for you…" Lauren said, her cheeks flushed.

Elliott circled the table and approached her. She took the serving spoon from her hand and set it back on the tray. She turned to Lauren to look at her. "You never told me that."

"It never came up," Lauren said evasively.

"A lot of things don't just come up. You have to bring them up, especially if they concern us." Elliott lifted Lauren's chin so she could look into her beautiful blue eyes. She could get lost in those eyes and often did. She loved it when their eyes locked just before one or both orgasmed.

"It wasn't important," Lauren said, her eyes darting back and forth between hers and something over Elliott's shoulder.

"I think it is," Elliott said quietly. "Did I ever give you the idea I was looking for something?" Elliott couldn't believe that, after four years, they were having this conversation. They could have talked about this early on in their relationship.

"No, of course not," Lauren replied quickly.

"But…"

"But sometimes I just—"

"Lauren. You are the most perfect lover I have ever had and ever will have. And you know why? Because I love you. I didn't love any of those other women. Making love with you is the most important, extraordinary thing in my life. You are everything I could ever want in a lover, because you love me. Everything you do makes me crazy, except for that thing with the feather. That just made me giggle." Elliott smiled, remembering the event. "I love you, Lauren. I don't want for anything in our sex life or in our life other than for you to keep loving me."

Lauren hugged her and said into her neck, "How is it, when I feel absolutely stupid, you make me feel like I'm the most important thing in the world?"

Elliott kissed her. "That's because you are." Lauren pulled her head back down, and the sweet kiss of moments ago was now anything but.

Lauren's mouth was hot and demanding, and Elliott responded equally. In seconds, shirts and bras were scattered around on the floor, pants were unzipped and frantically pushed down, and Lauren's fingers were buried deep inside her. Before she was too far gone, Elliott mirrored Lauren's actions, and within minutes they came, fast and hard and as one.

"Remind me to be an idiot again real soon," Lauren said, her breath hot on Elliott's neck.

Elliott was still trying to catch her breath and somehow manage to keep them both upright. She was afraid to move for fear they would topple to the wood floor. It wouldn't be their first time on the floor.

"Okay." That was all she managed to say.

They stayed together for several more minutes, when Lauren finally said, "I think dinner's cold."

"Who cares? You were hot." Elliott grinned. She moved her fingers slightly, and Lauren contracted around them again. God, that was sexy.

Lauren lifted her head and kissed Elliott again.

"Be careful. That's how this all started," Elliott teased. She wouldn't mind a repeat.

Lauren laughed and slowly separated herself from Elliott. Elliott instantly missed the warmth of her touch and reached for her again.

"Nope. As much as I loved what we did and may, at some time, want to do again, I need to eat." Lauren picked up Elliott's clothes and handed them to her. "Go wash your hands and get dressed."

"Are you worried about this deal?" Lauren asked just after they sat down. The lasagna was still warm, and the wine was perfect.

"No. It's rather cut-and-dried. It sounds pretty good." Elliott proceeded to give an overview of Auburn Pharmaceuticals as they finished their dinner. "Their lawyer, Adrienne Stewart, is a lesbian."

Lauren perked up. "Really?"

"Yes, really," Elliott said, looking at her. "Don't get any ideas. She had a huge ring on her finger." Lauren was a romantic and thought everyone should be as happily married as she was. That, and she was always playing matchmaker for Sloan.

"Party pooper," Lauren said. "Are you worried about Sloan?"

"No, not really. I'll keep an eye on her the next few days."

"How is Ryan doing, by the way?" Lauren asked. Ryan Smith had held Sloan's job before he relocated to Boston to be closer to his mother after his father passed away suddenly.

"He made partner last week," Elliott said fondly. She had been upset both personally and professionally when Ryan gave his notice, but she didn't begrudge his decision. They had kept in touch, and Ryan had put out a few feelers on Sloan before Elliott hired her.

"How was your day?" Elliott asked after dinner was over. "Slay any dragons?"

"Only one, I'm afraid," Lauren answered, pretending to be dejected. "LuEllen got full custody of her daughter, and the Marcus family decided counseling was better than jumping right into divorce court." Lauren's legal practice specialized in children and family services, and she had more clients than she knew what to do with these days.

Lauren and Elliott had met at a fund-raiser five years earlier, and their courtship had been anything but whirlwind. Lauren had been in a position similar to Sloan's but at a different company, and shortly after they got together she quit and opened her own practice. At first she'd suffered long hours and heartbreaking losses, but Lauren's reputation as a fair and talented litigator was now well-known.

They left the dishes in the sink and took the wine outside to the back patio. Elliott had changed into a pair of shorts and a plain white T-shirt, while Lauren was wearing dark-blue yoga pants and a sleeveless top. They sat on lounge chairs next to each other, close enough to hold hands. Water cascading into the pool from the fountain was relaxing, while the carefully placed accent lighting in the trees and bushes created an intimate scene.

Elliott gazed at the stars and gave thanks to whoever or whatever was watching over her. She had managed to save Foster McKenzie from bankruptcy and met the woman she planned to spend the rest of her life with when she literally ran into Lauren. She was happier than she ever knew she could be. Before Lauren, Elliott had thought she was happy. She had her pick of women and really didn't care if they wanted her or her money. She wanted them for only a few nights so it really didn't matter. But when Lauren didn't let her get away with her typical bullshit, Elliott knew she had met someone very special. Elliott was afraid she might lose Lauren when an old flame showed up demanding money, but Lauren didn't even flinch. That was when Elliott knew for certain that she was the one.

"What are you thinking?" Lauren asked, taking her hand and squeezing it.

"Just how lucky I am that you love me."

"I'm the one that's lucky. Why you put up with me and chased me, I'll never know." Lauren chuckled softly. It was their running joke.

"Because when you kissed me my toes curled," Elliott confessed.

"Really?"

"Yes, really." Elliott remembered their first kiss. They had gone to the theater, and Lauren had looked stunning in her little black dress, supported by spaghetti straps that exposed her smooth shoulders. The bodice was held snug by pearl buttons, and as she walked, the soft folds of the dress moved with her, falling to just below her knees. Her strawberry-blond hair was pulled back off her face and secured at the base of her neck, and her ears sparkled with diamonds that matched the jewels around her neck. A gold watch on her left wrist had completed her accessories.

After dinner, Elliott had driven Lauren home, and when Lauren had invited her in, she knew the night had only just begun. She remembered Lauren's lips were softer than she had imagined, and she savored every sensation. She gently nibbled, smiling when Lauren wound her fingers tightly in her hair and pulled her closer. Wanting more, Elliott reluctantly dragged her lips away and kissed the fine bones of Lauren's cheeks and along her jawline before returning to her enticing mouth. Lauren quickly invited her in for more. She let her hands roam over Lauren's back, and then she slowly reached forward to cup Lauren's breasts. She kissed her way down Lauren's neck, stopping to tease the racing pulse just above her collarbone, then continued on her journey to taste the bare shoulders that had tormented her all evening.

"I hadn't had much experience," Lauren said, and Elliott didn't sense any embarrassment in her voice. Lauren was a lesbian virgin when they met, and that had taken some getting used to. Elliott didn't want the burden of being Lauren's first. She didn't want to be subject to that kind of emotional commitment.

"Didn't matter. You knocked my socks off."

"It wasn't your socks I wanted off," Lauren said, running her finger back and forth across Elliott's palm.

"Really?"

"Really."

"Do tell."

"I wanted to unbutton your shirt very slowly. I wanted to touch your breasts and lick your nipples. I wanted to find out if your skin was as soft and warm as I dreamed it was. I wanted to unzip your pants and slide my fingers into you. I wanted to make your knees weak and your clit hard."

Elliott was having a hard time focusing. Her body was reacting in all the places Lauren was talking about.

"Then I'd listen to what your body was telling me. I'd find just the right places, discover if you liked it fast or slow, hard or feather-light. Then I'd take you there. To that place that only we share."

By the time Lauren finished, Elliott felt like she was one stroke away from orgasm. "Well," she said, her voice barely above a whisper. "If I'd known that," she threw her legs over the side of her chair, "I would have let you kiss me sooner."

Elliott took Lauren's hand and pulled her up, and Lauren followed her toward the pool. When she didn't stop to take her clothes off but just descended the steps, Lauren's pulse jumped. Last year, Elliott had installed the salt-water pool, the water making them buoyant, almost weightless. They had christened it that night and several nights later, but they hadn't had any playtime in the pool in several weeks.

The water was cool, but Lauren could swear she heard it sizzle when they entered. Elliott didn't stop until the water was just below her breasts. Elliott's kiss was searing, and Lauren wrapped her arms around Elliott's neck. Elliott quickly dispensed with her clothes, and nothing separated them but pure blue water.

Elliott put one hand on each of Lauren's ass cheeks and lifted. Lauren wrapped her legs around her as Elliott walked forward until her back was pressed against the pool tile. Elliott lifted her and set her on the edge of the pool. Seconds later, Elliott had her head between her legs and her mouth exactly where Lauren needed it.

"Elliott, God, you make me crazy. You know just what I need." Lauren lifted her legs, placed her feet on Elliott's shoulders, and let her knees drop open. This simple act gave Elliott access to whatever she wanted. Lauren raised her head, and her breath caught at the image of the love of her life right where she wanted to be.

It wasn't long before tremors started in her core and threatened to expand to every nerve ending. She wanted to explode, to release the love and sensations Elliott created in her. But she wanted the experience to last. She lived for these moments when they were one, giving and receiving pleasure. They were going too quickly, and she tried to focus on something else to stave off her climax.

Elliott must've sensed what she was feeling, because she pulled her mouth away just enough to look up at her and grinned. "What are you waiting for?" Elliott knew exactly what she was doing, and Lauren had told her so many times before.

"I want you to come with me."

"Next time," Elliott said, lowering her mouth and giving Lauren no chance to argue.

CHAPTER SEVEN

"Hey, Google," Sloan said into the microphone to wake up her iPad. She kept getting interrupted when she'd tried to do this research earlier in the day. The familiar bleep answered her. "Who is Adrienne Stewart, attorney in San Diego." Sloan was rewarded with 4,653 hits. She scanned the headlines, clicked on a few, and didn't uncover any new information she didn't have before she started. She narrowed her search by saying, "Adrienne Phillips marries Stewart."

Sloan's heart was pounding as she quickly skimmed these results. She didn't want to know who Adrienne married, but she couldn't keep herself from looking. The first article in, she hit pay dirt on the link from seven years ago. She read out loud.

Adrienne Phillips, age twenty-four, was married yesterday to Brenna Stewart. Ms. Phillips attended the prestigious Howard College on an academic scholarship and graduated summa cum laude. She graduated from San Diego State Law School and passed the bar shortly thereafter. She is currently an attorney in the public defender's office. Ms. Stewart, twenty-eight and hailing from Britain, is a kindergarten teacher at Fireside School for the Deaf. The couple plans to reside in San Diego.

Looking at a photo of Adrienne and her bride, Sloan had to admit they made a striking couple. Ms. Stewart was shorter than

Adrienne by four or five inches, yet she seemed to dominate the photo. She was stunning. Her hair was long and dark, her smile unforced.

"Jesus, Sloan, get a grip," she said, hitting the Home button on her browser and flipping the cover closed. She choked when she swallowed her drink too fast and cussed when it dribbled down her chin. Suddenly feeling closed in, Sloan opened the sliding door to her patio and stepped outside.

The night was cool, the breeze billowing the curtain behind her. She leaned against the railing, her forearms on top of the wide metal beam. To her left and right the lights of the city twinkled, but straight ahead, less than one hundred yards away, lay the Pacific Ocean. If the crashing waves didn't convince you the ocean was near, the salt scent in the air would.

One evening, on a night very much like this one, she and Adrienne had been lying on a blanket in the center of the lacrosse field. Sweat covered their bodies from their own strenuous activity, and Sloan was having a hard time catching her breath. Their clothes were disheveled because Adrienne refused to be caught with her clothes off. It had taken all of Sloan's powers of persuasion to get her to agree to a quickie out here, let alone get buck naked to do it. She improvised, and they both had an experience neither of them would ever forget.

Swimming in post-orgasmic bliss, Sloan had thought about what her life would be like without Adrienne in it. Instead of the idea smothering her, Sloan felt an odd sense of freedom. It had been five or six months into their relationship, and she realized that Adrienne made her happier than she'd ever been. She was demanding without being overbearing, supportive without being smothering, and she insisted on monogamy, which, surprisingly, Sloan had no trouble adhering to.

But those thoughts and any others she might have had that night flew out of her head when the lights overhead had turned on. They'd grabbed the blanket and scampered under the nearest bleachers.

Sloan smiled at the memory and how they'd laughed all the way back to Adrienne's room. Even though Sloan could easily afford an apartment off campus, students were required to live in one of the dormitories. They lived in different dorms, and since both had roommates, sleeping together was often out of the question. On those rare occasions either roomie went away for the weekend, they spent the entire time in a small twin bed. They were an item, a couple. Their time together had been magical, and Sloan had thought her life couldn't get any better. But then it had ended.

The ringing of her phone pulled Sloan out of her daydream and back to the present. She searched for her briefcase, pulled it out, and hit the answer button, silencing the ring and not bothering to look at the caller ID.

"Hello?"

"Hey, baby."

The woman on the other end of the line didn't need to identify herself. She was Nan Cummings, a woman Sloan had been seeing off and on for a few months.

She'd met Nan at a fund-raiser for one of Elliott's charities when they struck up a conversation waiting in line at the bar. Nan was beautiful, owned a very successful landscaping company, and was great in bed. She didn't demand anything from Sloan other than to make her come as many times as she could. Sloan had always been up for the challenge.

"Hey, Nan."

"You busy?" That was code for *Wanna fuck?*

Sloan thought for a moment, feeling surprisingly indifferent. Normally within fifteen minutes of Nan's call she was naked, with Nan's gorgeous legs wrapped around her. Maybe she was tired. Obviously, she was off-kilter after seeing Adrienne again today. She had thought about her all afternoon, and her uncharacteristic lapse in concentration several times today had shaken her. But that was history. Old history. And Adrienne was married. She had moved on, and Sloan made it a point not to mess with a married woman.

"Sloan?" Nan's voice now sounded questioning.

"I'm here," Sloan responded, a thousand thoughts running through her head. She obviously needed to clear it. A few hours with Nan would set her world right again. She put her glass on the counter and grabbed her keys and wallet.

Chapter Eight

"No!"

Adrienne's nerves were at their end point. She hadn't slept much the past few nights, dreams of Sloan and Brenna mixing together. Most were innocuous, but one involved her hiding one woman from the other. More than once she dreamed of having sex with one of them or both of them. Often she dreamed she had made a colossal mistake and cheated on Brenna. Dreams? No way. They were nightmares, and this morning Callie was being a temperamental three-year-old, refusing to put on her shoes. Adrienne's normally long patience had expired.

"Callie Elizabeth Stewart, get your scrawny little behind over here and put your shoes on," Adrienne commanded through clenched teeth. Brenna had been the one with patience in the family, not her, especially not this morning and not with everything on her mind. Today was the second meeting at Foster McKenzie, and Adrienne didn't have the advantage of surprise this time.

Callie finally settled down, and Adrienne was able to slide her pudgy little feet into her sandals. Callie had the same birthmark on her right knee as Brenna had, and Adrienne kissed it after she finished buckling the toddler's sandals.

"Bucket, bucket," Callie said, running back into her room. For a moment, Adrienne thought she was saying *fuck it* until she remembered that her mother was taking Callie to the beach this morning.

"Yes, get your bucket, sweetie, and let's get going. Grandma is waiting."

Callie came running down the hall like only a three-year-old can, her bucket in one hand, a small, bright-green shovel in the other.

Adrienne wished she could go to the beach. Between preparing for the Auburn Pharma meetings and her other clients, she hadn't had a day off in what felt like months. And she could certainly use one. Adrienne didn't actually go in to the office on the weekends, but she had her laptop open or case files scattered on the desk in her home office when Callie napped and after she went to bed at night. Tomorrow was Saturday, and Adrienne had decided to take Callie to the zoo. She couldn't very well work if she was chasing a toddler around the exhibits. But today she needed to make it through being in the same room with Sloan again.

After lunch, she and Robert were ushered into the same conference room as they'd been in last week. They both declined coffee, but Adrienne accepted a glass of water. Her mouth was dry, and it would give her something to focus on if she needed it.

She drummed her fingers on the table. For the third time in five minutes she looked at her watch. It was ten minutes past the meeting start time, and she couldn't help but wonder if this was a power play of some type. Was it Sloan's idea? A way to get back at her, make Adrienne feel inferior? Auburn Pharmaceuticals needed Foster McKenzie, and they definitely had the upper hand. Everything she'd read about Elliott Foster didn't give any indication that she or her firm would be that petty. Would Sloan? Adrienne didn't pretend she knew Sloan anymore. Twelve years was a long, long time. She had no idea what Sloan was capable of any more.

"We should give them another five minutes," Adrienne said, looking at Robert.

"But how will it look if we leave?"

"Like we have important things to do, such as save lives," she added. "We don't need to fall all over ourselves to get this money. It makes us look desperate, and we don't want to appear desperate."

"But we are," Robert said, looking as such.

"The first rule in negotiating is to not show all your cards. I told you that several times when we were prepping for these meetings. Robert, you're a nice man, a very nice man, and an honest one, but we should not let them know how badly we want this funding. If they sense blood, they may ask for a higher rate of return or a larger equity stake, or any number of stipulations. They'll ask because they know we'll give it to them." Robert Douglas was a brilliant scientist but a terrible businessman. If it weren't for Adrienne and the other executives, Auburn would be in worse financial shape than it was at present.

Robert didn't like her answer but accepted it and spent his five minutes staring out the window. Adrienne used it to take a closer look at the framed photos and certificates around the large room. There were the typical *Thank You For Your Donation* from the United Way and other notable charities, to a proclamation citing Foster McKenzie for its support in keeping the city green. When Adrienne looked at her watch again, seven minutes had passed. It was now seventeen minutes past their appointment time.

"Let's go, Robert." Adrienne gathered up her papers and notepad from the table and put them back in her briefcase. "They'll have to reschedule."

Robert followed her out, and Adrienne knew he wasn't happy. He would have stayed for the rest of the afternoon and evening, if that's what it took. She refused to play that game.

Adrienne stopped at the reception desk and gave the message to the blonde sitting behind the ornate desk. Obviously, people didn't walk out of a meeting with Foster McKenzie because the woman seemed shocked. Adrienne fully expected her to call her back before they reached the elevator and was more than a little surprised when no one did.

As she was driving back to her office, her phone rang. She pushed the little red button of a telephone receiver on her steering wheel, thinking it ironic that in a car less than a year old, the Bluetooth phone button featured a picture of a handset.

When the caller ID came up blank she answered with her name. "Adrienne Stewart."

"It's Sloan."

Her voice was clear in the interior of the car, and Adrienne would recognize it even if she hadn't identified herself. She didn't know what to say. Her choices were "I know," "Are you calling to apologize for standing us up," or a variety of other responses. Or she could simply say hello. She chose the latter.

"I'm sorry for being late to the meeting. We got hung up on another issue."

"That's understandable." Adrienne wasn't going to say something like it's okay or no problem, because it wasn't, and it was a problem. She and Robert had come all the way downtown, and now they'd wasted most of the afternoon. An afternoon she could have spent at the beach with Callie.

"We were surprised to see that you had left."

"We gave you almost twenty minutes. It was obvious you weren't going to make it and thought you'd rather reschedule," Adrienne said diplomatically. She really wanted to say it was rude not to send someone in to let them know they would be late.

"Elliott and I would like to apologize. We don't operate that way. There was a miscommunication. We'd like to invite you and Robert to dinner tonight, if you're available."

Adrienne thought before she answered. It was obvious this would be strictly a business conversation, and she was relieved. She'd thought about what she would say to Sloan on a more personal level but never settled on anything specific.

"I'll have to check with Robert and get back with you." She knew it was just a formality. Robert would drop everything to have dinner with his hopefully soon-to-be financier.

"Of course. Call me back one way or the other. If you can make it, we have a table at Huey's for seven thirty."

Adrienne had never been to the most popular and expensive restaurant on the shoreline. It had rave reviews and was *the* place to go for business or pleasure. As Adrienne waited for Robert to come on the line, a flashback of another dinner popped into her mind.

She was sitting across from Sloan in a restaurant very similar to Huey's. Adrienne had begged Sloan not to take them there, but she had insisted. Even in her little black dress, Adrienne felt outclassed and underdressed. Sloan had money and didn't mind spending it. She didn't flaunt it, but she always had the latest electronic gadget, the newest car, and the nicest clothes. She was always completely put together. Adrienne often wondered how rich people always looked...well...rich.

They were sitting in the far corner in a booth obviously meant for lovers. The small table, dark wood, oversize seats, and subtle lighting had an intimate feel. As Adrienne followed the hostess to their table, Sloan had her hand possessively on the small of Adrienne's back. It was a warm, wonderful feeling to know that she belonged to Sloan.

They talked about this and that and nothing at all, often spending long moments simply looking into each other's eyes. The waiter came and went with little fanfare, and before she knew it, dinner was over. The meal, company, and ambience were very effective foreplay, and Adrienne could hardly wait to get Sloan back to her dorm room.

Sloan obviously had similar thoughts, because they had barely closed the door when clothes started falling to the floor. Sloan's mouth was insistent and Adrienne answered with equal passion. Neither one of them was shy in bed, and they didn't fight for who was on top or up against the door, as was the case this time.

Adrienne's back was the one against the door, Sloan pressing against her. Sloan ran hot, passionate kisses up and down her neck, drifting farther south on each trip. Sloan's muscular thigh was pressed against her sex, and Adrienne squeezed her legs together, enjoying the connection. Sloan dropped her head and encircled one nipple, then the other with her tongue before capturing each one with her mouth. Her tongue danced across one nipple, while her finger and thumb mimicked the motions on the other. Adrienne gripped Sloan's hair, holding her in place while rockets of pleasure shot through her. She had a direct connection from her nipples to her clit, and Sloan took advantage of that sensitivity every time. Sloan put her hands on Adrienne's ass and lifted her slightly, giving Adrienne more direct contact with her hard, muscular thigh.

Adrienne was more than ready, her juices coating Sloan's thigh as she slid up and down it sensuously. Faster and faster Adrienne moved, and somehow Sloan's mouth never left her breast. She came fast and hard and had to stifle her moan with the back of her hand. Somehow Adrienne had managed to remember they were right at the door.

Breathing heavily, Adrienne slid off Sloan's thigh and let her feet settle on the floor. Her legs were rubbery and she was light-headed. They were both breathing fast and covered in a light sheen of sweat. They didn't have to work at it and it was lightning fast, but it was one of the most powerful orgasms Adrienne had ever had.

Adrienne took Sloan's hand, led her to her bed, and proceeded to return the favor. Sloan could arouse her with just a look, but making love to Sloan never failed to incredibly turn her on.

"Hello, Adrienne." Robert's voice over the phone speaker startled Adrienne from her thoughts. She conveyed the dinner invitation, and after being put on hold for another few minutes as Robert checked with his wife, they agreed to meet at the restaurant.

Adrienne was tempted to have Ruth convey their RSVP to Sloan, but she didn't want Sloan to even begin to think she was afraid of her. She picked up the phone and dialed.

Chapter Nine

Sloan exchanged her keys for a ticket from the valet, who didn't even try to remain professional about her car. Guys will always have a thing about cars, she thought. She didn't have time to go home, but what she'd worn to work today wasn't too far out of line for dinner. She gave her name to the maître d' and was escorted to their table. Elliott was texting and put her phone in her pocket as Sloan approached.

"Just chatting with Lauren," Elliott said, with the smile she always had when talking about her wife.

"How is she?"

"She's great. She's hiring another attorney next week to help with the client load."

"That's a high-class problem to have," Sloan commented. She'd offered to help Lauren on several occasions, and they'd become friends. Even though their areas of law were vastly different, Sloan could handle the basics well enough to help out.

"Yeah," Elliott said, sipping her water. "She works more than I do sometimes."

"Makes it kind of hard to have a life, I guess." Sloan couldn't even imagine being in a relationship and working. She believed you couldn't have it all. She didn't have room for anything else.

"Some days all we can do is collapse into bed and fall asleep," Elliott said.

Sloan didn't detect even a hint of unhappiness in her statement.

Lauren had told her the story of how Elliott had chased her until Lauren let her catch her. It was nothing short of romantic, if that's what you were looking for. She wasn't, but she didn't begrudge anyone that was.

"How's your sister doing?" Elliott's sister Stephanie had recently separated from her husband Mark, and the custody battle was getting nasty. Lauren had refused to represent Stephanie but had referred her to the best divorce attorney in town.

"Okay. Mark's being an ass, which is typical, and using the kids against her. He thinks it's Lauren's fault she filed for divorce."

"But didn't he cheat on her?"

"Yes, and probably more often than the time he got caught. But he thinks that if Lauren hadn't given Stephanie the name of her lawyer, they'd still be together. Stephanie simply asked for a name. Lauren didn't push her into anything. He just can't get that through his stupid head." Elliott shook her head.

Mark had worked at Foster McKenzie for years, but when Elliott had discovered he was stealing, she fired his worthless ass. Rumor had it he was hot after Lauren as well. What a piece of work, Sloan thought.

"As far as we know, Stephanie's attorney is getting ready to file the child-support request. He's refusing to pay anything."

"How do people do that?" Sloan asked. "I don't have kids, so I wouldn't know, but even I think that since these are your kids, why wouldn't you take care of them?"

"Ask every deadbeat dad, or mom for that matter, why. Most say it's because they can't stand giving their ex money. It's usually an ugly breakup to start with." Elliott stood, her attention on something over Sloan's right shoulder.

Sloan turned in her chair and stopped breathing. Adrienne was walking toward them, and she looked fabulous. She'd obviously made it home to change, because Sloan didn't think she would wear a sleeveless red dress, a strand of pearls, and heels that made her legs look like they should be designated a national treasure to the office. She wasn't dressed provocatively or inappropriately for a business dinner, but that was also not everyday wear. Her hair was up, a few strands that had escaped framing her face. Sloan's hands twitched when she remembered how soft those strands were.

"Adrienne, Robert, thank you for coming," Elliott said.

Elliott indicated the chair to her right for Robert, putting Adrienne to Sloan's left. Robert held Adrienne's chair as she sat down. Sloan had almost reached to do that out of habit—old habit—but stopped before anyone noticed. When she sat, her knees touched Adrienne's, and Sloan looked at her. Adrienne didn't return the look but said something to Elliott. Sloan shifted slightly in her chair, breaking the contact that would ruin her concentration if not her composure.

The waiter took their drink order, and Elliott began by apologizing for the miscommunication earlier in the day. Sloan caught a whiff of Adrienne's perfume and felt a little dizzy. It was the same scent she'd had on for their first meeting and what she'd worn all those years ago. Did she really still wear it, or had she bought a bottle specifically to torment her?

Elliott and Robert kept the conversation flowing during dinner, with Adrienne and Sloan chiming in occasionally. Adrienne never spoke directly to her, but then again, she didn't ask her any questions. Elliott inquired about Adrienne's practice and her time at the DA's office.

"It was great experience. Sometimes I still shake my head at the stupid things people do and the terrible things they do to each other," Adrienne commented.

"What made you go into private practice?" Elliott asked over coffee.

"I'd been doing quite a bit of pro bono work for various nonprofit agencies and just felt like it was the right time to branch out on my own. I shared an office with another attorney for a few months until I was able to get my own, and the rest is history, as they say."

Sloan could tell Adrienne was proud of what she'd accomplished, but she was humble enough not to let her pride show.

"I understand you and Sloan went to the same college," Elliott said.

Adrienne grew pale and glanced at her. "Yes, we did."

"Did you know each other?"

It was Sloan's turn to look at Adrienne. It was a natural follow-up question, an innocent one, but Sloan knew the color had drained from her face, and she couldn't breathe. She had no idea how Adrienne would answer.

"We had a few classes together." It was a benign reply meant to end the topic, and thankfully it did.

"Did you always want to be a lawyer like Sloan here? She told me that, since she always argued with her siblings, she might as well be a lawyer."

I can answer that question, Sloan thought, but kept her mouth closed.

"No. I was accepted at the Price Art School in Italy."

"That's an excellent school," Elliott replied, obviously impressed. "How did you get from Price to the DA's office?"

"My father became ill. I came back home to help my mother."

Sloan had wondered what had happened. Adrienne had talked about her family and how close they all were. The Phillips family was the complete opposite of hers. Adrienne had four brothers and one sister; she had one of each. Adrienne's family had huge, boisterous dinners with aunts, uncles, and assorted cousins; her dinner table was quiet and subdued. Adrienne told stories of how they teased each other all the time; she fought constantly with her siblings. Adrienne's parents were warm and loving; she couldn't remember hers ever touching each other or any of their children.

"What does your wife do?" Elliott asked.

Sloan didn't want to hear about Adrienne's wife. The woman she shared her life with. The woman she shared her bed with. She looked for an easy exit but didn't see one.

"I'm not married," Adrienne said.

"I'm sorry, my mistake," Elliott replied apologetically. "I saw your ring and just assumed. My wife Lauren is always scolding me for assuming."

"It's all right," Adrienne said softly. "My wife passed away almost three years ago."

Sloan froze, her coffee cup halfway to her mouth. Adrienne's wife had died? She was a widow? The heartbreak must be unimaginable.

"I'm so sorry for your loss," Elliott replied politely. Sloan didn't say anything. She couldn't say anything.

"Thank you," Adrienne said, a flash of sadness filling her eyes before she blinked it away. "She was the one who encouraged me to leave the DA's office. She decorated my office and helped me pick out stationery and all those other wifely things."

Sloan didn't want to think about *all* the wifely things they shared.

Elliott smiled. "Yes. I know all about those things. Lauren is my better half. What I don't have, she definitely does, and she reminds me constantly where I'd be without her." The chuckles around the table eased some of the tension. Sloan still hadn't said anything.

"What did she do, if I may ask?" Elliott said carefully.

"She taught kindergarten at Fireside School for the Deaf."

"Lauren would know exactly what to say at this moment," Elliott said. "But again, I'm sorry for your loss."

Much to Sloan's relief, Elliott changed the subject, and fifty minutes later they were shaking hands and saying their good-byes at the valet stand. When Adrienne turned to her, Sloan saw the lingering pain in her eyes. The lines around her eyes and mouth were a little more pronounced, the tension evident. Sloan wanted to pull her in her arms and take away the pain, but she knew she never could. Their time for such things had passed and could never be rekindled.

CHAPTER TEN

Adrienne fingered the ring on the third finger of her left hand while she drove home. She'd been afraid the wife question would come up. It often did because she couldn't bring herself to stop wearing her wedding ring. She'd tried several times, but her bare finger was almost worse than the emptiness in her heart. She supposed someday she'd move it to her other hand and ultimately put it away for Callie, but she wasn't in any hurry. When she had thanked Elliott for her sympathy and said that it was all right, that was a lie she had practiced to perfection. It would never be all right.

Adrienne was impressed with Elliott's directness in asking about Brenna. Too many people didn't know what to say so they said nothing, pretending Brenna never existed. When she had named Brenna's school she'd seen a flicker of recollection flash across Elliott's face. It was an expression she was familiar with. Brenna's death had made the local and national news and had stayed front and center for a week. People usually didn't remember the particulars, but they did remember the name of the school. The pain had lessened a bit, but it was a day she would never forget.

She was working on a motion when her phone rang. The caller ID showed it to be her mother, and Adrienne picked up on the second ring. Callie was with her mother today, Brenna's first day back at work after her maternity leave.

"Hi, Mom. How's everything going?" Adrienne asked, looking at the framed photo of her daughter on her desk.

"Adrienne, turn on channel fifteen. There's been a shooting at Fireside."

Adrienne looked at the phone, not certain she'd heard her mother correctly. "What?"

"Turn on channel fifteen. There's been a shooting at Fireside." Her mother sounded more agitated this time.

Adrienne's heart pounded, and her hands began to tremble. "Brenna." She stood and crossed the room and turned on the TV. Her legs felt like rubber, and she sat down in one of the chairs in front of the big screen. She didn't have to turn the channel; the story was on all of them.

Adrienne stared at the TV, searching every inch looking for any sign of Brenna. The voice of the commentator echoed in her brain.

"To recap, this morning at nine fifty-three, a gunman opened fire inside Fireside School for the Deaf. Police have not commented on how he entered the building, but we do know that several have been injured. It is unknown at this time if the injured are students or school employees. Officials at the scene say that the 911 call came in at nine fifty-five, with officers arriving within four minutes. Fireside is two blocks from our station here on Georgia Avenue, and our reporter Megan Hughes is on the scene. Megan, what updates can you give us?"

"Thank you, Beverly. Several ambulances and paramedics are in the building, but we haven't seen anyone come out yet. We don't know if that means there are no injuries, but one officer at the scene told me the gunman was in custody."

Adrienne grabbed her bag and her keys and started to run out the door. Two officers barely out of the academy stopped her just inside her office. They were there to escort her to the command center a block from the school. She was in a fog, sick with worry about Brenna. She'd called her phone every minute, and her worry grew each time it went directly to voice mail.

Whether it was protocol or they simply didn't know anything, the two men didn't say a word, and the ride across town took a lifetime. Adrienne scanned her phone for any news whatsoever and checked her ring tone several times, double-checking to make sure she hadn't missed a call from Brenna. She phoned her mother.

"Mom." Her voice was shaky, and she took a breath to regain some control. She didn't need her mother to be any more upset than she probably already was.

"Adrienne, have you heard from Brenna?"

"No. Two police officers are taking me to the command center. I don't know anything at this point other than what was on the news." She and her mother exchanged a few more words before Adrienne ended the conversation by saying, "Give Callie a kiss for me."

It was ordered chaos at the command center when Adrienne walked in. The police had occupied the vacant retail space in a small strip mall no more than fifty yards from the school. The officers escorted her to a small office in a corner of the large, empty room. Two women with badges and guns on their waist were in the room, along with Jane Reeds, the principal at Fireside.

"Mrs. Stewart, I'm Detective Donovan and this is Detective Klein," the taller of the two women said.

Adrienne ignored the introductions, panic starting to rise even faster at the delay. "Where's Brenna? My wife. Is she okay?" Adrienne instantly knew she wasn't when Detective Klein offered her a chair.

"I don't want to sit down. Where's Brenna?"

"Mrs. Stewart, please sit," Detective Donovan said gently.

Obviously they weren't going to tell her anything until she did what they suggested. "Where's Brenna?" She looked back and forth between the detectives and Jane, the answer clear on the woman's face.

"Mrs. Stewart, I'm sorry to tell you that your wife was killed during the shooting."

"What?" Adrienne had heard the detective the first time and didn't need or want her to repeat it. The words I'm sorry, killed, *and* shooting *echoed in her brain, and a crushing weight squeezed the breath out of her. The room began to spin.*

The first year after Brenna died was a blur. Her family was beside her, but only Adrienne could identify her body in the morgue. And then there were the funeral arrangements with flowers, music, note cards, and a viewing. Adrienne was grateful she and Brenna had talked about what arrangements they wanted; that unknown would have been absolutely unbearable. And she had a thirteen-week-old infant to take care of.

The plan had been that Adrienne's mother would watch Callie during the day, using the breast milk Brenna had provided the day before, but when Brenna died, Adrienne had to switch her to formula. The first few days Callie would barely eat, and when she did she threw up the milk within a few minutes. If it wasn't coming out of that end, it was the other, and Adrienne lost track of the number of diapers she went through that first few weeks.

Maria stepped in as much as Adrienne would let her, but not only was Callie her connection to Brenna, she also needed her as a reason to get up in the morning. Without her daughter, Adrienne would have probably stayed curled up in a ball under the covers. As it was, she moved Callie's crib out of the bedroom she and Brenna shared and into the guest room where they both slept, or tried to sleep, for the next eight months. Finally, Adrienne admitted that she couldn't live in a house filled with Brenna's memories. She sold it, and she and Callie now lived around the corner from her parents.

Most, but not all, of the anger had passed. She'd been angry at God for taking Brenna away from her and Callie. Angry at Brenna for going to work that day instead of staying home longer, angry at Brenna for her actions that day. They could afford for Brenna to stay home, but she loved her class, and as much as she loved taking care of Callie, she was anxious to return to her twelve kindergarteners.

Brenna had been at Fireside for eleven years. She glowed when she talked about each milestone her students achieved. On the first day of school, most of her class couldn't even write their own names, and by the last day they were reading.

Adrienne had yet to relinquish the anger that Callie would never know the woman who gave birth to her, hear her laugh, feel her arms around her, or know that her mother loved her more than life itself. She still struggled at times with the fact that the woman she'd been planning to spend the rest of her life with was gone—in an instant. Because of a man with a gun and a school full of children. Adrienne had felt nothing when Detective Donovan informed her the shooter had been killed in prison two weeks ago.

According to the police report, the gunman had come in just after class started that Monday morning. He broke through the exterior door just as the last of Brenna's students rounded the corner at the end of the hall. They had been walking behind Brenna like little ducklings, and when she saw the man she charged him. She was able to push him backward into the door before he shot her. She died instantly. The gunman fell back, hitting his head on the cement and stunning him enough for another teacher to grab the gun. Brenna was a hero.

Adrienne didn't care that the man was sentenced to life in prison or that Brenna was a hero. She didn't care that articles were written touting Brenna's commitment to her students, how her quick response had saved countless lives, or that she was posthumously named the national teacher of the year. Brenna was dead, and that was all that mattered.

Adrienne knew the stages of grief weren't linear. It wasn't as though you passed through one and then moved on to the next. Grief came in waves, often when she least expected it. She'd be mowing the lawn, and tears would be falling down her cheeks. She was in the middle of aisle five in the grocery store one day when she completely fell apart, as if she'd just been notified of Brenna's death. And more often than not when Callie was asleep in her arms, Adrienne missed Brenna the most.

Both Maria and Brenna's mother tried to convince Adrienne that her anger toward the gunman wasn't allowing her to move on, that forgiveness would allow her to heal. How was she supposed to forgive a man who'd ripped her heart out? Who'd left a child without her mother? The women meant well, but Adrienne would never *move on*. She'd put one foot in front of the other and breathe one more time, she would never forgive him.

Her hands were still trembling as she pulled into the driveway of her parents' home. Her father's truck was parked in its usual place, and the lights on either side of the garage door were burning brightly. She turned off the ignition and sat for a few minutes. Between seeing Sloan again and Elliott's innocent question, she was a wreck. She took several deep breaths before opening the car door.

Chapter Eleven

Sloan skimmed the Google results until she hit on an article that froze her fingers over the keyboard. A knot in the pit of her stomach formed and grew bigger as she read the article, then another, and another, and several more. She ached for Adrienne and the pain she must have experienced when her wife was killed. And to be left with a baby. Holy shit. Sloan scanned the articles again and found no mention of the child's name. All the news accounts simply referred to her as the thirteen-week-old daughter of Brenna Stewart.

Sloan finally had to shut her laptop and get up from her desk. She wandered around her apartment looking but not really seeing anything. She stepped out onto the balcony. *Adrienne is a widow. Adrienne is a mother.* She repeated both sentences in her head several times, as if saying them one more time would make those facts real. She did some quick math in her head. The child would be about three by now. Did Adrienne see her wife every time she looked at her daughter? Who was the father? Was he involved in the child's life, or had they used some anonymous donor? How had they picked him? Did you just walk into a sperm bank, choose somebody out of a book, and thirty minutes later walk out pregnant? Was it someone they knew? How did that work? Did they just ask some guy they knew if he wanted to donate?

"Jesus, Sloan, stop it," she said to the night sky. "Stop focusing on how the baby was made and on the fact that Adrienne is a widow.

Think about how much she's gone through." She was still having a hard time reconciling that Adrienne was married and now that she was a widow—and a mother. Could this week get any more mind-blowing?

She and Adrienne had never talked about children, but then again they hadn't talked at all about their future. Looking back on it, Sloan realized that they both somehow had known they would go their separate ways after they graduated. It wouldn't be due to geography but something other than that. They came from two very different places, and they had different dreams. Sloan never saw Adrienne by her side as she climbed the corporate ladder. She didn't see anyone by her side on the rungs of success. And she certainly wasn't moving to Europe. It had to end, and they both had known it.

She'd thought about Adrienne occasionally through the years, especially when she went into an art gallery or watched any movie starring Humphrey Bogart. The first movie they'd watched together was *The African Queen*, and it was still one of her favorites. She'd assumed Adrienne had found someone, or many someones, for that matter. She was more than a little attractive, and her smile could light up any dark place. She often wondered if she was happy or even alive. She never Googled her or searched for her on Facebook. That part of her life was over.

Sloan wondered what kind of woman Brenna Stewart was. She had to have been someone special to capture Adrienne's attention and her heart. She had to be kind and funny, smart and passionate about life. And, my God, she'd have to like having Adrienne's family involved in their lives. Did they all get along? Did they have family barbecues and birthday parties? Did they accept Brenna's daughter as a member of the family? Did Brenna make Adrienne happy? Did Adrienne introduce Brenna to Bogart and *I Love Lucy*? Did they fight and then have make-up sex? Did Brenna learn that Adrienne was ticklish behind her knees and that kisses on her palm made her absolutely crazy? Did Brenna kiss her… *Ugh. Stop!*

Sloan made several circuits around her apartment trying to erase the image of Adrienne, her head on the pillow, back arched, and Brenna's mouth between her legs. She was sure Adrienne had other lovers after her, but the thought of her making a commitment to another woman, taking a wife, was something altogether different. It was as if it were the final period of their ending. But that was years ago. So why was it still so painful?

Sloan didn't sleep much that night, tossing and turning, her head full of the evening's conversation and her subsequent web search. When she did doze off, images of Adrienne, Brenna, and a toddler filled her dreams. At 5:15 she finally gave up and got in the shower.

Sloan debated with herself all morning before finally making a decision. She had no idea if it was the right one, but when the woman on the other end of the phone answered, it was too late to change her mind. "May I speak with Adrienne, please? This is Sloan Merchant."

"Yes, Ms. Merchant," the woman said cheerfully. "Let me see if she can take your call. One moment, please."

Sloan mangled three paperclips waiting for Adrienne to come to the phone. When she heard her voice, she forgot everything she was going to say.

"Sloan?"

"Yes, uh, hi…" God. She sounded like a teenager again, asking a girl to the movies.

"Is there something I can do for you?" Adrienne said after a prolonged silence.

"Yes…uh…no. What I mean is my sympathies to you on the loss of your wife." There. She'd said it. She still wasn't sure if she should have called. This made it personal, and she needed to keep it professional. Then why in the hell did she call?

"Thank you," Adrienne said hesitantly.

"I just…I thought because we…"

"Thank you, Sloan. I appreciate it." Adrienne's voice sounded different this time, more personal than professional. Or maybe it was her imagination, or wishful thinking. Another long pause.

"Was there something else you wanted to talk about?" Adrienne asked politely.

"Um, no…um…That's all I wanted to say." For someone who

had been tongue-tied a minute ago, she suddenly didn't want to hang up. "It was rude of me for not saying so last night."

"Okay," Adrienne said. "Thank you for calling, Sloan."

The dial tone in her ear signaled the call was over, and Sloan dropped the receiver back in its cradle and fell back in her chair. Her hands were shaking, her heart racing faster than it should have been after making a simple condolence call to an old friend. But they were more than just old friends. Her reactions since seeing Adrienne again confused her. She couldn't focus on her work, and her mind and body kept remembering how it was when they were together. She had to get a grip.

Elliott stopped by later that morning when she was daydreaming out the window.

"Lauren wants you to come to dinner tomorrow night. She's cooking spaghetti, and she always fixes enough for a small army." Elliott sat in the chair across from Sloan. "She said she hasn't seen you in ages."

"I've been busy."

"And Lauren will definitely give you the third degree about that too."

"Your wife thinks everyone should be coupled up and married."

"Yes, she does, and she won't be happy until you are."

"Then you're going to have to unfriend me, because she's never going to be happy with me."

"Never?" Elliott asked, raising her eyebrows.

"Never."

"You don't see yourself settling down? I don't mean right away, but eventually?"

"Nope." Sloan was confident in her answer. She enjoyed her life. She enjoyed not having to answer to anyone, let them know she was going to be late or consult them if she wanted to buy a new car. If she wanted to eat a bowl of cereal in her underwear for dinner and drink orange juice right out of the container, she could. She liked leaving her hair gel and toothpaste out on the bathroom counter and tossing her clothes onto a chair when she got home from work. She couldn't remember the last time she put away the ironing board.

"Well, don't be mad at me when she keeps trying." Elliott rose from the chair. "Seven o'clock, and don't be late. You know how she hates for people to be late for dinner."

Sloan did know. She'd suffered the consequences once, and only once, and was always on time after that. For a petite woman, Lauren could wield a very big stick.

"What have you been doing with yourself, Sloan?" Lauren asked the next night, handing Sloan a basket of warm garlic bread from across the table.

"A little of this, a little of that," Sloan replied vaguely, and Lauren gave her that look—the one that said stop bullshitting me. "Really, nothing special. I go to work and the gym and play basketball twice a week."

"Are you training for another Ironman?"

Sloan had competed in several of the grueling events over the past year. Swimming was her weakest of the three events, followed by bicycling and her strongest, running. "Yes. The one in LA is in six weeks, and I'm working hard to be ready."

"What's your personal best?" Elliott asked, referring to the total time it took Sloan to complete all three events.

"Five hours, fifty-five minutes, and a few seconds."

"How far is each event? I keep forgetting," Lauren asked.

"It's a two-point-four-mile swim, a hundred and twelve miles on the bike, and a full marathon." Sloan had trained for almost a year before her first Ironman, finishing in just under six hours. That was three years, nine races, and one Ironman tattoo ago.

"Just hearing you talk about it exhausts me," Lauren said, chuckling. They ate in comfortable silence before Lauren spoke again. "Are you seeing anyone?"

Sloan saw Elliott hide a smile behind her glass of wine. She'd expected the question. Lauren never didn't ask. "No one special."

"Are you seeing any *one*?" Lauren emphasized the word.

"Lauren, honey, leave Sloan alone," Elliott said fondly, scolding her.

"I will not. I'm concerned about her."

Sloan chuckled. "I appreciate that, Lauren, but I'm fine. My life is right where I want it to be."

"That's okay, but what about tomorrow?"

"Tomorrow?" Sloan wracked her mind, thinking of what she might have forgotten about tomorrow.

"Yes, tomorrow. And the next day and the day after that? Who are you going to share your life with? Grow old with?"

"Lauren, Sloan is a grown woman and a very smart one. I think she can figure it out on her own."

"Thank you, Elliott. I appreciate it, and I appreciate your concern, Lauren. I do. But I'm happy with what I have in my life, the women in my life," she added. "If I ever need anything else, I'll be sure to go after it."

Later that evening, after Sloan had left, Elliott was untying her shoes when Lauren said, "I think you were that stubborn when I met you."

"I was not," she replied, placing her shoes on the shelf in her closet.

"Yes, you were. You just didn't know it."

Elliott stepped into their bedroom, ready to dispute her wife's opinion. "I was…" Her words stopped at the sight of Lauren in a very short, very transparent nightgown she'd never seen. "I…uh…" Elliott stammered as Lauren stepped closer.

After four years together, Lauren could still take her breath away, and she always would. She wasn't looking for a girlfriend or even a date when she met Lauren. She hadn't realized at that time, or for quite some time later, that she had met the woman she didn't know she'd been looking for. Their love was strong, exciting, and most definitely passionate. And now she recognized the look in Lauren's eyes. Lauren walked toward her, and her pulse kicked up a notch.

Lauren stopped just as their breasts touched. Elliott breathed in the familiar scent. It reminded her of everything that was Lauren—bold, challenging, and desirable. Her breathing picked up speed.

Lauren unbuckled Elliott's belt and slowly slid the leather out through the loops, held it up like a prized possession for her to see, then let it drop to the floor. Elliott never would have guessed that taking off a belt could be arousing. Lauren unbuttoned Elliott's shirt, starting at the top and working her way down, exposing her skin to the cool evening air. Elliott's nipples hardened in anticipation of what was to come. She wanted to take Lauren in her arms and kiss her, feel her body pressed against hers, but somehow she knew this was Lauren's show.

Lauren slid her shirt off her shoulders, and her hands followed the sleeves down her arms. Elliott's skin was on fire where Lauren touched her, and her knees trembled. Lauren was a master of seduction and excelled at foreplay to the point that by the time she finally touched her, Elliott was ready to explode. She took several deep breaths but almost choked on them when Lauren ran the tip of one finger down the center of her chest.

Lauren hadn't broken eye contact from the moment she stopped in front of her, an action that Elliott found incredibly sensual. Lauren was using it right now to get what she wanted, and Elliott was definitely not going to complain. What Lauren wanted, she got.

The pop of the snap on her pants, followed by the sound of the zipper descending, was like music building to a crescendo. Lauren put her thumbs in the waistband of the pants, pushing them down past her hips. Gravity took care of the rest. Lauren slid her palms inside her briefs and around to her ass, and Elliott stifled a gasp when Lauren slid the last garment off. Elliott wasn't sure how much longer she could remain upright. Her head was spinning, her heart hammering, and her clit was demanding attention. She stood there naked, practically quivering with the need to be touched as Lauren's eyes traveled slowly down her body and back up again. Their eyes locked, and Lauren's were burning with desire.

"You are so beautiful," Lauren said, her breath almost a whisper. Elliott knew Lauren was as aroused as she was. This evening was going to be special. Every time they made love was, of course, special, but something about this time was more intense and intimate, and Elliott could hardly wait to touch her.

"You're making me crazy, Lauren. I'll go out of my mind if you don't touch me."

Lauren indulged in another long, hot look at Elliott before she took her hand and led her to their bed. She motioned for Elliott to lie down, and the throbbing in her clit beat harder. Lauren straddled her lap, sitting just below Elliott's belly. She didn't move to lie on top of her, instead running her hands over her own stomach and breasts. Elliott stopped breathing as she watched, mesmerized.

Lauren wasn't wearing anything under her nightgown, and Elliott could feel her warm, wet center. With each pass of Lauren's hands the gown slid upward, giving Elliott a glimpse of Lauren's dark pubic hair. Lauren's nipples grew harder, clearly evident under the thin, silk fabric. Elliott swallowed several times and clenched her fists together to keep from replacing Lauren's hands with hers.

Slowly Lauren moved against her, her wetness coating Elliott's stomach. Elliott gripped the sheets as Lauren slid her gown up and over her head and tossed it to the floor. Lauren arched her back, her breasts rising like those of a goddess to be worshipped. Lauren tipped her head back and slowly slid her hands up her stomach and cupped her breasts. She flicked her nipples.

"Jesus, Lauren. You're making me lose my mind," Elliott hissed between clenched teeth.

Lauren looked at her and smiled. "You'd better not, because I want you to remember this."

Like there was any chance Elliott would forget *this*.

Elliott felt Lauren's clit harden as she rubbed against her, tweaking her nipples at the same time. Lauren controlled the tempo, while Elliott was helpless to do anything other than stare and watch the woman she loved please herself. Lauren knew how much that drove Elliott crazy and was doing it for her. Elliott's heart swelled with more love than she thought possible. Faster and faster Lauren moved, and Elliott's own orgasm was imminent. In this moment Lauren was breathtakingly beautiful. Her skin was flushed, her breathing ragged, and Elliott's name was on her lips. Finally, after Elliott didn't know how much more she could take, Lauren shouted her name as she climaxed.

Elliott sat up, pulled Lauren into her arms, and turned her onto her back. She buried her face in Lauren's wetness, tasting her, feeling her, taking her over the top a second and a third time.

"Oh my God," Lauren said breathlessly a few minutes later. Elliott hadn't moved but a few inches, the view of Lauren's glistening desire irresistible. "How does it keep getting better and better between us?"

Elliott couldn't answer the same question she was asking herself.

Lauren tapped her chest. "Come here."

Elliott didn't want to leave her favorite spot but wanted to feel Lauren's arms around her. She kissed her way to Lauren's mouth, surprised at the desire with which Lauren kissed her.

Lauren kissed her again so hard it took her breath away. "This is for you."

Lauren trailed hot kisses down her neck and across her breasts. She circled each one completely before taking a nipple into her mouth. Elliott fought back her own orgasm. "I thought what you just did was for me."

Lauren chuckled and slid her hand down Elliott's stomach and into her. Elliott gasped with pleasure and didn't hold back her climax this time. She groaned and arched her back as fireworks shot through her. She exploded, every nerve ending experiencing maximum sensation. A kaleidoscope of colors darted across her eyelids, each image more beautiful than the one before. She couldn't breathe, didn't want to breathe for fear this moment would end. Finally, her body took over her mind, and she slowly started to descend back to earth. She fell asleep floating in Lauren's arms.

Chapter Twelve

The next few meetings were more relaxed than the first one. Their dinner and subsequent conversations had given Elliott a chance to get to know her and Robert personally, not just as business associates. In her research, Adrienne had read that Elliott was far more likely to invest in the person and their vision instead of the pure financials of the deal. She'd briefed Robert on this point and had been pleased when he referred to something personal in their conversations. Adrienne had kept her personal comments carefully scripted. She didn't know if Sloan would grab any morsel of information or ignore it altogether.

"I'd like to see your operation," Elliott said.

Adrienne had expected the request, and Auburn was ready. They ran a clean, safe operation at all times, so it really didn't matter if Elliott showed up in thirty days or thirty minutes. The result would still be the same.

"Absolutely," Robert replied, his eyes sparkling. "We wouldn't want your investment without it. We run a tight ship, and we're proud of our reputation for integrity in everything we do."

Elliott turned to her. "What would work for you, Adrienne? We don't want any special treatment. But I would like to see your R and D center and talk to a few people."

"Certainly. You can talk to whomever you please. Everyone is a representative of Auburn."

The surprise on Elliott's face confirmed that she didn't expect to have carte blanche to talk to any employee. It was typical for the company to select their best and brightest to put in front of VIPs. Adrienne knew most of the employees and would put anyone, including the janitorial staff, on the hot seat anytime.

Elliott looked at her phone and tapped a few screens. "How about the week of the seventeenth?"

Adrienne and Robert did the same. "Our research-and-development operations are in Portland, and manufacturing is just outside Augusta, Georgia."

"We'll fly into Portland Monday morning, then on to Augusta on Wednesday."

Adrienne's stomach flipped when it became apparent that the "we" included Sloan. It tumbled again at the thought that she'd be spending at least five days with her and away from Callie.

Robert supported her work-life balance mandate, which limited her out-of-town travel to no more than two nights in a row and not more than twice a month. If it was any longer, she didn't go. She nodded her acceptance when Robert looked at her questioningly. Relief flooded his face.

"I'll have Ruth work out the details," Adrienne said, making a note in her phone.

Sloan hadn't said much during the meeting, but that didn't mean she wasn't completely aware of every word that had been spoken and the agreed-upon visit. Adrienne had felt her eyes on her most of the meeting, and she was glad she'd taken extra care getting ready this morning. She wasn't vain—raising a toddler saw to that—but she felt more confident when she was completely put together. Thanks to her parents taking Callie to the park yesterday, Adrienne had a fresh haircut and even managed to squeeze in a facial and a manicure.

Elliott glanced at her Brietling watch, stood, and pushed her chair away from the table. "Lunch should be ready. Sloan, will you take Adrienne on down? I want to talk with Robert about something. We'll be just a few minutes," Elliott said, already turning her back to them.

Sloan's heart raced even faster than it had been before the meeting started. The last thing she wanted was to be left alone with Adrienne, and the absolute last thing her nerves could handle was to be in an elevator with her. But unless she wanted to look ridiculous, she had no choice.

The anxiety-producing ding signaled the elevator had arrived. The doors opened, and Sloan didn't know if it was a good thing or a bad thing that the car was empty. She gestured for Adrienne to step inside, which she did without hesitation. Sloan, however, took a deep breath before she entered. *I can do this, I can do this. I have to do this.*

Her hand trembled when she pushed the button to the lobby. Her heart was beating so loud Adrienne had to be able to hear it. When the car hesitated, then began to descend, she squeezed her fists together and focused on the red numbers, counting down from twelve.

Neither of them said anything during the awkward silence. Sloan's throat was so tight she couldn't. The elevator jerked, then stopped. Sloan fought back instant panic.

"Did we stop?" Adrienne asked, looking at the numbers on the bank of floor numbers.

Sloan concentrated on her breathing. Was she breathing? She wasn't sure because she was light-headed. At least the lights were still on.

"Sloan?" Adrienne's voice penetrated her terror.

Sloan summoned whatever she had somewhere to reply. "I think so."

"Does this happen often?"

"I don't know. I take the stairs," Sloan added. *Inhale, exhale, inhale.*

"You take the stairs? Twelve flights?"

"Good exercise," she somehow managed to say.

Adrienne looked at her questioningly. "You don't like elevators, do you?" she asked, assessing the situation correctly.

"Not particularly." That was an understatement, to say the least.

"Since when?"

This was the first time either one of them had mentioned their past. But then again, they hadn't been alone together for years.

"Since I got stuck in one for three hours and nine minutes."

Adrienne looked at her for a few seconds before stepping in front of the control panel. "There should be an emergency call button somewhere here."

A bell started clanging when Adrienne pushed a red button, jarring Sloan's already frazzled nerves. Instead of freaking out, she concentrated on the round buttons on the panel, the sign that informed the occupants the location of the safety inspection, the maximum car capacity, the sixteen and one-quarter tiles on the floor, the dirty grout, the eight lights in the ceiling, and the missing screw in the handrail. A voice came through the speaker at Sloan's eye level.

"Hello, this is the security desk. Is everyone all right?"

The inside of the doors was mirrored, and Sloan saw Adrienne look at her as if judging how to answer the question. Sloan answered it for her. "Yes, we're fine." She pinned Adrienne with a look that said, *Don't even think about answering otherwise*.

"Okay," the anonymous voice replied. "We've called building maintenance. They're on the way. They should have you out of there in just a few minutes."

To Sloan, a few minutes was a few months too long. She concentrated on her breathing and tried not to look at Adrienne or her reflection.

"How long have you worked for Foster McKenzie?" Adrienne asked, her voice breaking the suffocating silence.

"Um…four years." Sloan hoped her voice was steady.

"Where were you before then? Another big corporate job?"

"I was counsel for a company in Little Rock."

"How did you get here?"

Sloan appreciated the questions. They helped keep her main focus off the fact that she was stuck in an elevator. "I was at a conference, and Elliott was one of the speakers. I asked a few questions, we had dinner, and—" Sloan held her hands up, waist high and palms out—"here I am."

"I hear Elliott is a great person to work for," Adrienne said, leaning against the back wall and crossing her feet at her ankles. Sloan hadn't moved from standing rigidly in front of the control panel.

"Yes, she's tough but fair and very smart."

Adrienne didn't ask any more questions for several minutes, which, to Sloan, felt like hours. When she looked at her, Adrienne was scrolling through something on her phone.

"Can you get a signal?" Sloan asked.

"Yes. I'm just checking my email. Might as well do something productive while we're stuck in here."

Sloan thought about doing the same, but she didn't want to give away the fact that her hands were shaking so bad she wouldn't be able to see the screen.

"At least we know each other. Can you imagine how awkward it would be if we were total strangers?"

Actually, Sloan thought it would be much better if Adrienne were a total stranger, at least for her. She could freak out and not have to worry about ruining her reputation or embarrassing herself in front of people she'd have to look at tomorrow. She remembered reading a book about how two strangers had passed the time in their stuck elevator. If this were another time, she and Adrienne would certainly find something to occupy their time. That thought made her skin hotter than it already was.

"Aren't we, though?" Adrienne asked quietly.

Sloan thought about her answer. She could agree, or she could say that she knew how Adrienne liked her eggs, how she loved to stay up late and watch B movies, go to baseball games, and put two sugars in her coffee and three in her iced tea. Or she could say that she knew that Adrienne liked to make love on lazy Sunday mornings and make out at the drive-in like a teenager. She could say all of that but didn't. "I suppose we are."

Another ten minutes passed, and Sloan was surprised she

hadn't lost control. She was more relaxed than she thought she'd be. She'd expected she'd be pacing back and forth in the small space or trying to escape out the ceiling. But that idea was foolish; it only happened like that in the movies.

"How are your parents?" Sloan asked, surprised at her own question.

Adrienne was keying something in on her phone, and her head shot up, their eyes locking. She frowned like she always did when she was thinking. Finally, she answered. "They're well, thank you."

"If I asked about the rest of your family, we'd be here all day," Sloan said, chuckling. She'd never met anyone in Adrienne's family but had heard enough stories to feel like she knew them. She, on the other hand, didn't have much to say about hers.

"It's not like we're going anywhere," Adrienne commented.

Sloan didn't know if that was an invitation for more conversation or an observation. She wasn't up to the former, so she stuck with the latter. Her phone vibrated in her pocket, and she almost didn't notice it. She glanced at the caller ID before hitting the answer button. She had no choice.

"Hey, Elliott."

"Where are you?" Elliott asked.

Sloan glanced up at the number that hadn't moved in thirteen minutes. "Between the eighth and ninth floor. We're stuck in the elevator." Sloan was surprised her voice was as calm as it was. Sloan had never confided to Elliott, or anyone for that matter, about her phobia. To her it was a sign of weakness, and she would certainly never tell her boss.

"How long have you been in there?"

Sloan looked at her watch. "About fifteen minutes," give or take a lifetime, she thought. "Maintenance is on the way. We'll be fine," she added. She and Elliott exchanged a few more words before she hung up. She turned to Adrienne and found her staring at her.

Adrienne studied Sloan and knew she was nervous because she was doing that thing with her fingers again. Sloan hadn't said as much, but it was obvious. At least to her it was, and even though it was painful to watch, it was interesting. Sloan had always been in control, never afraid of anything, sometimes so much Adrienne wasn't sure she felt anything. But she was anxious and nervous now, much more so than in their previous meetings. At first she thought it was because they were going to be together alone, but now it was clear she was trying valiantly not to panic.

When the car had first stopped, she herself was nervous, but not for the same reason Sloan was. If they were stuck for some time, what would they talk about? Would they discuss this deal, the weather, or global warning? Or since they weren't going anywhere, would they talk about the things they'd done when they were together? They knew too much about each other to say absolutely nothing. She'd been more than a little surprised when Sloan had asked about her parents. That was personal, and they'd both done an excellent job of keeping these interactions anything but.

She'd sent a few emails and a text to her mother, telling her she was stuck in an elevator with Sloan. Maria didn't know who Sloan was other than the attorney for Foster McKenzie. She might have to tell her mother someday, but not now. Her mother answered with a picture of Callie, and she couldn't help but smile.

"Feel free to share," Sloan said, the tension lines around her mouth more noticeable.

"My mom sent me a picture of Callie stuffing pretzels in her mouth," she said, smiling again.

"Callie?"

"My daughter." Did Sloan not know about her daughter? Surely by now she'd Googled her and unearthed all the grisly details.

Sloan nodded. "I didn't know her name."

She *had* Googled her. Adrienne looked at Sloan closely for any signs of pity, curiosity, or sympathy and saw none. Adrienne didn't know if she was relieved or disappointed. She waited for the typical follow-up questions, surprised when none came. I guess Sloan isn't interested enough to ask, she thought.

Tired of standing, Adrienne tore several sheets of paper from her legal pad and laid them on the floor. "I'm going to sit down," she said before dropping to the floor. She was thankful she'd worn pants today. "Care to join me?"

A look of panic crossed over Sloan's face before she answered. "No, thanks. I'm fine."

Adrienne knew she was lying but didn't call her on it. This wasn't the place, and it really wasn't her business—anymore. At one time, it had been, but not today, not for a very long time.

Adrienne's phone rang, and she had a brief conversation with Ruth and asked her to reschedule her afternoon. She had no idea how long they'd be in here and didn't want to leave someone sitting in her offices waiting for her. She pulled out her legal pad again, this time making a grocery list on the yellow paper. On the right side, she started writing down names of those who would be attending her mother's birthday party next month. Flipping the page, she started making notes for briefs on several of the cases she was currently working. Sloan continued to fidget.

She heard voices in the elevator shaft above them, and the guard checked in a few times through the intercom. Finally, after fifty minutes, the elevator jerked and continued its descent. Sloan's relief was more than obvious, and she offered her hand to Adrienne to help her up off the floor. Adrienne hesitated before taking it, remembering the spark that shot up and down her spine every other time they'd touched.

As she stood, Sloan stepped closer to get better leverage to help her. When she stood, their faces were only inches apart, their hands still clutched together. The tension in the car ratcheted up more than she thought possible. Their eyes locked, and Adrienne saw the familiar dark ring around Sloan's pupils and the kaleidoscope of colors in her irises. Memories flooded her senses, and Adrienne saw desire flare in Sloan's eyes. Out of habit, or pure instinct, she shifted her eyes to Sloan's lips. They were as full and sensuous as she remembered, and when Sloan's tongue peeked out and wet them, Adrienne swayed toward her.

Chapter Thirteen

The doors slid open, and Adrienne jumped back so fast her head hit the wall with a thud. Stars danced in front of her eyes, and she knew they weren't associated with love.

"Are you two okay?"

Elliott was standing just outside, concern in her voice and on her face. Adrienne felt flushed and used the excuse of picking up her papers and briefcase to avoid any further eye contact with her. Sloan practically sprinted out of the open doors, and Adrienne wondered if it was to get away from her and what had almost happened.

What had she almost done? She was about to kiss Sloan; that's what had almost happened. Adrienne chastised herself. *What in the hell was I thinking? She's a business associate.* Adrienne needed to get out of there. No way could she sit across the table from Sloan and pretend she hadn't been an instant from kissing her. But she hadn't, Adrienne reminded herself. Yet if the doors hadn't opened at that moment…

"Adrienne?" Elliott asked when she didn't answer her question.

"Yes, I'm fine, but I think I'll take a rain check on lunch. I don't have much of an appetite anymore." It was the truth, as well as a plausible excuse, and Elliott didn't try to change her mind. Even though she had nothing to do with it, Elliott apologized for the elevator malfunction. The only thing she saw from Sloan was her retreating back as she quickly turned the corner.

"Did you freak out?" her friend Char asked Adrienne several

hours later. She'd called Char on her way back to the office, needing a drink for more reasons than she wanted to admit.

"No, but I can't say the same for Sloan."

"What did she do?" Char was sitting on the edge of her chair, her knee bouncing up and down. Char was always in motion, which was why she probably weighed in at one hundred pounds on her five-foot-four-inch frame. Her thick brown hair probably accounted for ten of those pounds.

Adrienne hesitated and took a sip of her cocktail before answering. "Nothing really. She just said she hated elevators and always used the stairs." For some reason, Adrienne felt protective of Sloan's obvious fear and anxiety.

"What did you all talk about?"

"Not much," Adrienne said vaguely.

"I guess if you don't know the person, what would you talk about?" Char commented.

"Actually, I do know her. Or at least I did."

Char's head turned so fast Adrienne thought she was possessed. "You know her?"

Adrienne knew that tone actually said, *and you had better tell me everything*. "We knew each other in college."

Char waved her hand in a circular motion, indicating for her to keep talking.

"We dated in college."

This time Char looked at her, clearly exasperated. "You might as well tell me everything because you know I'll drag it out of you before the night's over. So, save us both from a forty-questions-and-answers session, and spill." Char settled back in her seat.

Adrienne proceeded to do just that, but only the CliffsNotes version. She glossed over how it had ended. She didn't have all night to get into every detail, however much Char begged. She had to pick up Callie from her mother's.

"And she hasn't said anything about it?"

Adrienne shook her head.

"Not even when you were stuck in the elevator?"

She shook her head again but added, "But neither have I."

"Wow, that must have been awkward."

"That's one way to describe it."

Char looked at her again, this time sarcastically. "What is another way?"

"What do you mean?" Adrienne asked, trying to gain some time to think.

"What else happened in that elevator? And before you make up some flimsy denial, remember, I am your BFF and I know you better than you think I do."

Unfortunately, Adrienne had admitted to herself years ago, that was true. There was no way out of this unless she got an emergency call from her mother about Callie. "I almost kissed her." Her voice was so low she wasn't sure she'd said the words.

Char's expression told her otherwise. "You what?"

"You heard me."

"I thought you said you two hadn't talked about it? Oh, that's right," she said sarcastically, "kissing *is* a form of communication."

"Shut up, Char," Adrienne said much too harshly. Char didn't deserve to be snapped at. Adrienne reached over and laid her hand on Char's arm. "Sorry. I didn't mean to bite your head off."

"What is going on, Adrienne?"

"Nothing. I mean it. Nothing is going on," she added to help dispel Char's disbelieving expression. "It was just, I don't know… the moment…maybe it was habit. But it is not going to happen again."

"Why not?"

"Why not?" Adrienne asked incredulously.

"Yeah, why not? I mean this deal will be over in a few weeks, so why not?" Char asked.

If it were only that simple, Adrienne thought. "I can't start up with Sloan."

"Again, I ask, why not?"

"Because we're history. I have a child. And we have a business relationship," Adrienne answered, more flustered than she wanted to admit.

"So? Pick up where you left off, and don't make the same

mistakes you made the first time. Just because you have Callie doesn't mean you can never date again, or just get laid."

Adrienne was getting frustrated at her dear, dear friend. Char was single and had none of the emotional baggage she carried around, and sometimes Adrienne just wished all the pain would go away. But if it did, then that meant she hadn't loved Brenna enough to keep her memory alive.

"First of all," Adrienne said, slipping into her lawyer mode, "it didn't end well, and we can't just pick it up and move on. Second, I know Callie doesn't stop me from getting laid, but Brenna does." She held up her hands. "I know, I know. Brenna is dead, and she would want me to be happy and move on, including being with someone else. I know it wouldn't harm Callie if I fell in love again and got married, blah, blah, blah. I know all that, but it's not going to happen. So don't push me on this, Char," Adrienne said firmly. "I can't handle that right now."

She couldn't now and didn't know if she ever would. Adrienne loved Brenna, and that would never change. She would never love anyone the way she loved her, and to settle for second best would be just that—settling. It wouldn't be fair to her, to Callie, and certainly not to the other woman. The thought of touching another woman made her feel like she was cheating on Brenna. Intellectually she knew what that was all about, but physically it made her stomach churn.

And then there was Sloan and those last few seconds in the elevator. What in the hell was that? It had to have been habit. Kind of like when you say *I love you* to your significant other on the phone and then almost say it at the end of a conversation with your boss or a friend. Of course, that was it. It had to be.

"Okay, sure, honey," Char said, giving up. "I know how much you loved Brenna and how much she loved you. Yes, that love comes once in a lifetime, but there is other love that is just as wonderful."

"How do you know all this? You're a bank teller," Adrienne asked, humor trickling back into her voice.

"I watch reruns of *Oprah* and *Dr. Phil*."

"*Dr. Phil*? His show is about how people treat each other badly, not about something like this."

"I know, but it just sounded good."

They both laughed and bumped shoulders. "You are an idiot, and because you're my best friend I accept that and will continue to be your BFF." No truer words have never been spoken, Adrienne thought.

"You know I love you," Char said seriously.

"Yes, I do, and I love you back and appreciate what you're trying to do." She called for the check. "I've got to go pick up my bundle of joy and try to convince her peas are delicious and that bedtime is seven thirty, not eight or nine." She slid off the stool and gave Char a tight hug. She held it a little longer than normal, conveying how much she did appreciate Char's concern.

"Peas are disgusting," Char said as she walked out the door and to her car.

CHAPTER FOURTEEN

Sloan kept asking herself all the way back to her office just what in the hell had almost happened? She'd survived being stuck in an elevator—again relatively intact and without freaking out—but had topped the entire nightmarish episode off by almost kissing Adrienne. What in the hell was she thinking? Actually, she hadn't been thinking; she'd just reacted. She'd spent fifty minutes within five feet of Adrienne, smelling her perfume, seeing her smile, watching her long, slim fingers flying over the keyboard of her phone. Imagined, no, remembered how they felt caressing her. That was the only thing that kept her mind off her situation. It wasn't a smart thing to do, but she'd had no choice. And it had worked.

She'd fought the memories of Adrienne creeping into her consciousness from the moment she saw her in the conference room. Was that only a few weeks ago? She remembered the night they met, the first time they made love, when they snuck away to the coatroom at a mutual friend's wedding, and the time they had to be absolutely quiet because their tent was three feet from their neighbors'.

They had agreed to go camping at the Canyon Point campground one weekend in September with several other students. There were eight people in total, including one other couple. Each of the couples shared a tent, and the other four drew straws to see who would double up with whom. Their assigned space was small, and they were practically right next to each other. She and Adrienne were still in the early-have-sex-all-the-time stage, and the evening they arrived was no different.

"This tent is small," Adrienne commented while hammering the stakes into the ground.

"Then I guess we'll have to sleep really close together," she replied, raising and lowering her eyebrows à la Groucho Marx.

"No," Adrienne said, but she was grinning too. "With everyone almost on top of each other, no way. It is not going to happen."

Sloan didn't try to change her mind. She knew Adrienne enjoyed sex just as much as she did. She'd just wait and see how it played out.

Steve, an engineering major, had brought beer but declared that no one could even touch the cooler until all the tents were set up. Sloan noticed that as complicated as some of them were to assemble, that was probably a good idea. And it was good motivation to get it done sooner rather than later, as the sun was setting fast.

Steve proposed a toast, and almost in unison, everyone popped their top. She was sitting across the fire from Adrienne, and the flames dancing on her face made her that much more beautiful. They took turns telling stories about their wildest sexual adventure, and after two hours of verbal foreplay Sloan was more than ready. By the looks Adrienne had been directing her way, she was as well.

"I'm headed to the bathroom," Sloan said, looking around for the flashlight. Since they were all in tents, the facilities were down the road. Her clit throbbed a little harder when Adrienne said she'd come along.

They held hands as they left the glow of the campfire, and as soon as they were out of sight, Sloan pulled them off the path.

"What are you doing?"

"Getting us a little privacy," Sloan replied, squinting to see in the dark. She didn't want to turn on the flashlight and give away their location if she didn't need to. Finding a good spot, she turned, pulled Adrienne into her arms, and kissed her.

Adrienne, always willing, wrapped her arms around her neck and deepened the kiss. Sloan wasn't sure who did what next, but shirts were up, bras opened, and hands everywhere. She sucked on Adrienne's nipples as Adrienne pinched hers. Somebody moaned and somebody shushed, reminding each other that sound traveled easily up here in the soundless night. Impatient fingers opened buttons and unzipped zippers, and fingers touched warm, wet flesh. Sloan loved the way Adrienne surged into her fingers as they played with her sensitive places, and she didn't disappoint this time either.

"God, Sloan, how do make me so wet so fast?"

Sloan knew it wasn't really a question, but she answered anyway, whispering in Adrienne's ear. "Because you know how good it feels when I touch you, when I play with your clit until you beg me to make you come. You like the feel of my fingers stroking you and teasing you before I slide my fingers inside your warm, wet center." Sloan described what her fingers were doing, the double action making Adrienne wetter.

"Oh, Jesus, that feels good." Adrienne dropped her head back against a pine tree, exposing her neck for Sloan to kiss and lick and run her tongue up from her breasts and back down to circle a hard, swollen nipple.

"You have no idea," Sloan said before nipping at the hard tip and driving her fingers inside Adrienne. Adrienne rose on her toes and ground her clit into Sloan's hand.

"Wait," Adrienne suddenly said, trying to put some distance between them. "I want you to come with me." She shifted her body, and her hand quickly found its way into Sloan's shorts. "Oh, God," Adrienne moaned as soon as she touched her.

"Double that," Sloan said breathlessly. Between Adrienne pulsing in her hand and against her fingertips and her own arousal, it wouldn't take long.

"Faster," Adrienne said, her hips mimicking her command.

Sloan obeyed, knowing just how Adrienne liked it. They were absolutely in sync. Long, hard, fast strokes followed by short thrusts resulted in gasps of pleasure from them both. Sloan felt Adrienne climb closer and closer to orgasm, and when she peaked, she came with her.

Stars exploded behind her eyes, and she swirled in a vortex of sensation. Her head pounded, and the only sound that existed was

Adrienne whispering her name. Hearing Adrienne call her name when she totally lost control made her come again.

It took more than a few moments before Sloan could think, and a few more before she could speak. When she did, she simply said, "God, it's good between us."

When they finally arrived back to the campfire, they were met with a series of catcalls and good-natured teasing about how long it took for them to simply go to the bathroom. Everyone knew they never made it to the latrine, and nobody cared.

Later that night, after everyone had gone to bed, Sloan lay on her back, and Adrienne curled against her. Crickets chirped in the night, and what sounded like an owl hooted far away. Her mind wandered, not spending too long on any subject, but she always kept returning to the woman in her arms.

She and Adrienne were so very different. Her family barely spoke to each other, whereas Adrienne's seemed to constantly be in each other's business. Sloan wondered what it would be like if her family gathered for loud, boisterous holidays or birthday parties for distant cousins. Hell, she didn't even know if she had any distant cousins. Sometimes she felt all alone in the world. Yet when she was with Adrienne she felt safe, secure, and protected. She didn't want to think about her life when they went their separate ways.

"I hear your brain churning," Adrienne said.

"Just thinking about how much fun I have when I'm with you."

"That's because you're an uptight stick-in-the-mud without me."

"Uptight stick-in-the-mud?"

"Okay. Maybe that was a little harsh. Let's just say cautious and overanalytic."

"It's the would-be lawyer in me. And my parents. We didn't show much emotion in my house. Everything had to be just so. My dad was a surgeon and ran his house like his OR. He was in charge with no questions asked." Sloan felt a pang of something missing in her life, but if you don't have something, how can you miss it? Adrienne climbed on top of her. They had zipped two sleeping bags

together, but it was still a tight fit. They were both naked, so it was a very nice fit.

There was a full moon, and even through their tent, she could see Adrienne's face inches from hers. She had that look, and Sloan's pulse quickened.

"You show a lot of emotion when you're with me," Adrienne said, nipping at the outside of her lips and drifting down to her jaw.

Sloan's hands automatically went to Adrienne's waist, and Adrienne shifted again, their legs straddling each other. Her heart started to beat faster.

"That's just biology," she somehow managed to say when Adrienne's mouth captured her nipple. She felt Adrienne smile against her breast. "I thought you said this wasn't going to happen." Sloan reminded Adrienne of her earlier decree.

Adrienne lifted her head and looked at her, eyes gleaming. "I lied."

Sloan didn't have much time to think before Adrienne had her mouth where her fingers had been earlier. Adrienne knew just what she needed and when, and slowly and methodically she used her tongue to drive Sloan out of her mind. She traced the outside of her lips before moving to the inside. She was careful to stay away from her clit, causing the anticipation to build to the point it was almost painful. Somehow the sleeping bag had been cast aside, and the image of Adrienne on her knees between her legs illuminated by the full moon was the most erotic image she had ever seen.

"Adrienne," she said, on the verge of orgasm, but was then pulled back when Adrienne took her mouth from her. She raised her head and looked down. "What? Why did you stop?"

Adrienne didn't say anything but put her finger up to her lips, the universal sign of quiet. Sloan got the message and clamped her mouth shut. It felt like forever before Adrienne put her tongue exactly where Sloan needed it.

Sloan was not a quiet lover. If something felt good she said so, so it was difficult for her to keep her mouth shut, especially when something felt this good. She put her hand over her mouth when Adrienne sucked on her clit and took her over the edge.

Voices outside her office rudely reminded Sloan that she was at work, not in her bedroom. Her heart was pounding, she was sweating, and she was more than a little turned on at the memory. She didn't want to remember, not like this. Not when so much was on the line. After this deal was done, maybe, but not now. No, definitely not then either. Adrienne had a dead wife and a child. No thanks. No way was she going to get mixed up in that.

Her afternoon dragged, and Sloan found herself reading the same email three times. She cursed and read it out loud, forcing herself to pay attention. She had to repeat that trick she'd learned in law school several more times before the day was mercifully over. She had no plans for dinner and quickly ran through her options. Joanne was a possibility, but that would then make Sloan feel like she'd need to have sex with her to make up for the other night. However exciting Joanne was, she wasn't interested in obligatory sex. Nan was another possibility, but she was all about sex, and surprisingly Sloan wasn't interested.

She ran through her other options and settled on a long run. She was on her way out when Elliott stopped her.

"Got a minute?"

"Sure. What's up?" She followed Elliott into her office. They sat in the comfortable chairs in the corner.

"Is something going on between you and Adrienne Stewart?"

Sloan's heart stopped, and she felt like every other organ in her body had stopped as well. "What do you mean?" The best defense was sometimes offense.

"I mean you looked pretty rattled when the elevator doors opened. And you couldn't wait to get away from Adrienne." Elliott had unknowingly hit the nail on the head.

"I hate elevators," Sloan replied, hoping Elliott would accept that as an answer. She didn't.

"I know that and was worried about you. But there was something else."

Sloan had no more than five seconds to decide if she should tell Elliott everything or continue to evade the question. She took a deep breath. "We…uh…knew each other in college." Elliott didn't say anything, just waited for her to continue. "We…uh…dated." Again Elliott remained quiet. "We were…involved." There, she'd gotten it out. Sloan waited for the other shoe to drop.

"How involved?" Elliott's voice was hard.

An image of Adrienne over her, under her, and between her legs flashed through Sloan's brain. She felt her face flush. Before she had a chance to answer Elliott asked, "That involved?"

"Yes."

"Why didn't you say so when I first asked?"

"It's not relevant."

"Not relevant?" Elliott asked, her eyebrows rising.

"It was a long time ago, and it's over. It's been over. She married someone else and had a baby with her, that kind of over." *Then why did I almost kiss her?*

Elliott studied her for several moments that felt like hours. Elliott could read people better than anyone Sloan had ever met. She had a spooky intuitiveness and a finely tuned bullshit meter. She kept repeating her explanation over and over in her head while she forced herself not to break eye contact. Fortunately, Elliott must have believed her.

"You should have said something to me at your first opportunity. I don't need to tell you that business and pleasure do not mix, and they certainly don't when it affects Foster McKenzie."

"No, Elliott, you don't. I understand, and it's not a problem. I can also guarantee you it won't become one."

All the way home Sloan hoped she hadn't just lied to her boss.

Chapter Fifteen

How's my girl?" Adrienne's father asked when she came into the kitchen. Joe Phillips was a big man, standing well over six feet six, and had weighed two sixty the last time he checked. He barely fit in the vehicle he delivered mail in. To people who didn't know him, he was more than a little intimidating. Those that did knew he was firm but fair with his children and that Adrienne and her sister Frankie would always be his little girls.

"Good. How was your day?" Adrienne placed her keys and phone on the counter, then kissed her father's grizzled cheek. It was only four, but his five o'clock shadow was rough and scratchy on her lips. He was completely bald, preferring to shave his head versus the wiry bristles that had returned after chemo years ago.

"Great. Callie and I made cookies when I got home. She was a little crabby after getting up from her nap, and I gave your mom a break."

Adrienne's dad was a fabulous grandfather. He would sit and read the same book to Callie for an hour if she wanted him to.

Midway through her second year at college she had come home for a long weekend, and his excitement in seeing her had quickly turned to angst when she dropped a bombshell into his lap.

"Dad, I'm a lesbian."

"What?"

This was the hardest conversation Adrienne had ever had with her dad. She'd planned to talk to her parents separately, and the conversation with her mother went better than she expected. Maria had calmly asked several questions, and after Adrienne answered them she assured her mother that this was her decision and that she had not been brainwashed or seduced by an older woman. After assuring Adrienne that she would love her no matter what, her mother asked for two things. First, not to ever refer to her girlfriend as her lover and, second, to tell her father after dinner that night. Her parents kept nothing from each other, and Maria was uncomfortable with knowing this all-important aspect of their daughter for too long before Jon did.

"I'm a lesbian. I'm attracted to women."

"I know what a lesbian is, Adrienne," he said, obviously exasperated. "I may be old, but I'm not stupid."

"No, sir, you're not. I never intended to—"

"Are you sure?"

Her father's response surprised her. He'd always told her he just wanted her to be happy in whatever she did, but Adrienne didn't think this was what he meant. She had to give him credit. Some of her friends' parents had thrown them out of the house. "Yes." Her voice was firm and steady. She was surer of this than anything else.

"But you dated boys in high school."

She shrugged. She'd anticipated this comment. "I guess it's because it was expected."

"We never pressured you to..." he said quickly.

"I know, Dad. It's not that."

"Then what is it?" he asked sincerely.

Her father sat patiently as she struggled to find the words to explain how she'd felt that something in her life just hadn't been right. Going away to college had exposed her to entirely new experiences, friends, and viewpoints, and it wasn't long before she began to realize what it was. When she'd gone to a lesbian bar, she felt at home. When she kissed a girl, she was afraid her heart would explode from the excitement. The first time she touched a woman, her hands were shaking so bad she was surprised she was able to do it at all. Her first orgasm with a woman was unlike any she'd had before. Of course, she didn't tell her father any of that.

"It's just right," she said finally.

Adrienne watched a myriad of emotions move across her father's face. He was the most important man in her life, and she wanted his blessing. If not, then his acceptance. If he was unable to give either, she would be devastated.

"I'm concerned," he said, echoing the expression on his rugged face. "This is a very big decision, and you're so young." When Adrienne stared to interrupt, he held up his hand. "Please let me finish. This is a very big decision, a life-changing decision. One that will set a course for the rest of your life. I can't say I'm surprised. Adrienne, you've always been a step different from everyone else. You never followed the status quo, never had the same interests as the other little girls and boys. When all the other kids were trying to fit in, you took pride in being on the outside. You never wanted the same clothes, or hairstyle, or anything else that made you look just like everyone else. You were always an individual, so I'm not surprised that you've chosen a different path when it comes to this."

He sat back in his chair. "But I am your father, and I am concerned for you. I'm afraid for you, afraid you'll be ridiculed and harmed because of this. I don't know much about this, but I do know that it's not a choice. I know that your mother and I raised you to look at all sides of an argument and consider different points of view. I know you didn't make this decision lightly. You've grown into a strong, courageous woman that I'm proud to call my daughter. I love you, and I will always love you, and I will love whomever you choose to spend the rest of your life with."

Her father had been true to his word and had welcomed Brenna into the family as he had the women and men her brothers and her sister Frankie brought home. He was at the hospital when Callie was born and held Adrienne upright at Brenna's funeral. He was her rock, her go-to guy, and her sounding board.

"And how many cookies did she con you out of?" Adrienne asked, grabbing one of the treats and putting it into her mouth. God, that was good. Her mother's chocolate-chip cookie recipe was her favorite.

"One."

Adrienne looked at him skeptically. She knew her daughter and how she had her grandfather wrapped around her pudgy little finger.

"Okay, two. But I made her have a glass of milk with them." That was his excuse that made it all better.

Adrienne didn't fault her father, just gave him a nudge with her hip. "I should let her spend the night, and you can battle her to go to bed," she teased him.

"She'll go right down," her father said, boasting. "We had a talk and she promised me."

"She promised you?" Adrienne asked skeptically.

"Yes. Callie and I have a connection," he said, rinsing his hands in the sink. "We have an understanding."

"Dad, she's three years old. She doesn't understand anything."

"She understands me. Just wait and see."

Her father was convinced, and for her sake, Adrienne hoped that what he said was true.

"You look tired, sweetie. Is something else going on other than this deal?"

Damn, her father could read her like he was inside her head. He always could, and it used to make her crazy. Now she appreciated it because she didn't always know how to broach a subject when she needed advice or a sounding board.

"Talk," her father said, taking her by the elbow and leading her to the couch. He sat down beside her. "Your mom has Callie in the pool. Neither one knows you're here."

She debated about telling her father about Sloan. He didn't know about their relationship, and she was uncomfortable talking to him about her life before Brenna. He had to have known she dated before Brenna; it was several years after her coming-out discussion before she brought Brenna home.

"The attorney for Foster McKenzie is a woman I knew in college," she said hesitantly.

"Knew? As in *knew*?"

She was certain of exactly what he was referring to. She nodded, not wanting to actually say the words.

"Is that good or bad?"

Adrienne answered honestly. "I'm not sure."

"I take it you're not still friends?"

For not having more than a high-school education, her father was very astute. "No."

"Did you know about her before you approached them?"

"Yes."

"Did she know it would be you in these discussions?"

"Judging by the expression on her face when she saw me, I'd have to say no. Probably because I changed my name when I married Brenna," Adrienne added, trying to help her father understand.

"So how is it going?"

Adrienne wasn't sure if he was referring to the negotiations of the deal or negotiating with Sloan. "The deal is going as we expected."

"And with the woman?"

"I'm not sure. Today we got stuck in an elevator together."

"Oh, dear. That must have been awkward."

"Alone. For almost an hour."

"Hmm." Her father nodded. "What's her name?"

"Sloan Merchant." Adrienne drew in a breath. Just saying her name made her head spin again. Images of Sloan flashed in front of her eyes. The time Sloan had laughed at the antics of a friend's puppy, the time she stood up to the professor who was bullying a student in their economics class. The times she reached for her in the dark. Sloan had been almost bigger than life. At least she had been for Adrienne.

Sloan had been everything she wanted in a lover, a friend, a partner. But that was a lifetime ago, before that fateful day in May. Before her heart was ripped out of her chest by the way Sloan left.

But she was a very different person now. Pain and heartbreak had changed her by clearing her rose-colored glasses. She'd never loved anyone like she'd loved Sloan until she met Brenna. Brenna hadn't let her run or close herself off from the world until Adrienne had felt she had no choice but to fall in love again. The result had been wonderful and glorious, and when Callie was born, Adrienne had known she could never be happier.

"Have you two talked since you, uh, broke up?"

She shook her head.

"What did you do, in the elevator?"

"Had a very civilized conversation."

"Did you expect something different?"

She really hadn't known what to expect and said so. "I think she was trying hard not to panic. She said she hated elevators and kept looking at her watch and fidgeting."

"What did you talk about?"

Her father was better than your average man in asking questions to get information about matters of the heart.

"We were a little stilted at first. I think she felt just as awkward and uncomfortable as I did. I asked her about her job and she asked about mine, that sort of thing. She asked about you and Mom." Her father seemed more than a little surprised. "I'd told her all about you two," Adrienne said, a little sheepishly. She'd talked to Sloan about her family but had never mentioned her to them. "Her family is nothing like ours, and she always found it interesting how close we all are. She often described hers as cold."

"But not so close that you ever shared with us you were seeing her." Her father was obviously trying hard to keep the hurt from his voice, but Adrienne suspected he felt bad.

"It wasn't like that." She tried to explain but felt herself blush at the conclusion her father had seemingly reached.

"It wasn't serious," she said, then cringed because that sounded worse. "Mom sent me the picture of Callie stuffing pretzels into her mouth, and when I laughed, Sloan wanted to know why. I told her about Callie."

"Would you have told her if you weren't stuck there together?"

"If it ever came up in conversation."

Her father looked at her dubiously. "What was the chance of that?"

"Slim to none," Adrienne answered quietly.

"And why is that?"

"I doubt she'd ever ask, Dad."

"Does she know about Brenna?"

"Elliott asked about my ring at dinner one evening." Adrienne fingered her wedding ring. "I told them Brenna had died."

"And nothing about Callie?"

"What was I supposed to say, Dad? A crazy man murdered my wife and left me with a twelve-week-old baby?" Adrienne was appalled at her tone. "I'm sorry, Dad. I didn't mean to snap at you." She felt terrible. She kissed him on the cheek.

"You know, if you put it away for Callie, it might not be so awkward," he said, pointing at her wedding ring.

He was really saying it had been three years, and it was time to take it off and move on. It was a conversation her mother had had with her several months ago. She wasn't ready, didn't know if she would ever be ready. Then why did she almost kiss Sloan?

"What happened in that elevator?"

"I almost kissed her." Adrienne's voice was little more than a whisper. She knew that was the last thing her father expected to hear.

"And?"

"And I almost kissed her," Adrienne repeated, like that explained everything.

"You almost kissed her or she almost kissed you?"

"I almost kissed her."

"And how do you feel about that?"

Her father was a trouper for having this conversation with her. When she was a teenager he'd often talked to her about teenage boys and didn't spare any graphic descriptions to make his point.

"It came as a complete surprise."

"Do you still have feelings for her?"

"No," she said quickly. "I love Brenna. I'll always love her.

Sloan and I were over a long time before Brenna." She had no doubt about that.

"So what's the problem? Besides the fact that you're working with her for a while. But that'll be over in a few weeks."

"So? So?" Adrienne asked, surprised at her father's question. "I'm in love with Brenna."

"Brenna is dead," her father said, his voice soft. Like that could soften the word *dead*.

"I know she's dead." Adrienne tried to control her temper. No one understood that just because her wife had died she hadn't stopped loving her. "And I know she'd want me to move on and find someone else to love. But I don't want to. Brenna was the love of my life, the mother of our child. No one can take her place." This was the same argument she'd had in her head dozens of times.

"No, no one can take Brenna's place. I have no idea the pain you must have felt when she died, the pain you still feel. But that does not mean you have to stop living too. You are a healthy, young woman with the rest of your life in front of you."

"With a three-year-old." Like that needed to be said. The sound of Callie's laughter came through the window.

"So? Widows with children get remarried all the time."

"Good God, Dad. When did we get on the topic of getting married? That's quite a leap from an almost-kiss."

"Would you have preferred I say that widows with children still have sex?"

Adrienne blushed again.

"I didn't think so. Look, honey," her father said, scooting closer to her. He took her hands between his big ones. They were rough and callused from years of delivering mail and doing home improvements. "You're starting to come alive again. Your body is telling you something, and you need to listen to it. Just like when you started to realize you were a lesbian. You weren't afraid to venture down that path to see where it would take you. I'm just saying this is kind of the same. You were leaving behind what you knew and had the courage to find yourself. You're afraid you'll leave Brenna behind, but you won't. She'll always be in your heart, and you'll always have her in Callie."

Adrienne fought back tears. "How did you get to be so smart?"

Her father gathered her in his arms and kissed the top of her head. "I've read every book I could get my hands on. If I can't take the pain away, I have to help you deal with it."

His deep voice rumbling in his chest comforted her. It took her back to the many times they had sat in this exact same place during her childhood. He was always there for her, and now that she was grown and had a child of her own, he still was.

She sniffed and squeezed him tight, before pulling away and sitting up. She looked him in the eyes and saw nothing but love. "I love you, Dad. Let's go get our girl."

CHAPTER SIXTEEN

I invited Adrienne and Robert to the holiday party," Elliott said a week later over lunch.

Sloan swallowed her spoonful of soup too fast. It was hot and made her eyes water as it scalded her throat on the way down. "Sounds good" was all she was able to say.

The annual Foster McKenzie holiday party was a don't-miss on the holiday party circuit. Elliott and Lauren hosted it, and employees and select business associates were invited. Sloan had always had a good time, and now, six weeks later, she slowed her breathing as she walked up the steps to Elliott's front door.

Several cars stood in the circular driveway, and another dozen or so lined both sides of McComb Drive. Sloan caught herself looking for the one with a car seat in the back. At least she thought a three-year-old would still be in a car seat. But what the hell did she know about kids? Other than they took up all your time and were noisy and messy, she had no clue. She'd never babysat as a teenager, and she'd never spent any time around youngsters.

She thought she saw a shadow of something in the backseat of the Audi two cars away, but it was too dark to see clearly. She rang the bell and dried her palms on her pants. She hadn't been this nervous since the first time she met Elliott.

She'd changed clothes three times before settling on a pair of navy trousers and a long-sleeved, cream-colored silk top under the matching jacket. Her outfit was somewhere between casual and work wear. She'd never spent as much time as she had on her appearance tonight.

The invitation was plus one, and Sloan was characteristically alone. She didn't have a "one" to bring. She hadn't seen Joanne for several weeks, and she wasn't seeing anyone else.

She'd overheard Teresa tell Elliott that Adrienne had accepted but didn't know if she was bringing her "one" or not.

Light flooded the entryway when a tuxedo-clad man opened the door. "Good evening."

His voice was deep and smooth, and Sloan wondered if it was natural or he practiced it.

She stepped inside and heard soft music coming from the speakers overhead and the sound of voices from the room to her right.

A server greeted Sloan as she stepped into the room of people. She bypassed the flute of champagne and accepted a glass of water instead. This was a business gathering, after all, and she needed her complete wits about her this evening.

Sloan made small talk with several people she knew, all the while searching the room for Adrienne. She lost track of what Mitch in Accounting was saying when she saw Adrienne talking with Lauren across the room.

Both women were beautiful in their own right, but together they were stunning. Sloan barely registered the blue skirt and top Lauren was wearing, her attention completely focused on Adrienne.

Her hair was up in the style Sloan had always liked. It accentuated her long, smooth neck that she suddenly wanted to lick. A necklace reflected the overhead lights, but Adrienne was too far away for Sloan to see what the bauble was that had settled in the V of her dress. And OMG, what a dress.

A pale shade of green, it reminded Sloan of the color of Adrienne's eyes. It was fitted without being tight and fell to a respectable distance above the top of her knees. Her polished toenails peeked out from the tips of a pair of very fashionable shoes. Sloan had no idea who made them and didn't care. What she did care about was how they made her legs look. She knew how long they were and that they fit perfectly around her waist. She flushed at the image.

"Sloan?"

Mitch's voice interrupted her thoughts, and she asked him to repeat his question. At least she thought he'd asked a question. She forced herself to concentrate on what the man was saying and not stand there and gape at Adrienne like a schoolgirl and her first crush.

It took several more minutes for Sloan to find an appropriate lull in the conversation so she could escape. She walked across the room and out the French doors to the patio, desperately needing some fresh air.

A soft breeze blew in from the ocean, and the crash of the breaking waves was an invitation. Sloan slipped off her shoes, stuffed her trouser socks into each respective loafer, and stepped into the sand. It was smooth and cool, her feet sinking as she walked.

With each step the sounds of the party faded away until the only sound was the waves and her own thoughts. She'd been acutely aware of Adrienne the entire evening. It had started the minute she'd walked into the sprawling house. Without seeing her, Sloan knew Adrienne was there. She sensed her, felt her presence. It had always been that way when they were together. They didn't have to be in the same room for her to know Adrienne was near.

A sliver of moon peeking out from the clouds provided Sloan with enough light to see. Elliott and Lauren's house was about one hundred yards from the water, giving them privacy yet stunning views of the Pacific Ocean.

Sloan stopped. A long-forgotten but familiar feeling filled her. She lifted her head and focused on someone in the distance, walking along the shoreline away from her. Sloan knew it was Adrienne.

It wasn't the way she carried herself or the relaxed way she strolled in the sand or even her long hair blowing in the breeze. No, it was more than that. Much more. It was an innate connection Sloan would have sworn was no longer relevant. Warmth surged through her, and she stood and simply watched.

Adrienne took several more steps, hesitated, then suddenly

turned around. It was dark, but Sloan knew she was looking right at her. For several moments, neither one moved. Sloan expected Adrienne to continue with her walk, but when she started heading her way, Sloan's breath quickened.

Adrienne's heart raced when she knew Sloan was on the beach with her. She'd come outside at Lauren's insistence, to get away from the noise and commotion and all the people. Other than Sloan, Elliott, Lauren, and Robert, she hadn't known anyone and was feeling a bit overwhelmed. Lauren had welcomed her immediately, and they had chatted for a few minutes several times throughout the evening, and Lauren relayed Elliott's invitation to the Children's Education Fund charity event the following week. Lauren's father was a mail carrier, just like her dad, and they had several other shared interests. But Lauren had hostess responsibilities, so she couldn't stay in one place too long.

Adrienne just needed a few minutes to herself. She'd been there for about fifteen minutes, and Elliott had graciously introduced her around. She was talking with Lauren and Teresa when she felt Sloan come into the room. She was stunned that she still had any connection with Sloan. When they were together during meetings or talking on the phone about some element of their deal, she had always been completely aware of her. That was to be expected. But for her to know the exact moment Sloan entered the room was more than a little unsettling.

She'd caught Sloan looking at her several times throughout the evening and felt a vague sense of arousal. She hadn't experienced the feeling since Brenna. Every woman knew what that was—the innate awareness that she is desired. Other than a polite introductory hello, she'd managed to avoid talking with Sloan tonight, and she didn't want to talk to her now.

This wasn't the first party she'd attended since Brenna died, but she was unsettled and on edge. Adrienne had been to business functions before, but Elliott and Lauren obviously viewed this evening as more social than that. As a result, several times she'd been faced with answering questions about her marital status and

Callie. She hated the instant look of pity in eyes when they realized she was raising Callie alone, due to tragic circumstance versus her choice.

Someone had once told her that maybe she should say she was single instead of widowed. It was the same thing, they'd argued. Adrienne didn't even try. That was acting as if Brenna never existed, that their eight years together never happened. It had been hard enough removing her name from the deed to their home, their banking accounts, and other official documents. She'd broken down and sobbed when she had to update Callie's records at the pediatrician. The instructions were to cross out any incorrect or irrelevant information. Irrelevant? She'd spoken with the office manager about the wording on the form, and the following year it had changed.

As much as she wanted to continue walking, Adrienne knew she had to return to the party. It was one thing to leave early but downright rude to disappear for the remainder of the party. Sloan stood between her and the path back up the house. Maybe, if she was lucky, Sloan would walk the other way or simply let her pass. As she stepped closer, it was obvious that luck wasn't on her side tonight.

"Enjoy your walk?" Sloan asked when she was a few feet away.

"Yes, it's very beautiful here. Elliott and Lauren are very lucky to have this place." Adrienne envied the location but shuddered to think about the upkeep and trying to keep track of Callie in such a large house. If she ever got out and into the water…

"Cold?" Sloan asked, noticing her shiver.

"No." Adrienne didn't explain.

"Walk with me?" Sloan asked when Adrienne started past her toward the path that led back to the house. "For just a few minutes?" Sloan sensed her hesitation.

Adrienne paused, then instead of giving an answer she took a step in the direction Sloan had indicated. Sloan quickly fell into step beside her.

They didn't talk but walked silently along the shoreline. Suddenly Sloan grabbed her hand and pulled her away from a rogue wave that threatened to drench their legs. Adrienne's heart hammered from the surprise, and her pulse raced at the sensation of Sloan's hand in hers. Other than her mother and a few close friends, Adrienne hadn't felt the touch of another woman in a long time. And it had been even longer since it had been Sloan.

They walked several more steps before Adrienne pulled her hand free. She murmured a polite "Thanks" while fighting the sensations coursing through her.

"Elliott and Lauren know how to throw a good party," Sloan commented, breaking the tension between them.

"Do you go to many of them?" Adrienne asked. She could do benign conversation.

Sloan chuckled before answering. "Lauren took me on as a project."

"A project? Why's that?"

"When Elliott hired me, I moved here not knowing a soul. Lauren thinks it's important to have a bit of work-life balance, so I was invited to everything from dinner to her monthly book club."

"Is Elliott a workaholic?" Adrienne asked.

"She would be if not for Lauren. She has her charities and other philanthropic causes, but she loves her job. With our global operations, she could very easily work twenty-four seven. I get the impression she did before she met Lauren. Now she's the first one out of the office on some days."

A pang of longing hit Adrienne in the stomach when she remembered being just like Elliott. All that had changed with Brenna, and even more so when Callie was born. She'd had to drag herself out of the house in the morning and hurried home as soon as she could. In the evening, they would put Callie down and snuggle on the couch and reconnect. More often than not, Brenna would be asleep in minutes.

"What?" Sloan asked.

Adrienne didn't realize that she'd laughed. She was remembering how she'd been so sleep-deprived she was usually nodding off a few minutes after Brenna. "Nothing." Adrienne didn't want to share that memory with anyone, especially Sloan.

"So, was Lauren's project successful?" she asked instead. "Have you read any good books lately?"

"*Fifty Shades of Grey*," Sloan answered quickly.

Adrienne stopped and looked at Sloan, surprised. That wasn't the answer she'd expected.

"What?" Sloan asked, a teasing look on her face. "I was curious if I was missing anything."

"And were you?" Adrienne held her hand up. "Never mind. Don't answer that." She continued walking.

Sloan laughed, the sound low and warm. Adrienne stumbled, and Sloan caught her before she fell face-first into the water. When she got her feet back under her, Sloan's arms were around her waist, their bodies close. Their lips were inches apart.

Flashbacks of the hundreds of times they'd stood like this made Adrienne's legs weak, and she clung to Sloan for support. Her heart was banging in her chest, and she was suddenly hot all over. The rapid beating of the vein in Sloan's neck indicated that she was affected by this moment too. The movement of Sloan's lips caught her attention. She stared at them while Sloan spoke.

"You know I don't kiss and tell."

Adrienne's knees almost buckled at the insinuation in Sloan's words. Was it more than a double entendre? Was Sloan saying that if they were to act on this moment that she wouldn't tell anyone?

Adrienne was almost overcome with desire. Sloan was an exceptional kisser and attentive lover, and she'd always left Adrienne wanting more. One more kiss, one more touch, one more orgasm. This would be simple but not uncomplicated. This opportunity was right here, right now. She could do this and never look back. But she could also never look forward. She had no future, no tomorrow with Sloan.

It had been forever since she'd lost herself in the warm kiss of a woman. An eternity since she'd felt like a woman, not a mom or daughter or sister who needed looking after. She was a woman, with natural desires and needs that had gone unfulfilled far too long. No one would know, and Sloan could take her where she needed to go.

It had been over ten years and a lifetime ago, but for some reason, she still trusted Sloan.

Seconds ticked by, and Sloan's hot, ragged breath on her face was intoxicating. She felt Sloan tremble under her hands, and the pulsing desire between them was palpable. Sloan hadn't budged. It was definitely her move to make. She wanted to pass Boardwalk, Park Place, pass Go, and not even worry about collecting $200. She just wanted to feel again. Feel alive, wanted, desired. But she was afraid of what would happen. The last time she felt anything, it had been her heart tearing apart.

Guilt and desire warred for position in her head, both dominating her next move. She stopped listening as Sloan slowly lowered her head.

When Sloan kissed her, Adrienne's desire exploded like fireworks over a calm lake. Waves of longing and memories of other times fueled her body's reaction to Sloan's lips. Her body surged into Sloan's, every nerve ending, long dormant, coming alive, stunning her with its intensity.

She remembered so much about Sloan: the texture of her hair, the tense muscles in her back, the way their bodies fit perfectly together. Sloan's kisses were tentative at first, but Adrienne needed more, so much more. She dragged her lips from Sloan's and fought to take a breath. Her head was spinning.

"God, I've missed you," Sloan said between kisses on Adrienne's sensitive neck.

Adrienne froze, then stumbled backward, her arms empty. She covered her mouth with her hands. Shock rocketed through her.

Sloane took a step forward, her hand outstretched, trying to regain their connection. "Adrienne."

Adrienne took an equal step backward. "No." Her voice was little more than a whisper. "No." She repeated the word this time with much more conviction.

"Adrienne," Sloan said again.

"No, Sloan." Adrienne squared her shoulders and dropped her hands. "We are not doing this. What we had…"

"Was amazing."

"Is over," Adrienne said firmly. "That was history. This is today, and we are very different people in very different circumstances."

"But…"

"No."

Chapter Seventeen

Somehow Adrienne managed to return to the house. She said her good-byes to her hosts and a few others before she almost ran to her car. Being in it after closing the door and locking it was like having a coat of armor slide around her. She felt safe here, the familiar surroundings stabilizing her. An empty sippy cup from the movie *Frozen* sat in the cup holder, a CD of the famous movie's soundtrack peeking out of the player. A pair of Callie's socks lay on the front seat, a bag of unopened Ritz crackers in a cubby above the gearshift.

Her hands were shaking so badly she had trouble putting the key in the ignition. She finally succeeded, and when she turned the key, the dash lit up. A picture next to the speedometer gauge was now clearly visible. Somehow she held back her tears until she was around the corner.

Adrienne pulled over, looked at the picture, and let the tears flow. She had no idea how long she cried, but as she did, the images of the photo were clear. It was one of her favorite pictures, taken minutes after their daughter was born. Callie was wrapped in a pink hospital blanket, Brenna looked exhausted yet exuberant, and Adrienne was still in her delivery-room scrubs. It was their first family photo. Their last one, taken twelve weeks later on Brenna's first day back at work, was in a frame on Adrienne's nightstand.

Drying her tears with a McDonald's napkin, Adrienne relived those few precious, yet nightmarish minutes on the beach. Being in Sloan's arms had felt so right. Sloan's kiss soothed her but inflamed her long-dormant desire. Sloan was the first woman she'd kissed since Brenna's death, and the only woman she wanted to kiss. It was right but very, very wrong. Right in the sense that Brenna had been dead for almost three years and it was time to move on.

She and Brenna had talked about just this scenario when they were updating their wills shortly after Callie was born. Brenna had made her promise to be happy if something happened to her, neither one of them thinking that would be the case almost before the ink was dry on the paper. Real life was nothing like a conversation at the kitchen table, regardless of how serious and well-intended.

She still loved Brenna. How could she move on? Tonight her body had betrayed that love, and she struggled to make sense of what she'd done. How could that be? When she was with Brenna, no woman had ever turned her head. No woman ever made her look twice or wonder how it would be to be unfaithful to Brenna. She'd barely recognized the few times a woman had flirted with her, and except for a very suggestive note on the back of a business card, she would have completely missed that invitation. She and Brenna had a good laugh over it and made love as if it were the first time.

Her reaction had to be because of her history with Sloan. Like a song could take you back to a different place and time or a scent could bring back visceral memories. Just because the smell of fresh-baked brownies made her want to sit at her grandmother's table didn't mean she was going to visit her, a box of brownie mix in her hand. She didn't have to react to this instinct. She was in control of her actions, not the other way around.

Blowing her nose, Adrienne pulled herself together and headed home. She was relieved that Callie was spending the night with her parents. The last thing she wanted to do was explain her puffy red eyes. At least something was going her way tonight.

CHAPTER EIGHTEEN

Adrienne did her best to hide the dark circles under her eyes before heading over to her parents' house the next morning. She hadn't slept much the night before. Memories of her and Sloan on the beach had kept intruding. But in her dreams, she hadn't pushed Sloan away.

"Touch me, please," Adrienne said, sliding Sloan's hand from behind her back to her breasts. It didn't take much encouragement for Sloan to do exactly as she said. Adrienne's dress was thin and her nipples hard and responsive under Sloan's caresses. She ran her hands down Sloan's back, tugged at the bottom of her blouse, and pulled it from her pants. She slid her hands under the silky material. Sloan's skin was hot, and she murmured something against Adrienne's neck. It didn't matter what it was; it only mattered that she was finally able to touch her.

Sloan slid the shoulder of her dress down, her lips following its path. Adrienne shuddered at the light, delicate kisses. Sloan moaned when Adrienne ran her fingernails across Sloan's sides and then cupped her breasts. She brushed her thumb across Sloan's nipples, alternating between soft then hard, the way she remembered Sloan liked it.

"We need to stop or take this somewhere else."

Sloan's breathing was ragged, and Adrienne soared at the thought she could still cause a reaction like that. Adrienne looked around and spotted a lifeguard stand a few yards away. It was enclosed at the bottom for storage, the perfect place for a few minutes of privacy. That was all she needed, knowing the instant she touched her she would explode. She grabbed Sloan's hand and pulled her toward the stand.

Adrienne kissed her like it was the last kiss they would ever have. She unbuckled Sloan's belt, then her pants, and as soon as her hand could fit, she slid into her.

"Oh my God," someone said, and Adrienne thought it was probably her.

Sloan was warm and wet, and when she spread her legs, that was the only invitation Adrienne needed.

Her arousal was evident. Sloan's lips were soft, her clitoris hard with anticipation.

Adrienne teased Sloan's opening, then slid in and out, grazing Sloan's clit as she did. Sloan bit her shoulder. Staying inside, Adrienne dropped to her knees, pulling Sloan's pants and boxers down with her. She inhaled the scent of Sloan's desire, which took her back to another time.

Sloan grabbed her hair, and Adrienne knew what she wanted. What they both wanted. She withdrew her fingers and with both hands splayed Sloan open to her. The clouds chose that moment to shift, and Adrienne could see the glistening wetness waiting for her. Slowly Adrienne lowered her head.

"Oh God, Adrienne." Sloan spread her legs wider and bent her knees.

Adrienne repeated the tasting, flicking her tongue harder and harder with each pass.

"Don't stop," Sloan growled, her voice barely loud enough to be heard over the roaring in Adrienne's ears.

Adrienne slid two fingers into Sloan and focused all her attention on the swelling hard nub of flesh. She slid her free hand around to caress Sloan's ass. Then Adrienne did something she'd never done before. She wet her finger with her own juices before touching Sloan's tight opening. Sloan froze. After a few moments, Adrienne felt the area begin to relax.

Slowly, she slid her finger a little deeper, matching Sloan's thrusts. She soared outside herself, as if she were looking down on this scene. Sloan's head was back, her legs far apart, Adrienne's face buried in her pussy, with one finger in her vagina and the other in her ass. The image was more than erotic. When Sloan climaxed, Adrienne came one second behind her.

The dream had been so vivid she had to look in her bathroom mirror this morning to see if she had teeth marks on her shoulder. She did that right after she had her own orgasm, imagining Sloan's fingers instead of her own.

Adrienne declined her mother's offer to keep Callie for the remainder of the day. It was a typical Sunday, and she had several errands to run that would take twice as long with a wiggly toddler along. But Callie would provide the distraction she desperately needed to keep her mind off reliving last night's events.

Three stops and ninety minutes later, Adrienne was only halfway through her list when she made a quick U-turn and headed to the park. She wasn't getting anything done and felt guilty for leaving Callie with her parents so often during the past few weeks. Other than Auburn Pharma, she had several other clients who needed her attention. Unfortunately, Auburn was taking up all of her time, and she used her evenings and weekends to play catch-up. She tried to get out of the office by six at the latest to get home, feed Callie, give her a bath, and squeeze in a few minutes of playtime before bedtime. Once her daughter was settled, Adrienne pulled open her briefcase and went back to work. Often she woke to a crick in her neck from falling asleep in the chair reading a brief.

A bench adjacent to the toddler playground was vacant, and when Callie ran to play with two other little girls, Adrienne sat down to enjoy the warm afternoon and watch her daughter have fun. Suddenly a wave of exhaustion overcame her. It wasn't the typical end-of-the-week tired, or the nagging exhaustion from being a single, working parent. She was bone weary. Her nerves had still not recovered from having to work with Sloan again, and she was constantly fighting off memories. She certainly hadn't been sleeping worth a damn either.

Adrienne often thought how different her life would be if Brenna were still alive. She suspected they would probably have another baby in the house by now and smiled at the flashback of Brenna pregnant. Adrienne never believed in the saying that a woman glowed when she was expecting until the day Brenna had told her she was pregnant. They had agreed to wait one more day than the expected number of days past Brenna's insemination before she peed on the stick.

It was a Tuesday, and Adrienne had come home from work to find Brenna waiting for her in the driveway.

"Hey, honey, how was your..." Adrienne closed her car door, but Brenna had grabbed her and practically hugged the stuffing out of her.

"Hey, what's this all about?" Adrienne was finally able to say. "Did we win the lottery or something?" Brenna let loose of her as quickly as she'd grabbed her, and Adrienne had to put her hand on the car to steady herself.

"I threw up this morning."

Adrienne was confused. On the one hand, Brenna looked so excited she could hardly contain herself, and on the other, she'd been sick this...Adrienne's heart stopped, and the same dizzying, mind-blowing sensations she'd felt when she first met Brenna washed over her now. Her brain was sprinting, but her mouth took longer to catch up. Brenna must have grown tired of waiting for her to say something, instead handing her a white stick about the size of a tongue depressor.

Adrienne knew Brenna hadn't put it in her mouth, and as much as she'd wanted this moment, she was having a difficult time looking at it. Their life would change in more than a million ways. It would no longer be just the two of them. They would be a family, and she was suddenly scared shitless. The overwhelming sense of responsibility of being a mom finally hit her. Panic rose in her throat and just as quickly disintegrated like a puff of soft breath on a dandelion.

The first thing Adrienne saw was that her hand was shaking. The second was the bright blue plus sign in the middle of the stick.

The third was the look of sheer joy on Brenna's face. After that, nothing mattered. Not how loud the shriek of joy was that came out of her mouth. Not the sight they must be to their neighbors as she pulled Brenna into her arms and swung her around like a top. And certainly not the way she kissed her tenderly, then passionately right there in their driveway. If Bruce, their neighbor to the north, hadn't cleared his throat, they might have stayed that way forever. But her forever had ceased with one bullet.

"Mommy?"

Adrienne blinked several times, pulling herself back from her fantasy life. Her heart jumped when she realized Callie was standing in front of her. How long had she been there? What had she been doing while Adrienne transported herself back to another time? *My God. She could have wandered off and...* The thought of what could have happened when she wasn't paying attention to her child made Adrienne almost vomit.

She scooped Callie onto her lap and hugged her. Callie squirmed, trying to escape. Adrienne quickly looked around to see if anything was amiss, if anyone was crying or hurt or, God forbid, a stranger in a trench coat was loitering around. She knew that last one was a stereotypical view of a child predator but the only thing she could think of in her moment of total panic.

"No, Mommy. I want to stay and play," Callie said firmly. She didn't whine or throw a fit but simply stated what she wanted. She took after Brenna in the temperament department.

"Did you want something, sweetie?" Adrienne asked, loosening her hold on the child.

"I wanna swing," Callie said and pointed her chubby finger. Pink polish was on her nails, courtesy of her sleepover at Grandma's.

Adrienne followed Callie's direction to the swings across the playground. She was relieved that Callie had asked and hadn't just wandered over there.

"Of course you can swing. I'm proud of you for asking," Adrienne said, hugging Callie before setting her down on the ground. "Race you."

All thoughts of Brenna, Sloan, and bad guys disappeared with the sound of her little girl's squeals of laughter beside her.

❖

Sloan's head pounded and her stomach lurched when she dared to turn over. A sharp pain sliced through her right eye when she opened it, and she immediately slammed it shut, groaning at the effort. She lay still for several minutes as the events of last night rewound behind her eyelids. She remembered everything leading up to talking with Adrienne on the beach and the four cocktails that followed. Everything after that was more than a little foggy. She did remember she'd at least had enough sense to save her drinking until after she reached home.

Her body insisted that she lie quietly for a few minutes as her head cleared. The noises around her were familiar. The sounds of the city outside her window and the soothing hum of the fan rotating over her bed. The usual melodic ticking of the antique Big Ben alarm clock on her nightstand felt like an ice pick stabbing just above her right ear this morning.

Risking another shot of agony, Sloan put her hand over her eyes and opened one of them, then the other. That slight move made her stomach jump, and she took several deep breaths to calm it. She thought it ironic how any movement made her need to puke, but unless she wanted to deal with a disgusting mess, she had to get to the bathroom if she did.

Her stomach settled, Sloan removed her hand from over her eyes and risked the full force of the morning sun on her obviously overindulged body. Fighting down another wave of nausea, she rolled over onto her side and slowly sat up. The room spun, and she placed both feet on the floor in a ridiculous attempt to steady the world around her.

She was still dressed in the clothes she'd worn to the party, including her shoes, and had an awful taste in her mouth. She wasn't even fit to be around herself. She slowly and carefully made her way to the adjoining bathroom, hustling the last few steps before the liquid contents of her stomach emptied into the bright-white porcelain toilet.

"Oh my God," Sloan moaned, sitting back, her butt on the hard tile floor, back against the wall, and holding her pounding head in her hands. She couldn't remember the last time she'd drunk enough to make her feel this bad. It had to have been in college or maybe the evening after scoring her first big job after graduating from law school. It didn't matter, because if anyone could see her now, she would be completely humiliated. And all over a woman. *This* was why she didn't get involved. *This* was why she kept things light and easy. *This* was why she ended things before they got too serious. This loss of control was not worth it.

She remembered last night and the touch of Adrienne's hands on her and the feel of her body pressed against her again. It had felt so right. It always had and surprisingly still did. No one had ever felt as good as Adrienne. Sloan had no self-control when it came to Adrienne, and she didn't want to even try. She needed Adrienne's lips on hers, to feel her body mold against her, hear the moans of pleasure and desire Adrienne could never hold back. This waiting had been agony, her need more powerful than she'd ever experienced. Sloan had known what was around the corner if she kissed Adrienne. If she touched her. And that knowledge had driven her forward.

Everything had ceased to exist when their lips finally met. The world around them had disappeared. Lingering emptiness Sloan was not aware was cloaked around her had drifted away like the outgoing tide, replaced by a euphoria she could only describe as the crashing of the waves around them.

She kept the kiss tentative and exploring, fighting the need to plunder and take. When Adrienne had responded, need overtook common sense, and Sloan had pulled Adrienne against her. Adrienne had looped her arms around Sloan's neck, lifting herself closer, her breasts pressing against Sloan's.

Then Adrienne had pushed her away.

Carefully getting to her feet, Sloan managed to strip and step into the shower without a repeat visit to the porcelain god. She sat on the bench in the corner and let her head loll back as the cool water sprayed over her body, rinsing off the general nastiness of a night of too much alcohol, too many emotions, and way too many memories.

Why had Adrienne come back into her life? Why had she let Adrienne get to her again? How had she let Adrienne worm her way back under her skin to the point that, if she wasn't thinking about her, she wanted to be with her? She was good at maintaining an emotional distance. She had mastered the art after she left Adrienne sleeping in her bed that last time.

Sloan didn't want to leave. She wanted to take off all her clothes and crawl back into bed and press her naked body against Adrienne. Adrienne would be warm, soft, and inviting. Even when sleeping, Adrienne would mold her body into hers, snuggling up to Sloan during the night. They fit together perfectly, like God or someone had intended.

Sloan stood at the foot of the bed watching the steady rise and fall of Adrienne's breathing. She wanted to feel Adrienne's warm breath on her skin, inhale her life-affirming air as they kissed, touch her skin as she explored her body as if for the first time. Her fingers itched as she remembered the secret places of Adrienne's desire, the ones that made her tremble and beg for release. She needed to feel Adrienne's body respond, hear Adrienne call her name when she came.

But this wasn't about what she wanted or needed. It was what she had to do. She had to leave. They'd said their good-byes last night. Actually they'd said their good-byes every night for the past few weeks. They both knew this day was coming, and by tacit mutual agreement, both of them knew their time together would end. Sloan was going to law school in California, and Adrienne was flying to Italy in three days. They were going their separate ways, both of them mature enough to realize that a long-distance relationship was just not in their deck of cards. After one last light kiss on Adrienne's cheek, Sloan quietly closed the door behind her.

It was a moonless night, and Sloan's feet dragged as she walked the thirty yards to where her car was parked. It was such an effort she could have sworn she was slogging through mud up to her knees. With every step her heart cracked open a little wider, and she forced herself not to look back. Her life was moving forward, and with it came commitments she could not renege on; it was far too late to turn back now.

The familiar beep of the alarm and unlocking of the two doors made it all real. She was leaving Adrienne's bed for the last time. Her car would never again be parked in the space next to Adrienne's red Toyota. Sloan closed the door and let her head fall back, closing her eyes. She didn't want to see the stairs leading up to Adrienne's door for fear she'd climb them and never come back down.

Taking a deep breath, Sloan turned the key, and the powerful engine roared to life. She had to use her side mirrors to back out, as her rear window was blocked by what she'd packed for the next chapter in her life. What couldn't fit had been shipped to her new apartment and would arrive the day after she did, but first Sloan had to manage a three-day drive across the country.

The first day Sloan didn't even try to stanch the tears that flowed freely down her cheeks. The second, she alternated between sniffles and downright sobs. By the time she pulled into her new parking spot, her eyes were dry, her heart closed and locked. She'd symbolically thrown the key away somewhere in Colorado.

Feeling marginally human, Sloan dressed in a pair of cutoff sweats and a too-thin-to-wear-in-public T-shirt. She managed to keep down a glass of water and a piece of dry toast and, refilling her glass, opened the patio door, fully intending to spend what was left of the day in the sun. A little vitamin D would do wonders for her recovery. Her disposition was another matter altogether.

As much as she didn't want it, every time Sloan closed her eyes, images of Adrienne floated to the surface. In one she was standing next to Lauren, their heads close together as if sharing a confidence. In another she was in the middle of a group, laughing along with several others. But the one that continued to take Sloan's breath away was Adrienne bathed in moonlight, walking on the beach toward her.

After the pounding in her head subsided to a dull throb, she wished she could say the same about the throbbing between her legs. It was getting more and more difficult to think about anything other than Adrienne, which was certainly not doing anything to dampen her almost-constant state of arousal. Sloan thought of calling someone, then changed her mind when her stomach rolled. She was in no condition for anything. Instead, she pulled out her briefcase, fired up her laptop, and tried to concentrate on the dozens of unanswered emails that had arrived in her in-box since she'd last checked Friday afternoon.

CHAPTER NINETEEN

Oh, my, Adrienne. You look beautiful," Maria said when she walked through the front door. Callie was already in bed, hopefully asleep. If not, and she heard her grandmother's voice, she'd be tottering down the steps any moment.

"Thanks, Mom." Adrienne gathered up the matching jacket to her dress. Twenty minutes ago she'd pulled her Vera Wang from the back of her closet, still wrapped in the clear plastic wrap from the cleaners.

Elliott had invited her and Robert to the Children's Education Fund benefit tonight; however, Adrienne would have gone without the invitation. The Children's Education Fund was one of Brenna's favorite charities, and since she had become a mother and understood the challenges that she faced as an adult with a good job and a steady relationship, she could only imagine how difficult parenting could be for a teenage girl who didn't have her resources.

It had been two weeks since her disastrous kiss on the beach with Sloan, and she wouldn't be surprised if she saw her tonight. She'd thought about sending her regrets, but this event had been important to Brenna. Thus it was important to her. She'd even toyed with the idea of having one of her friends masquerade as her date for the evening, but that sounded ridiculous and cowardly.

She grabbed the small matching clutch, slid her feet into her black pumps, and took one last look at herself in the mirror in her bedroom. Her makeup was flawless, much heavier than her normal everyday wear. Hell, she'd had to wipe off the eyeliner twice, not used to putting on the damn stuff. She'd bought a new shade of lipstick, justifying the high cost as a business expense. She'd bought the dress seven or eight months ago for a similar event, so it should have fit her perfectly. Now it was a little loose, but she couldn't do anything about it.

"Have fun," her mother said after bussing her on the cheek, careful not to touch her made-up face. What she really meant was "have some fun." She knew her mother worried about her and how she hadn't started dating again or done anything other than work. The last three years were nothing like she had envisioned them to be, but it was what it was, and as with every other challenge she faced, she kept her head up and pushed on.

Leaving her keys with the valet, Adrienne tucked the ticket into her bag, checked to make sure her phone was on vibrate, and entered the hotel. The event this year was held at the Dana, a beautiful waterfront location on Mission Bay. The benefit was so successful it outgrew its venue each year.

Adrienne followed the signs to the event, trailing couples as they traversed the lighted stone path surrounded by the hotel's lush, perfectly manicured landscaping. Passing a sprawling lawn area and an inviting swimming pool, she noticed several people in formal wear stepping off a boat docked at the adjacent marina.

She entered the ballroom with its eighteen-foot-high ceilings, floor-to-ceiling windows providing a spectacular view of the water. Last year she had seen Elliott and her wife Lauren at this event but had never been in a positon to speak with them. They made a striking couple: Elliott long and lean, with a look of contentment that Adrienne envied. Lauren was the perfect complement, looking equally happy as she stood beside her wife. In that moment, overwhelming sadness had engulfed Adrienne, and it had been all she could do to get through the evening without sobbing. That was how she had pictured her life with Brenna. As it was, she had left much later than she wanted to and much earlier than she should have. She'd made it home and shooed her mother out the door before breaking down. Now, twelve months further along in her journey as a widow, Adrienne hoped she was strong enough to not have a repeat experience.

The crowd was boisterous, the room energized as the who's who of San Diego rubbed elbows with their peers and those who desperately wanted to be. It was a traditional black-tie affair, and this year was no different. The men dressed in Armani, Hugo Boss, Calvin Klein, and a variety of other designers Adrienne had no clue of, or interest in. It was a tuxedo, and she'd never understood how the basic suit could have such various styles. The women's attire, on the other hand, formed a rainbow of color—reds and blues predominant—with a smattering of white gowns scattered throughout the large room.

Adrienne accepted a glass of sparkling water from a passing waiter but declined an hors d'oeuvre from another. She'd attended several of these events but had never been able to juggle a purse, a beverage, and a plate of food and shake hands simultaneously. And because her stomach had been in knots all day, she wasn't interested in eating at all.

Someone called her name, and she turned to see Robert's wife Georgia coming her way. Georgia was as large as Robert was thin, and seeing them together always reminded Adrienne of the nursery rhyme about Jack Spratt, who could eat no fat, and his wife could eat no lean. She shook her head, quickly erasing that image from her mind, and greeted the woman who had been nothing but friendly and welcoming to her every time they met.

"Adrienne, you look beautiful," Georgia said in her thick Texas drawl.

"Thank you, Georgia. You as well. That's a beautiful dress."

"Oh, it's just something I had in the back of my closet."

Adrienne knew that to be true. She'd seen Georgia wear this dress when she'd attended their son's wedding last year.

"Your pearls are stunning," Georgia told her.

"These old things," Adrienne said, fingering the strand of Mikimoto white South Sea pearls draped around her neck. They were a gift from Brenna on their first wedding anniversary, and other than a few other times that she'd worn them, she'd left them tucked away neatly in their blue box on the top shelf of her safe for the past three years. She'd pulled them out not only because they were the perfect accessory to her dress but because she needed a piece of Brenna with her tonight.

Georgia slipped her hand through Adrienne's elbow. "Let's go get something to eat. I'm starved," she said, pulling Adrienne toward the buffet table. Ten minutes later, Georgia waved to someone, excused herself, and waddled across the room to greet a woman in a hideous orange dress.

Adrienne sipped her champagne, looking at her program to see what table she'd been assigned. The event tonight consisted of a mixture of a silent auction, speeches, and videos of the girls the foundation had helped over the years—gut-wrenching, heartbreaking stories of those who still needed their help—the good food and open bar designed specifically to encourage the guests to pull out their American Express cards.

"I saw your name on the attendee list."

Adrienne went completely still. Sloan's voice over her left shoulder sent chills down her spine—the good kind. She had a hard time catching her breath, and her knees felt a little weak. Instead of focusing on the silent slide show filling the screen around the room, her mind flashed back to the many, many times Sloan's body had pressed against hers, whispering sweet nothings and hot somethings into her ear. A shudder ran through her, and her nipples hardened.

Adrienne carefully turned around, not used to the height of the heels on her new shoes, and once she did, what little breath that was in her lungs evaporated. She had never seen Sloan in formal wear, and she was striking.

Her jacket was jet-black with a mandarin collar, worn over a crisp white shirt. Instead of a tie, a black onyx stud held the collar closed. Smaller black studs peeked out down the front of her shirt. The material looked like finely spun silk that would be as soft as a rose petal. Without thinking, Adrienne reached out but stopped herself an instant before she touched Sloan. She opened her mouth to say something, but closed it just as fast, so shocked by her actions she couldn't speak. Before, she would have touched Sloan without the slightest hesitation. Now she had no right, nor should she. She curled her fingers into a fist and squeezed tightly before dropping her hand to her side.

Adrienne darted her gaze around the room, paying special attention to her feet, the tension in the air thick between them. She could see Sloan's chest rising and falling quicker than it had been before. Gathering herself together, she forced herself to smile and finally looked at Sloan.

What was reflected in Sloan's eyes was so powerful it almost made her take a step back. Her look was intense, her pupils dilated, an inferno of desire raging behind her eyes. Adrienne could feel the tension in Sloan's body. She was familiar with this sexual energy between them, but its magnitude and intensity was almost overwhelming.

"Sloan, there you are, darling."

A voice belonging to a blonde who took the phrase *little black dress* to an entirely new level stopped next to Sloan. She put both perfectly manicured, ruby-red nails around Sloan's arm, stood on her toes, and kissed her.

"I've been looking for you all night. I knew you'd be here. Oh, my, don't you look yummy. Armani?" The woman practically purred and leaned closer so that more than just her hands was touching Sloan's suit.

Jealousy burned through Adrienne at the familiarity between this woman and Sloan. Obviously, she and Sloan weren't business associates. Nor were they simply two people who supported the same cause.

Sloan took a step to the side, tactfully disengaging herself from the woman by pulling her arm free and putting more distance between them.

"Hello, Shauna." Sloan's greeting was anything but warm.

The woman didn't seem to take the hint and moved in, obviously staking her claim to Sloan. Or what she thought was her claim.

"Sloan, you never called." She pressed her body to Sloan's side, stroking the material of her jacket in the same spot Adrienne would have if she hadn't stopped herself in time. This woman obviously had a more recent right to do so than Adrienne did.

Sloan's jaw clenched, and Adrienne felt a petty sense of superiority that Sloan wasn't the slightest bit interested in this woman. "We talked about this, Shauna. Excuse me." Sloan's voice was hard and firm, and she was barely looking at the woman.

Sloan reached for Adrienne's hand and pulled her with her as she walked away, but not before Adrienne saw a glare of pure hatred in the woman's eyes directed at her.

Sloan held her hand as they hurried across the room to one of the four bars strategically placed in the corners. Sloan ordered a Crown and Coke, then looked at her, silently asking if she would like anything.

"I'll have what she's having." Adrienne needed something strong to help her wrap her head around what had just happened.

Sloan only let go of her hand when she reached into her pocket, pulled out some money, and left a generous tip in the brandy snifter on the bar. Then she took her hand again, and they walked several steps away before she stopped.

Taking a swallow of her drink, Sloan looked at their clasped hands and, clearly realizing what she was doing, quickly released her. "Sorry." She tilted her head in the opposite direction to indicate Shauna. She looked at Adrienne's hand and then up at her. "Sorry about that too. I wasn't about to leave you standing there with her."

"I was expecting her to pull out her dagger and stick me with it. But then I realized there was nowhere she could have hidden a tissue, let alone a knife."

Sloan's look of confusion told Adrienne that she had no clue what Adrienne was talking about.

"Never mind. Obviously…she can't take no for an answer."

"No, she can't."

"A pest?"

"More like a stalker," Sloan said quickly, a hint of anger in her voice. "Again, I apologize. I don't think she'll bother you anymore this evening," Sloan commented, looking around the room as if trying to determine the location of the woman.

"I can take care of myself. It's not the first time I—" Adrienne snapped her mouth shut, realizing what she was about to say, but not before Sloan picked up on it. Her face warmed when Sloan smiled that sexy smile that could always bring Adrienne to her knees.

"What can I say? I was just a chick magnet back in college."

"You still are," Adrienne said, her voice husky and serious.

"Yeah, well, that kind of trouble I can do without."

Sloan took another swallow of her cocktail, surveying the crowd. She reached out again, this time taking Adrienne by the arm, and pulled her close. Adrienne's heart beat double time with excitement and dread.

"That guy behind you kept backing up, and he was going to step on you any second." Sloan nodded toward something behind her, and Adrienne saw the man she was referring to. He was so busy talking to the people in front of him, he wasn't watching where he was going—or backing up, as was the case.

"Thanks. That would have hurt." Adrienne smiled.

Several minutes passed, neither of them saying anything, the silence almost deafening. Adrienne reminded herself this was a charity function and she should mingle. But that message stopped about halfway between her brain and her feet.

Sloan smelled wonderful and looked even better in her tuxedo. Standing next to her, Adrienne felt the first, second, and third inkling of arousal. Sloan was what she would describe as devilishly attractive, and Adrienne had caught more than a few women eyeing her as if she were dinner or maybe, if they were lucky, a nightcap. What had that woman called her? Yummy?

"Adrienne, I'm glad you could make it," Elliott said. Lauren was beside her, holding her hand.

"Thank you for the invitation. The Children's Education Fund was one of my wife's favorite charities. We came every year."

"Really?" Lauren asked. "I don't recall ever meeting you." She frowned as if she was trying to remember a forgotten conversation.

"We were never in the same place at the same time. You can't be expected to meet every one of the hundreds of people who attend this event," Adrienne added.

"No, you're right." Lauren sighed. "It's just that I try to make it a point to meet everyone I didn't meet the year before." Lauren was on the board of the foundation that oversaw distribution of monies to the Children's Education Fund. "It's good for business," she said, winking at Adrienne.

The lights dimmed three times, signaling that everyone should take their seats because the program was about to begin. Adrienne found her table and sat down between the western division head of FedEx and the president of the Greater San Diego Bar Association. Their wives sat on either side of the two men. She held her breath, waiting for the other five seats to be filled, hoping Sloan wouldn't occupy one of them. Finally, another man and two other couples sat down just before the house lights dimmed.

The music rolled, and a loud, booming voice came over the speakers introducing the president of the Children's Education Fund. Half listening to the speaker, Adrienne glanced around her. She recognized several city leaders, the quarterback for the San Diego Chargers and his wife, several elected city officials, and more than a few local celebrities. As she skimmed the occupants seated at the table right across from hers, she saw Sloan sitting directly in front of her and looking right at her. Granted, fifteen people and two tables were between them, but it was as if they were sitting inches apart. This was going to be a long evening.

Dinner was better than average at these feed-four-hundred-people events, and as the speeches droned on, Adrienne debated with herself if she should leave as soon as it was politely possible. On the one hand, she wanted to stay and talk to some interesting people and simply enjoy herself. On the other hand was Sloan. No matter how hard she tried, her eyes kept drifting back to Sloan. What was thrilling and unnerving was that when she did, more often than not, their eyes met.

Speeches over, donations requested, and dinner cleared, the DJ began. He selected different songs until he hit the right combination of music that got the attendees on their feet. Two by two, couples made their way to the dance floor that had been set up in the front corner of the large room. One very brave gay couple walked confidently to the center of the floor and, with practiced ease, moved into each other's arms.

The couples at Adrienne's table joined them, as did several at Sloan's, leaving Adrienne an unobstructed view between them. Adrienne was about to get up and mingle when a familiar song floated through the speakers, and she almost doubled over in pain. It was the song she and Brenna had dubbed as their song. It was the one played at their wedding and the one for their first dance as a married couple. Adrienne's hands started to shake, and her skin felt like it was on fire. She needed to escape, run out of the room and keep running until the pain receded yet again. But she didn't think her legs would hold her. The room started to spin, and suddenly she was back in that dark, lonely place of the instant she knew Brenna was dead. She gasped for air, not able to breathe.

"I've got you," a familiar voice said as someone pulled her onto her feet. A solid arm wrapped around her waist and steadied her as they both started walking. Fog filled her brain and lights were flashing behind her eyes, and Adrienne stumbled before the voice pulled her closer. "I've got you. You're going to be all right," it repeated. Then she was wrapped in a cocoon of strength and warmth.

Slowly, very slowly, the fog lifted and the flashing lights receded, and Adrienne became aware of her surroundings. She was on the dance floor, her feet moving without conscious thought. The music was…she stiffened. The song!

"It's all right. I have you."

Sloan's voice blew away the remaining cloudiness like a soft, cool breeze. Sloan was holding her right hand, her left gripping Sloan's neck like a lifeline. Sloan held her close, their bodies touching as they moved across the dance floor. Sloan's mouth was close enough to her ear she only had to whisper.

Song after song they stayed that way, neither of them speaking or putting any distance between them. Sloan's arms were strong and held her tight, but Adrienne knew that if she were to step away,

Sloan would let her go. She started to relax, and her mind shifted from pain and memories to awareness of right now, this moment.

Sloan's hand was firm as it held hers—that same hand that could caress with a gentleness that touched her heart and drive into her until she begged for release. The arm that now held her safe had also kept her close in the dark as they slept. Their bodies fit together perfectly, their breasts touching, their bellies snug against each other, fabric the only thing separating them now. Their legs scissored in the familiar way lovers' do. Adrienne's face was pressed against Sloan's neck, and the familiar scent of her cologne took her back to that time, all those years ago, when it was just the two of them.

Adrienne felt the strain of tension in Sloan's body. Adrienne knew Sloan, her body's reaction. Sloan wasn't afraid Adrienne would continue with her meltdown. No, this was something entirely different. Sloan was working hard to contain her desire for her, and Adrienne suddenly didn't want her to. Her feelings caught her off guard, and she fought them. One minute she was grieving for Brenna like it was yesterday, and the next she was breathless with desire for Sloan. Her body was alive with sensation, as if awakening from a long sleep. Slowly at first, then with increasing intensity and urgency, rolling waves of longing crashed through her. Her own breathing became shallow, and Sloan pulled her even closer.

Heat shot through Adrienne down to her core, and her body responded in an all-too-familiar way. Tingles of electricity teased her skin where Sloan touched her. The rocking motion of the dance provided foreplay to something more. Her visceral reaction was staggering, her clit hot and swollen. Adrienne trembled with want and need. She lifted her head and met Sloan's burning eyes.

Passion, desire, need, and a variety of other equally sensually descriptive words flashed through Adrienne's brain. Her heart soared. Sloan wanted her; there was no mistaking that. Thick, dark lashes framed the large brown eyes that bored into her soul. The connection was powerful and as tight as it had been all those years ago. Adrienne's body melted into Sloan's. An instant later, Sloan's words shocked her.

"Feeling better?"

Adrienne would have sworn Sloan would have said something else. Something more personal like "Let's get out of here." She didn't know if the pounding in her brain was disappointment or admiration of Sloan's restraint.

It took the better part of a minute for Adrienne to reply, her nerves and emotions in a jumble. "Yes, thank you." Sloan loosened her grip, putting some space between them. Adrienne immediately reacted to losing contact by surging toward Sloan again. After a moment, Sloan stepped back once more.

"Adrienne?" Sloan's voice was tight.

"No." Adrienne's meaning was clear that nothing was going to happen between them. "I think I'd better go," Adrienne said, her mind a jumble of confusion and embarrassment again. One minute she was mourning her dead wife, the next wishing Sloan would take her to a dark corner and make her forget all about her pain. God, she was fucked up.

"I'll walk you to your car."

"No. Stay and enjoy yourself. I'll say my good-byes to Elliott and Lauren. I have to get home anyway."

Somehow Adrienne managed to locate the valet stand and drive home, her mind a whirl of images and sensations.

CHAPTER TWENTY

Excuse me?"

Elliott signaled the waitress for more coffee. Sloan had agreed to meet with Elliott Monday morning at Eggstatic, a trendy eatery a few miles from the office. Her appetite wasn't up to her typical plate of bacon, eggs, and pancakes, and she hoped the bowl of oatmeal she ate stayed right where it was. At least Elliott had waited until Sloan pushed her bowl away before broaching the subject she knew would come up.

"Are you and Adrienne involved?"

This was the third time Elliott had asked the question, and Sloan had a hard time dodging each one. Elliott's eyes never left Sloan's. Elliott was direct in her dealings with clients, and her employees were no exception.

Sloan swallowed the bile tickling the back of her throat. "No," she answered, just as direct.

"I saw you two on the dance floor." Her tone wasn't accusatory, but Sloan felt it nonetheless. Elliott was looking at her as if she'd been in Sloan's pocket with her and Adrienne Saturday night.

"We danced, yes." Sloan didn't confirm or deny what Elliott might be thinking. Elliott raised her eyebrows. "Are you trying to ask me something, Elliott? Because it's not like you to dance around a subject."

"Did something happen between you two?"

"No." Other than the kiss on the beach that had sent her into another world and wanting to drag Adrienne into a corner off the dance floor and drop to her knees. She wasn't lying, not really. Adrienne had made it clear there was nothing between them, and Sloan had refused to take advantage of her vulnerability the other night; therefore, nothing had happened. Admittedly she was splitting hairs, but Sloan had graduated from one of the top law schools in the country and could rationalize just about anything.

Elliott looked at her for several long moments. Sloan was tempted to fill the silence, but that was a sure sign of guilt—even if she didn't feel guilty. She maintained eye contact until Elliott finally said, "I need you to go to Tampa."

Sloan wasn't expecting Elliott to let the subject drop. "Tampa? What's in Tampa?"

"One of Auburn's suppliers. Actually, it's in Crystal River, about ninety miles north of Tampa. I was scheduled to meet Robert there Tuesday and Wednesday, but something's come up. You know what we're looking for. It's more of a cursory visit than anything else. I'm comfortable with this deal. Just dotting a few *t*'s and crossing the last *i*."

Sloan's mind raced through what she remembered of her calendar for the week. She didn't know exactly what meetings she had, but Beth, her assistant, would miraculously make them disappear and reappear on a later date.

"Is this about something you saw when you went to Portland and Augusta?" Sloan asked.

"No. This is something different. Robert was talking about it during one of our meetings last week, and I'd like to see it myself, but I can't. Teresa will have your flight and hotel arrangements." Elliott reached for the check, signaling that the conversation and breakfast were over.

Her itinerary was inside an orange transparent folder on her desk when Sloan arrived twenty minutes later. She had to make a stop at the Walgreens to replace her every-four-hour dose of Tylenol with Alka-Seltzer to shake off the remaining yuck of Saturday night. After leaving the charity, she'd again drunk way too much. This wasn't a good sign that every time she saw Adrienne she needed to get drunk in an attempt to forget her.

Sloan dropped two of the chalky-white tablets into the water and immediately felt a little better when she heard and saw the familiar tablets fizz. The bubbly concoction of sodium bicarbonate, citric acid, and a few other ingredients Sloan couldn't remember was marketed for relief of minor aches, pains, fever, headache, heartburn, stomachache, indigestion, and a hangover, while neutralizing excess stomach acid. That just about covered her symptoms. It had been a miracle cure in college, and she hoped it still would be more than ten years later. It was probably all in her head, she thought, and chuckled at her own play on words, the pounding in her head subsiding slightly.

Sloan quickly reviewed the schedule for her trip to Florida. She'd depart from San Diego airport Wednesday afternoon and meet Robert in the lobby of the facility in Crystal River Thursday morning at eight thirty. Downing the liquid medicine in four swallows, Sloan flipped to the next section in the packet, which contained information about Crystal River. She reminded herself to thank Teresa for the helpful data. Sloan liked to have at least some idea of where she was going.

Scanning the material, she deduced that the small town wasn't exactly a hotbed of entertainment. Sloan wasn't interested in the one shopping mall or in spending her free time at the Manatee Lanes, the local bowling alley. Reading on, Sloan learned that Crystal River was the self-professed Home of the Manatee—large, plant-eating mammals sometimes known as sea cows. That was an image she didn't need stuck in her head but a fact cited in Wikipedia. She'd have to remember that important detail if she ever auditioned for *Jeopardy*.

At least Adrienne wouldn't be there since she didn't see her name in any of the meeting information. Evidently, she had one small god in her life who saw fit to keep Adrienne home. The last thing she needed was there to be only one good hotel in a small town and Adrienne in the room down the hall.

Sloan looked around, double-checking that she was alone in

her office before releasing the belch generated by the mysterious cure-all drink. It wasn't ladylike, as her mother would say, but given the way she'd felt yesterday and today, Sloan didn't care. If the medicine worked, and she hoped it did, it didn't matter. Besides, it wasn't like she was onstage accepting an Academy Award, for heaven's sake. She hiccupped, wiped her nose, and settled in for another long day behind her desk.

❖

Adrienne parked in the short-term parking garage, grabbed her suitcase, and ran to the elevators. She'd been on time this afternoon until Callie had barfed all over her just before she handed the squirming toddler to her mother. Not only had she packed just enough clothes for the trip, but Callie's lunch had ended up in her hair, some sliding down the V of her T-shirt and between her breasts. Of course, Callie hadn't given the slightest indication she might vomit and was happy and giggly right after she did. The joys of motherhood, Adrienne thought as she hurried home to shower and change.

The security line was mercifully short, the TSA agents friendly and accommodating, and she arrived at her gate just before the last boarding call. The gate area was empty, and she showed her boarding pass to the smiling gate agent, who told her to have a nice flight. A very gay flight attendant welcomed her aboard, and she found her aisle seat in row twenty-one and sat down. It wasn't until several minutes later that she took a deep breath and started to relax.

"Tight connection?"

Adrienne almost jumped when the woman beside her spoke. She'd been so caught up in not missing her flight that she hadn't noticed anyone else on the plane. She turned her head and looked into a stunning pair of blue eyes. In her peripheral vision, Adrienne could see that the woman had a beautiful face to go with her extraordinary eyes that seemed to pull her in. In a nanosecond Adrienne thought of sandy beaches, crystal-clear water, warm sunshine, and hours of languid sex. She shook her head to toss that thought out of her mind.

It was a five-hour flight, which would be much longer if those were the thoughts in her head.

She smiled and the woman smiled back. Adrienne's heart skittered. *WTF?* Seeing Sloan again and the kiss on the beach must have opened the firehose of her pent-up libido. "Something like that," she replied. Adrienne didn't think her seatmate, however gorgeous, would really want to know the details of her daughter's gastrointestinal upset.

"Are you going or coming?" the woman asked as the flight attendant gave the required safety instructions.

Adrienne gasped, and she hid her reaction in a small cough. If she continued to react to every word that was even slightly sexually related, she was in big, big trouble.

"Going, business," Adrienne added.

"What business are you in?" the woman managed to say as the captain's voice came over the intercom, informing them they were number four in line for takeoff.

"I'm an attorney. I represent a client vying for investment capital. The investor is touring a facility in Crystal River." That was way too much information, but the penetrating blue eyes made her nervous, and she often babbled when she was nervous.

"Brilliant and beautiful," the woman said, leaning a little closer, her voice quiet and husky.

Adrienne tried not to react to the obvious come-on. She was flattered, as any woman would be, and before Brenna she would have been all over it; however, she was not interested in stepping back into the dating pool. From what she'd seen and heard from her single friends, the term *cesspool* was sometimes more applicable.

"You wouldn't have thought so if you'd seen me an hour ago," Adrienne managed to say.

"I seriously doubt it," Brilliant Blue Eyes stated. "Why do you say that?"

"Because I had toddler vomit in my hair and down the front of my shirt," Adrienne replied. She wondered if her subconscious was sabotaging this connection or, again, she just wasn't ready. After the kiss with Sloan on the beach and her reaction to this attractive stranger, she had no idea what was going on.

"Well, you clean up very nicely," Miss Dazzling Blue Eyes said after more than a cursory look at the parts of Adrienne's body she could see in the tight seating area.

Adrienne's body tingled where the woman looked at her. She felt her nipples start to harden and reached for the briefcase she'd stowed under the seat. She pulled out a stack of folders and a pen. She needed to get her mind off the thoughts and images spinning around in her head and other things swirling around in the lower parts of her body.

What in the hell is going on? One minute she never noticed another woman, and now she was reacting to the stranger beside her. Did this woman think she would have a quickie in the cramped lavatory? The thought made Adrienne's heart race, adding to her confusion and general WTF of the last ten minutes.

"Thank you," Adrienne said feeling her cheeks blush. "Unfortunately, I've had lots of practice."

"How old is your barf beast?"

Adrienne looked back at the woman. She expected to see repulsion on her face but instead saw humor. "Three."

"Boy or girl?"

"Girl."

"What's her name?"

"Callie." Adrienne watched for any sign that the mention of her daughter threw cold water on this woman like it had for so many others. She'd been hit on before, and mentioning Callie was a convenient way of giving the woman a polite out. Not with this woman.

"Is she as beautiful as her mother?"

Adrienne's pulse raced as Miss Amazing Blue Eyes focused on her. She took a deep breath to calm down and get her brain back together. "Yes, she's the spitting image of Brenna."

Adrienne watched as the woman comprehended her statement, then looked at her left hand. The obvious inference that she was involved with someone and the sparkling ring on her finger was a one-two punch that effectively slammed the door on the woman's interest. Adrienne didn't know if she was disappointed or relieved. The roar of the engines revving as they headed down the runway ended their conversation.

❖

Sloan accepted the complimentary cocktail that the very cute flight attendant in first class offered her. Elliott had insisted she fly first class due to the inconvenience of the short notice. Who was she to refuse? Her mama didn't raise no fool.

Miraculously, the seat beside her was empty. With the limited number of flights and the abundance of frequent-flier programs, usually every seat in the plane was full. She sipped on her drink and gazed out the window. She had been surprised to see Adrienne turn into the aisle and hurry to her seat. For an instant Sloan had thought her seat was immediately to her right, but when Adrienne kept moving she found she was disappointed. She'd looked a little frazzled, and considering that no one had been boarding in at least five minutes, it was obvious she was running late.

Sloan's ears popped as the plane gained altitude. The familiar ding and the flight attendant informing the passengers it was safe to turn on electronic devices should have been her signal to get some work done. She had an in-box full of electronic documents to review, and a briefcase of those that had arrived in paper form. She was hoping to get through most of her work during her five hours of uninterrupted time.

In the beginning of her career it had been exciting to go somewhere on someone else's dime, so to speak. She loved staying in nice hotels and eating in fabulous restaurants. She had also been ridiculously impressed with herself when people would look at her and see a successful lesbian traveling on company business. Now it had just become a chore that she tolerated. If she thought about it too much she'd probably begin to hate it, and as often as she had to maneuver through airports and deal with cranky taxi drivers, inexperienced Uber drivers, and stale hotel rooms, that would not be a good thing.

The flight attendant greeted her by name and offered her a second drink, which she readily accepted. By the time she reached Tampa, retrieved the rental car, plugged in her destination in the GPS, and hit the road, any effects of the alcohol would be out of her system. That, and it was after five in many parts of the world.

She debated whether to go talk with Adrienne. She couldn't deny that a surge of excitement had shot through her when she saw her board. She had only one reason for being on this flight, and that was to be with Robert at the site. Sloan wondered if Adrienne knew Elliott wasn't coming and she would be the one they showed around. Elliott hadn't mentioned if she'd informed Robert, but then again she didn't need to tell her if she had. She was the representative of Foster McKenzie, and that was all that mattered.

Movement out of the corner of her eye drew Sloan's attention. For an instant, she thought it might be Adrienne coming to talk with her. More than likely it was a fellow passenger heading to the lavatory.

Heat filled her core when Sloan remembered a trip she herself had taken to the small, cramped bathroom.

It was spring break their senior year, and they were on their way to Belize. Nothing but nine days of sun, sand, and privacy. Sloan had picked Adrienne up earlier that morning, her overnight bag stowed in the trunk.

"Is that all you packed?" Adrienne asked skeptically as Sloan hefted her suitcase into the trunk. "We're going to be there for a week."

Sloan closed the lid, then held open the passenger door for Adrienne to enter. Before she did, Sloan pressed her body against Adrienne. Heat flared between them, as it always did when they were together. She kissed her long, and passionately, the meaning unmistakable.

"Other than a swimsuit, the only thing I plan on covering my body with is sunscreen and you."

It was just after the beverage cart moved to the row in front of theirs when Adrienne leaned into Sloan. Her breasts pressed against her arm, and she felt Adrienne's hard nipple. "Come with me," she whispered seductively, her breath hot against her ear.

Adrienne sensuously slid from the middle seat across Sloan to step into the aisle. She pressed her ass into Sloan's lap, and Sloan couldn't suppress a groan. God, she loved Adrienne's ass, and the things she could do with it drove her out of her mind. There was no mistaking where they were headed and what they were going to do when they got there. Sloan's legs were weak as she followed Adrienne toward the rear of the plane.

Luck was on their side that no one was in line, and they ducked into the lavatory on the left. It was early into the four-hour flight, and their chance of being interrupted was slim. The flight attendants were busy serving passengers, and no one had seen them push the door shut behind them.

Adrienne locked the door and immediately reached for her. Her lips were hot and her hands busy, and as much as Sloan was expecting this, she was momentarily stunned. She'd had a lot of wild sexual experiences, but this was a first. She hadn't expected it from Adrienne, and like a match thrown into a puddle of gas, she exploded with need.

While Adrienne unbuttoned her shirt and opened the front closure of her bra, Sloan's shaking hands fought with the thin belt around Adrienne's waist. Adrienne accomplished her goal first, and Sloan gasped when her mouth fastened onto her breast and sucked—hard. The room was too small for Sloan to collapse when her knees gave out from pleasure, so she leaned back against the louvered door instead. She gave up trying to get her hands into Adrienne's pants and let her take the lead instead.

Lately Adrienne had initiated sex more often, her creativity expanding as her confidence grew. Sloan, a take-charge lover, hadn't felt uncomfortable in the least, and Adrienne's new attitude had added an entirely new dimension to their lovemaking.

Adrienne slid her hand down the front of Sloan's shorts and slipped her long fingers into her without hesitation. Sloan moved one hand to the back of Adrienne's head and the other to the grab bar on the wall for support. She rested her head back against the door and simply enjoyed the sensations bursting through her. Adrienne's tongue and lips were magical, her fingers on her clit breathtaking.

Sloan opened her eyes and saw their reflection in the small mirror. In any other situation, having sex in a public bathroom might have seemed cheap and disgusting, but the sight of Adrienne sucking her breast and having her hand in her pants threw Sloan over the edge. She started to moan as her orgasm wracked her, and Adrienne's free hand clamped over her mouth. Sloan was not a quiet lover and completely lost control when she came, and Adrienne needed to remind her exactly where they were.

As soon as she started to come down from one of the hardest orgasms of her life, Sloan turned them around, sat on the toilet, and pulled Adrienne's shorts off, careful not to let them touch the floor. She hurriedly placed one of Adrienne's feet on her shoulder, and Adrienne let her leg fall open, giving Sloan access to everything that was Adrienne. Sloan was overcome with the need to inhale her sweet scent, taste her again, feel her hot, wet center pulse against her tongue.

Quickly, passionately, thoroughly, almost feverishly, Sloan buried her face between Adrienne's legs. Warm thighs enclosed her in a cocoon of pleasure so exquisite Sloan almost came again. She forced herself to focus on Adrienne, her needs, the way she lifted herself to get closer to Sloan's mouth, the way she moved her hips in the familiar cadence leading up to her orgasm, the way she reached down and spread open her lips for her. God, this woman was hot, sexy, beautiful, sensuous, and every other adjective Sloan could think of to describe her. However, as Adrienne neared orgasm, Sloan's brain shut down, and she simply absorbed and memorized everything about this moment.

After they had pulled themselves together, washed their hands and faces as best they could in the very small space, and stepped out, several people were in line. Looks of shock, astonishment, and envy greeted them. One guy winked at Sloan as she passed by. What the hell, she thought. What was the worst thing that could happen to them? They were twenty-one years old and living life to the fullest. They were in love and invincible.

The plane hit some turbulence, shaking Sloan out of her hot, steamy, wet dream. Her breathing was shallow, her clit throbbing, and a bead of sweat slid down the side of her face. She looked up and saw that the first-class lavatory was unoccupied. Her hands shook as she unbuckled her seat belt and slid across the empty seat.

"Are you all right, Miss Merchant?" the flight attendant asked, concern on her face. "You look a little flushed."

I'm fine. Just so turned on I could come with one touch. "I'm fine. Thanks. I'll take a glass of ice water, if you wouldn't mind," Sloan said, slipping into the lavatory and pushing the door shut behind her. If she didn't calm down in the next two minutes, she'd have to dump the water down the front of her pants.

"Good God. What in the fuck is going on?" she asked her reflection in the mirror. "I'm thirty-six years old, but I'm reacting like a sixteen-year-old teenage boy." She ran the water in the microscopic sink, splashed some on her face and the back of her neck, and let it run over the inside of her wrists. After a few minutes, Sloan tidied up and pulled open the door.

She had just stepped out into the aisle when she looked up and froze. Adrienne was exiting the lavatory in the midsection of the aircraft. She saw her a second after Sloan glanced at her and froze too. Sloan's heart pounded in her ears as she stood there unable to move. They stared at each other, and Sloan knew Adrienne was thinking about another time they'd stepped out of an airplane restroom together.

Sloan had no idea how long she stood there, but finally a man approached Adrienne, and she was the first to look away. Sloan took advantage of the interruption and hurried back to her seat, forcing herself not to look down the long aisle while she did.

Chapter Twenty-one

Adrienne couldn't remember the last time she'd rented a car, and she was rapidly losing patience. Uber and a taxi were her means of transportation whenever she traveled, at least domestically. The few times she'd gone to Germany or Asia, she'd hired a driver. Here, she had no alternative but to drive to Crystal River, so she glanced around one more time. The line to the counter crawled forward, and every moment she stood in the rental-car terminal was one more minute she might have to face Sloan.

The incident in the plane—hell, she didn't know what to call it: incident, event, episode, flashback, scene—none of them aptly described that split second when she saw Sloan exiting the first-class lavatory. Shock had hit her first, and then memories had flooded over her so intense she couldn't breathe. She was twenty-one again, free of responsibilities, happy, her whole life in front of her. She knew what she wanted and was on her way to get it. Everything was going according to plan, and the only thing on her calendar was nine days in the sun with the sexiest woman on the planet.

Reality was so very different now. She had a huge responsibility, and her name was Callie. Adrienne believed she was happy, at least as happy as she could be with Brenna gone. Her life had taken a different track from art school to law, but she had a challenging and fulfilling career. The only things that slightly resembled art were the drawings Callie made that adorned her refrigerator. Her calendar for these next few days obviously involved Sloan, and she had to get through them before heading back to Callie and her brother's birthday party on Saturday.

Finally, keys in hand, Adrienne stowed her bag in the trunk and sat in the driver's seat. She pulled out her small pump spray of Lysol and doused every control button, the transmission shifter, seat-belt latch, and even the steering wheel. She wasn't a germophobe, but who knew how many hands had touched this car, and God only knew what they had touched. The last thing she needed was to catch something and take it home to Callie.

After programming her destination into the GPS, Adrienne exited the rental-car lot and followed the directions coming from the car speakers. Once she was on Highway 589 heading north, she set the cruise control. For the next seventy miles or so she'd be on this road, and not having to concentrate on turning or watching for road signs, she let her mind drift back to the one thing that had been occupying it for weeks—Sloan Merchant.

She'd stopped wondering why Sloan was on her flight. That was pretty clear. She was either accompanying Elliott or coming in place of Elliott. Either way, Adrienne hadn't been prepared to see her, let alone spend two days with her. But that was all it was—two days. Not even forty-eight hours. More like two six- or seven-hour days. Would she be expected to entertain Sloan? She'd planned to invite Elliott to dinner with their supplier's medical director, James Bartlow, tomorrow night, so she would have to invite Sloan instead. She could do that. Besides, James would be there as a buffer and could easily carry the conversation.

Three toll booths and seventy-eight miles later, Adrienne pulled into the hotel parking lot. It wasn't the Ritz or a Hilton, but it was new and well-lit and had an open parking space right next to the front door. She was so emotionally exhausted, all she wanted was clean sheets and a hot shower.

The room was surprisingly spacious and tastefully decorated, and Adrienne smelled fresh paint when she closed the door behind her. She laid her overnight bag on the rack and went about disinfecting every knob, dial, and button in the room. She paid particular attention to the TV remote. She'd seen a report on the

Discovery Channel several months ago about the cleanliness of hotel rooms. The remote control had more germs and bacteria than any other surface, including the toilet.

Adrienne hung her clothes in the closet. They had a few wrinkles, but they'd probably hang out by morning. The clock on the nightstand read ten fifty-five. Adrienne had called her mother when she landed, and Maria said Callie was running a slight fever but was fine. After several questions, Adrienne relaxed, knowing her daughter was in good hands. Her mother, for crying out loud, had raised six kids. She knew more than a little about what to do for a toddler with a fever. She stepped into the shower, hoping to wash away the angst of seeing Sloan today and the anticipation of the next two days as well.

CHAPTER TWENTY-TWO

Sloan had lost interest in what the man in the gray suit was saying about eight slides ago. Hadn't he heard that the best presentations included no more than ten slides? The appendix could consist of fifty, but after looking at the slide number on the one currently on the screen, she knew he had it totally backward.

Sloan had met James Bartlow earlier this morning, shortly after arriving at the supplier's facility. He was no taller than five feet five inches, and his waistline was probably fifty-five inches. He resembled the Pillsbury Dough Boy—pasty, with a limp handshake. Sloan felt the urge to wash her hands after shaking his.

Adrienne was waiting for her in the lobby, and they'd exchanged pleasantries, swapping explanations as to why they, not their respective bosses, were there. They hadn't said much since, and the forty-minute tour had focused on the technical elements of the operation, not idle chitchat. Now, almost an hour into a slide deck that looked like no end was in sight, Sloan's mind and eyes wandered.

They were sitting around a large oval table, Sloan at the far end, Adrienne several seats to her left. A spiral-bound report sat in front of everyone at the table. The smell of coffee was in the air, and six coffee cups were on the table. The blinds were drawn, the lights low as everyone focused on the large screen in front of them. Sloan focused on Adrienne.

The first thing she'd noticed this morning was Adrienne when she walked into the lobby of the facility. She was wearing a pair of tan chinos and a jade-green, long-sleeved blouse that brought out the color of her eyes. Her makeup was light, her hair pulled back into a clip at the base of her neck. Her shoes shone and matched the thin belt that circled her waist. But Adrienne looked tired. Her eyes were missing that interested, engaged sparkle Sloan knew so well, the dark circles under her makeup visible. It appeared that Adrienne had had as crappy a night as she'd had. Sloan was secretly glad.

From her vantage point she could look at everyone around the table without anyone else knowing it. All eyes were forward, including hers, but not only did she have the best view of the speaker, but she also had an unobstructed, unobserved view of Adrienne.

Sloan noticed that Adrienne looked as distracted as she was. She spun her pen in her fingers, kept glancing at her phone, and several times replied to a text message. She fiddled with her wedding ring, and Sloan wondered if she would ever take it off or wear it for the rest of her life.

She had no idea what Adrienne must have gone through when her wife died. No idea the kind of love Adrienne must have had to willingly commit to spend the rest of her life with one woman: to love, honor, and cherish, forsaking all others. God. Sloan could barely make it a few months without growing thoroughly bored.

Adrienne had the best posture in the room, and Sloan sat up a little straighter just because she was looking at her. Adrienne's hair shone, and the light reflecting off the screen accentuated her chin, her straight nose, and the curve of her lips. Adrienne had a small scar on her neck that hadn't been there when Sloan had nibbled, licked, sucked, and explored every inch of her years ago. Her face was thinner, and she wore a look of sorrow and determination. Adrienne had matured into a beautiful woman in the years since they'd been together.

Several heads turned her way, and Sloan realized that someone must have asked her a question. She made some excuse about not hearing it completely and asked Bartlow to repeat it. She felt Adrienne's eyes on her. She'd been caught not paying attention and refocused her attention on the information being shared with her.

After a catered lunch and another two hours of mind-numbing data and tour of an adjacent building, they were finished for the day. As the six men and two women filed out, Adrienne invited her and Bartlow to dinner. The man eagerly accepted, and Sloan faked her enthusiasm when she asked for directions to the restaurant.

The Hurricane Seafood Restaurant was about fifteen miles from the supplier, and Sloan used the time to answer her messages. She pulled into the parking lot just as she was finishing her conversation with Elliott. Elliott had asked her several questions that she couldn't answer, but Sloan suspected they were in the information covered today. She made a mental note to read the report tucked into her briefcase.

Adrienne and Bartlow were waiting in the bar of the restaurant, each with a glass in their hand. Sloan knew Adrienne's contained water or club soda, as she hadn't seen her drink anything stronger than that at any other dinner since this deal began. Bartlow, however, was halfway through what looked like a dark beer.

Bartlow greeted her as if they hadn't just left each other not twenty minutes ago. He signaled the waitress, and Sloan ordered a Crown Royal and Coke, her beverage of choice in just about any situation. Bartlow was telling Adrienne something about his dog when Sloan joined them and finished his story while she waited for the waitress to return.

As she sipped her drink, Adrienne and Bartlow discussed the pros and cons of different dog breeds and which were more suited to young children. Sloan focused on the crowd as she half listened to them.

Just as their dinner was served, Bartlow's phone rang. He mumbled something about his wife and excused himself from the table to take the call in private. Other than "please pass the salt," neither of them spoke after he left.

Sloan glanced up as Bartlow returned and saw he'd lost all color in his face.

"James, are you all right?" Adrienne asked, concern in her voice.

"I'm sorry. I've got to go. That was my wife. I have to get home. Her water broke. We've got to get to the hospital."

Earlier Bartlow had informed her and Adrienne that his wife was due with their second child "any day," as he phrased it. Given the way Bartlow's stomach hung over his pants, Sloan wondered how that conception had happened. She doubted he could find his penis to go to the bathroom, let alone… She shuddered.

Bartlow hurried out, leaving Sloan and Adrienne alone at the table. The silence dragged on until the awkwardness made them both speak at once.

"Tell me about your daughter."

"I want to thank you for the other night," Adrienne said, referring to the fund-raiser. She held her hand up to keep Sloan from saying more. "No. Please let me say this. I had a bad moment, and you were there to help me."

"Adrienne…"

"Please, Sloan." Adrienne took a deep breath, as if composing herself. "Please. I don't want to talk about it."

Sloan studied Adrienne across the table. The dinner lighting and the candle flickering on the table flattered Adrienne's features. She was beautiful without any enhancements and, if possible, was more beautiful as a grown woman than she'd been years ago. As much as Sloan suspected her "bad moment" had been about Adrienne's wife, she let it drop.

"Tell me about your daughter."

An expression of relief floated over Adrienne's face before she said, "Callie?"

"Do you have more than one?" Sloan replied and was rewarded with one of Adrienne's dazzling smiles. Her stomach fluttered.

"No, thank goodness. One three-year-old is enough, thank you."

"So, tell me," Sloan asked, "who carried her? You or your wife?" Sloan stumbled over the word "wife." It was surprisingly difficult to ask about Adrienne's wife in such an intimate context.

"Brenna is her birth mother." Adrienne answered as cautiously as Sloan had asked the question.

"How big was she?" Sloan hoped that was an appropriate question. At least she thought it was something mothers discussed about their babies.

"Six, two. Six pounds, two ounces," she added, probably due to Sloan's confused expression.

"How was it with a newborn?"

"Exhausting." Adrienne answered without hesitation. "Even though Brenna got up with Callie in the night, I couldn't sleep through that type of disturbance." Adrienne smiled, presumably at the memory.

Sloan couldn't believe she was having this inane conversation with Adrienne, asking such lame, stilted questions.

"I used to sleep through anything, but motherhood changes that," Adrienne replied. "And everything else, for that matter," she added.

"How so?" Sloan just wanted Adrienne to keep talking.

"Your life is no longer your own. You belong to another human being, one that is totally dependent on you for everything from food to warmth to shelter. And don't forget about the boogie man under the bed. That's one I never found in the Mommy library." Adrienne pointed her fork at Sloan for emphasis.

"Mommy library?" Sloan asked, liking the way Adrienne's face lit up as she talked about her daughter.

"That's what Brenna and I called the dozens of books we read while she was pregnant. After Callie was born, I bought dozens more just to try to figure her out."

"And have you?"

"Nope." Adrienne shook her head. "And she's only three. God help me when she's thirteen."

Sloan couldn't help but laugh with her. "Tell me about Brenna. She sounds like she was a wonderful woman. She must have been to catch you." This time Sloan felt a stab in her heart.

Adrienne hesitated so long Sloan wasn't sure she'd answer. The longer Adrienne's silence, the more Sloan realized she really didn't want to know about Brenna. Didn't want to know about their life together. Didn't want to know how they made each other happy, how they were so in love and everything that went with that. The thought of Brenna touching Adrienne, her mouth on her, discovering her secret places, causing her to come made Sloan's palms damp. Sloan was about to change the subject when Adrienne finally spoke.

"She was. She was kind, funny, smart, and an absolute pool shark. We'd go out or to a bar, and she'd end up bringing home at least twenty dollars more than we went in there with from her winnings on the table."

"Where did she learn how to play?" Sloan had spent her fair share of time leaning over a pool table with a cue stick in her hands.

"Her father. Paul was just as good. They had a table in their basement, and Brenna and Paul would play at least one game a night, sometimes two or three if her homework was done."

"Does she have a big family?" Sloan felt a hint of relief that they weren't getting too personal.

"Four brothers."

"Wow. I'd say." Sloan finished the last bit of her steak. "Are her parents still alive?"

"Yes. They live about fifteen minutes from us."

"Does Callie get to see them a lot?"

"Not so much when she was an infant." A shadow crossed Adrienne's eyes. "It was hard for them when Brenna died. She was their only daughter, and Callie looks just like her. Now that she's a little older and able to do things, they take her to the park, the zoo, that sort of thing."

"How long were you and Brenna together?" Another stab, this one sharper.

"Eight years."

"I can't even imagine what it was like for you when she died."

"No, nobody can unless they live through it themselves." Adrienne voice was flat, and her eyes had lost their sparkle. Sloan wanted to return it to its rightful place.

"What's Callie's favorite thing to do?"

Adrienne thought for a minute before answering. "Well, right now, she's into dinosaurs. Lives, eats, and breathes dinosaurs.

Sheets, her towel, every toy in the box, even her backpack has dinosaurs on it. I took her to the museum a few months ago when they had an exhibit of some of the creatures. She squealed nonstop and ran across the room and started climbing over the protective wall around the Tyrannosaurus Rex."

Sloan couldn't help but join Adrienne's laughter about her daughter's antics. "She sounds like a pistol."

"She is just like her mother," Adrienne stated wistfully.

"Who watches her while you're at work?"

"My mom. She's with her now." Adrienne glanced at her watch, her wedding ring sparkling in the overhead light. "They probably read ten books by the time Callie went to bed. My mother doesn't know how to say no."

"I'm not sure about that. She raised you pretty good."

"Oh, she said no to me a lot," Adrienne said, smiling and shaking her head. "But it's different with grandchildren. Robert says it's just fun. No responsibility, no worries that you'll damage them for life or turn them into an ax murderer. Just plain fun and enjoyment."

"An ax murderer?"

"Or some other sociopath or irresponsible adult," Adrienne added, smiling. "Being a parent comes with all the pressure and responsibility to raise a responsible adult."

"Especially when you're doing it alone." Damn, Sloan thought. That was a stupid thing to say. Why did she have to steer the conversation back around to Brenna?

"Especially."

An awkward silence encircled them before Sloan finally thought of a safe topic. "Do you remember Maggie Williams?"

Adrienne lifted her eyes from her plate and frowned. "Maggie from English Lit?"

Sloan shook her head. "She married a longshoreman and has a pack of kids now."

"Maggie? Maggie, who slept with every woman on campus? That Maggie?"

"One and the same," Sloan answered. She knew firsthand that

Maggie was a lesbian. At least she had been the five or six times they'd been together.

"Wow. I never would have seen that coming."

They ate the rest of their meal talking about people they knew in college, friends they ran around with, and laughed as they reminisced about some of the stupid pranks they'd pulled. If they'd gotten caught…they speculated on their fate if that had happened.

The waiter had just dropped off their check when Adrienne's phone rang. She ignored it, but when it rang again she glanced at the caller ID. She excused herself to answer it, mumbling that it was her mother.

Adrienne came back to the table, her face pale, her hands shaking, clearly upset.

"What is it? Is everything all right?" Sloan asked. It was obvious something was definitely not.

"I have to go," she said, quickly gathering up her purse.

"Adrienne? What is it?" Sloan repeated. Her heart started to beat faster, her adrenaline kicking in.

"It's Callie. She's in the emergency room. I've got to get back."

Sloan tossed five twenties on the table as Adrienne spun around and hurried out of the restaurant. She caught up with her as she was opening her car door.

"I'll drive you," Sloan said without thinking. Adrienne looked at her with a startled expression. "You are in no condition to drive, and certainly not an hour back to Tampa in the dark. Come on," Sloan said, reaching for Adrienne's arm and directing her around the rear of the car to the passenger door.

"I need to get my things," Adrienne said fifteen minutes later, as if remembering.

Sloan didn't know if Adrienne was staying at her hotel or somewhere else, but she was positive it was in the opposite direction from where they were headed. "Don't worry about it. We'll get them sent back to you." Sloan dialed her phone.

"Elliott, I need a favor." Fifty-eight minutes later, Sloan pulled the rental car into the parking garage of the executive terminal at Tampa International Airport.

A man in a black suit and extremely shiny shoes was waiting for them when they entered the terminal. "Miss Merchant, this way. We're ready to go."

A Cessna Citation, its cabin door open, was sitting just outside a large hangar, the lights of the runway and the surrounding building reflecting off its sleek white exterior. Adrienne stopped when she realized where they were headed.

"What is this?" It was the first words she'd spoken since getting into the car.

"It's going to take us back to San Diego."

Adrienne gasped, looking stricken. "I can't afford this!"

"Don't worry about it. You need to get back to Callie, and we don't have time to wait for the first flight out tomorrow."

"But—"

"But nothing." Sloan took Adrienne's hand and led her up the short stairway into the plane.

The interior was immaculate, and Sloan knew Adrienne saw none of it, her worry about Callie consuming her complete attention. She did manage to find a seat and buckle in. Ten minutes later, they were airborne.

Adrienne was distraught with worry. Her conversation with her mother had been brief, Maria simply informing Adrienne that Callie's temperature was 104 degrees, and she was being admitted to Children's Hospital. Every possible, conceivable, awful scene imaginable played out in her mind. She could not lose Callie. First Brenna and then Callie. Adrienne couldn't go on if Callie died. She closed her eyes and started to pray.

"Hey."

Adrienne felt a warm hand on her arm and opened her eyes. Sloan was sitting to her left, and as she glanced around, Adrienne didn't recognize where they were.

"Don't think like that," Sloan said, her voice calm.

"Where are we?" Adrienne asked. They were in a small plane, but that was all she knew.

Sloan glanced at her watch. "Probably somewhere over Mississippi by now."

"How did we get here? Whose plane is this?" What in the hell was going on? Had she been so out of her mind with worry that she had no idea how she'd got here?

"I made a few phone calls and called in a favor."

"A favor?" Adrienne asked, incredulous. The seats were expensive leather, the carpet plush and thick, the lighting subdued, and there was very little noise. "Some favor," she commented.

"Don't worry about it," Sloan said, dismissing her concern. "All that matters is that you get to Callie as soon as possible. You should rest. We have about three hours left."

Adrienne sat back in her seat as exhaustion threatened to suffocate her. But she was too keyed up and worried about Callie. No way was she going to rest. "Can I call my mother?" Adrienne asked. A plane like this had to have a phone.

"Sure," Sloan said, and pointed to the small box on the ledge next to the window. "It's in there." She got up and went to the back of the plane to give Adrienne some privacy.

Adrienne dialed her mother's cell phone. She held her breath.

"Mom, how is she?" Adrienne asked, not even waiting for her mother to say hello.

"They're still trying to get her fever down."

Adrienne was overcome with relief that Callie was fighting. "What's wrong with her?"

"They're not sure. They're running tests."

"What happened?"

Adrienne listened as her mother explained the chain of events that had led her to take Callie to the hospital. "I just knew something wasn't right," Maria said.

A mother's intuition, Adrienne thought. If so, why hadn't she herself sensed something wrong?

"Where are you?" her mother asked. "It sounds like you're in a can somewhere."

"I am. I'm in a plane flying back now. Sloan said we'll be landing in about three hours."

"A plane? How did you get a flight so fast?"

Adrienne wanted to smile at her mother's question, but she was too worried. "Sloan called in a favor, and it was waiting for us at the airport."

"Sloan?"

"Sloan Merchant. She works at Foster McKenzie. She was with me here in Tampa."

"Well, when Callie gets home, you'll have to bring her by so we can thank her properly. Now you need to get some rest. Won't do Callie any good if you worry yourself sick. She's in good hands here, and your father and I are with her."

Her mother's tone told Adrienne she had nothing left to say other than, "Yes, Mom. I'll try. I'll call you later to see if anything's changed." Adrienne placed the phone back in the box and shut the lid.

"How is she?" Sloan asked, returning to her seat beside her.

Adrienne didn't realize she was chilled until she felt the heat of Sloan's body next to her. "No change," she answered.

"Do they have any idea what's wrong?" Sloan asked cautiously.

"She said they're running tests. You'd think with modern medicine they'd be able to figure out why a little girl has a fever."

Sloan put her hand over hers. Adrienne's long, slim fingers instinctively interlocked them with hers. "Where is she?"

"Children's Hospital," Adrienne said, envisioning the large granite structure in her head. Children's Hospital was the premier pediatric and adolescent facility on the West Coast. Brenna had always insisted that a large part of their annual charitable contribution go to the hospital. Patients came from all over the country to Children's, their reputation world-renowned.

"She couldn't be in better hands," Sloan said.

Adrienne sighed as much as in frustration as in exhaustion.

"You need to get some rest." Sloan's voice held more than a note of concern.

"That's what my mother said."

Sloan chuckled. "And mothers always know what's best for their children. I can't even begin to imagine what you must be going through," Sloan said, this time enveloping her hand between both of hers. "I know you want to be with her. We're getting there as fast as we can. But your mom is right. You need to rest. You'll be no good to Callie if you get sick, or when she starts feeling better to see you looking like hell."

Adrienne managed to chuckle. "I see you haven't lost your knack for flattery with the girls. You were always very good with that."

Sloan leaned back a few inches, and Adrienne could see her full face. She didn't quite recognize her expression. Concern, yes, but something else she couldn't put her finger on. Her eyes were that same shade of brown, but they were much more intense than ever before.

"I only speak the truth."

Adrienne's stomach flip-flopped, and she immediately felt guilty. She should be focusing solely on Callie. She should be thinking of nothing else but her sick child, and certainly not herself.

"I know, but I can't sleep. I'm too worried imagining her, my little girl, in that great big white hospital bed." Adrienne unsuccessfully fought back a sob.

"Shh." Sloan put her arm around Adrienne and pulled her close. "Not to brag, but I used to know what to do to put you to sleep. But this isn't the time or the place, so this will have to do." Sloan moved Adrienne's head to the crook of her shoulder.

Adrienne could feel Sloan's heart beating faster and knew hers was as well, her mind flashing back to all the times she was barely able to keep her eyes open after they'd made love. Sloan's touch, the way she played her body, the way she drew every ounce of passion and sensation from her had always completely exhausted her, and she often lay back unable to do anything other than breathe.

Her eyes began to drift closed. Right before they did, she heard herself say, "You always knew exactly what to do."

CHAPTER TWENTY-THREE

Adrienne, sweetie, wake up."

Adrienne heard her name called from a distance. Someone was nudging her. She didn't want to wake up. She was warm and safe in this cocoon. The voice called her name again.

"Adrienne. We're beginning our descent."

Her eyes snapped open when she realized where they were. She sat up, quickly disentangling herself from Sloan. She rubbed her face and ran her hands through her hair.

"What time is it?" She looked around, trying to get her bearings.

"It's three thirty local time. We should be landing in about ten minutes."

"How long did I sleep?"

"Not long. How do you feel?"

Adrienne exhaled. "A little better," she said honestly. She was still in a bit of a fog, but she'd slept more than just a few minutes. Her body told her that much. Obviously, she'd needed it.

"Why don't you go freshen up before the captain turns on the seat-belt sign. You'll find a few spare toothbrushes in the lavatory. Feel free to use whatever else you see in there."

Adrienne laid her hand on Sloan's thigh and felt the muscles tighten. "Thank you," she said softly, their eyes meeting. Something familiar but new passed between them.

"You can drool on my shoulder any time," Sloan teased her. "You always have."

Adrienne flushed, and she couldn't help looking at the place on Sloan's shoulder where she'd slept. It was completely dry. She slapped her lightly on the leg. "I do not," she said before unbuckling her seat belt and heading toward the lavatory.

She used the toilet and, as she washed her hands, looked in the mirror. Her face was pale and drawn, her eyes red. If she looked like this after a few hours of good sleep, she could only imagine what she'd looked like before. She had to pull herself together. Her mother would have a fit, and even more to worry about, if she showed up at the hospital looking like shit. Her mother, who had done so much for her and Callie, did not need to add her to her worry list.

She washed her face, drying it with the soft, plush towel hanging neatly through the ring on the wall. She ran her fingers through her hair and gave up, then tugged the band off her wrist and pulled her hair up into some semblance of a bun. Adrienne looked at herself again and immediately took it back down, the look too severe for her tired face. She found the toothbrush Sloan had said was on the shelf and, after brushing her teeth, felt a little more human. With one more look in the mirror, Adrienne opened the door to prepare for landing.

A large black car sat waiting for them when they descended the stairs and stepped onto the tarmac. Sloan held open the door for Adrienne to slide inside. Adrienne glanced at her watch, did a calculation, and saw that it was four a.m. in San Diego, the sun still deep below the horizon. Mercifully traffic was light, but they still arrived at the hospital a lifetime later than Adrienne had thought possible.

As the car pulled into the circle drive, Adrienne's level of anxiety rose. She murmured a quick thank you to Sloan before getting out of the car. Then she hurried across the sidewalk and through the automatic door, looking around for someone to tell her where her daughter was. She heard voices to her left and turned and saw Sloan talking to a woman in dark-blue scrubs sitting behind a desk. A second later, Sloan approached her.

"She's in room 714," she said, taking Adrienne's arm and leading her toward a bank of elevators.

"You don't have to come with me."

Sloan held up her hand, silencing Adrienne's comment. "Come on."

The elevator ding was the only sound in the elevator lobby, and to Adrienne's sensitive ears it sounded like the ringing of a church bell on a quiet Sunday morning. They stepped inside, and Adrienne leaned against the back wall, gripping the railing to steady herself.

"Sloan, you don't have—"

Sloan held up her hand again. "I'm not leaving you," she said, her voice a little forced yet gentle.

Adrienne didn't have a chance to think about what that meant before the elevator doors opened. As they stepped onto the dimly lit floor, Sloan took her hand. Her touch was warm, comforting, and righted her world just a little.

As they walked down the hall, Adrienne couldn't help but notice murals of Disney characters painted on the walls who seemed to be skipping along behind them. Any moment she expected a chorus of one of the songs from the movie *Snow White and the Seven Dwarfs* to come over the speakers in the ceiling.

A man in white scrubs with ducks splashing in the water printed on them looked up with a calm, reassuring smile. Adrienne opened her mouth but couldn't speak, her guts twisted inside at the fear she might be too late.

"We're looking for Callie Stewart. This is Adrienne Stewart, her mother. We just got in from Florida."

The man's smile widened, and Adrienne momentarily thought that she wouldn't be greeted this way if something serious had happened to Callie.

"Ms. Stewart, of course. Your mother said you were on the way. Come with me. Callie is in 714," he said, rounding the corner of the large desk. Adrienne followed him, Sloan's hand still holding hers.

"How is she?" Sloan asked from beside her.

The man turned and, instead of answering Sloan, who had asked the question, spoke to Adrienne. "I've been on shift since seven last night, and there's been no change. She's stable. In some respect that's a good sign, but her fever is still high. Your mother hasn't left her side, even though we've encouraged her to get some rest. The doctor makes her rounds at six. She can tell you more."

They arrived at a sliding glass door, a large decal of Donald Duck waving them inside. She was suddenly more nervous than she'd ever been. She hesitated, a lump the size of a fist seeming to lodge in the back of her throat. Her feet were frozen to the floor, which made no sense whatsoever. She needed to be inside with her daughter, not standing out here. She felt Sloan step closer to her.

"It's okay," Sloan said. "You heard the nurse. There's no change. That's a good thing. She hasn't gotten any worse."

And she hasn't gotten any better, a voice in Adrienne's head screamed.

"What can we expect?" Sloan asked.

"She's hooked up to several IVs getting general antibiotics and fluids. She's on a heart monitor, just to be safe," he added quickly at the look of fright that must have been on her face. "She's pale and her breathing is a little labored, so she has an oxygen cannula." He pointed to the space between his upper lip and his nostrils.

A flashback of Brenna lying on a cot, a white sheet covering her up to her neck, in a dimly lit room paralyzed her. She could not live through this again.

"Adrienne?" Sloan's voice was soft but insistent. "Come on. Callie's waiting for you."

Those few words snapped her out of wherever the hell numb place she was, and she stepped into the room.

Her eyes immediately went to the sleeping figure on the bed. She inhaled, quickly putting her free hand to her mouth. Callie looked so small and frail that Adrienne couldn't hold back a sob of anguish.

"Adrienne," her mother said as she pulled her into a tight, warm hug. Adrienne pushed her tears back again. She needed to be here for her daughter and her mother.

Her mother unwrapped her arms and cupped Adrienne's face. "She's going to be okay, Adrienne. I know she is. She's a fighter."

It was all Adrienne could do to nod, because if she opened her mouth the only thing that would come out would be sobs.

"Go on," her mother urged her. "Hold her hand. Talk to her. She can hear you. I know she can."

Adrienne stepped closer to the bed, afraid to touch Callie. To her frazzled nerves, the beeping of the heart monitor was excruciatingly loud, and she could swear she heard the drip, drip, drip of the yellow fluid into the tube snaking into her daughter's arm.

Adrienne's hand was shaking as she reached for Callie's small one. She lifted it and brought it to her lips, the little hand weighing no more than a butterfly. She kissed her palm, then laid it against her cheek.

"Callie, honey. It's Mommy." Adrienne's voice was hoarse. She cleared her throat. "Callie, honey, I'm here. Grandma's been taking care of you until I could get home. But I'm here now, and I'm not leaving until you're all better."

Adrienne's head shot up from her daughter's face when the heart monitor started beeping faster.

"She knows you're here," the nurse said. "Talk to her for a few more minutes, and then let her get some rest."

Adrienne didn't hear the nurse leave the room, but when she looked up after singing Callie her favorite bedtime song, he was gone. And so was Sloan.

❖

"Excuse me. Excuse me."

Sloan stopped and turned around when it became apparent that the insistent voice was directed toward her. It was Adrienne's mother, and if Sloan had any doubt as to how beautiful Adrienne would be as she matured, looking at the woman standing in front of her now completely erased it.

Mrs. Phillips was several inches shorter than Adrienne, with more than a few strands of her salt-and-pepper hair escaped from a messy bun. Crow's feet on either side of her tired but sharp, clear green eyes gave her face a sense of experience rather than age.

"You're Sloan Merchant?" the woman asked tentatively.

"Yes."

"I'm Maria Phillips, Adrienne's mother. Thank you for bringing my daughter home. I don't know what you did or how you got her here so quickly, and I can't thank you enough. And please thank whoever else helped bring her home."

Sloan had never seen anyone express such sincerity. She liked her immediately, and not just because she was Adrienne's mother. She was a proud, strong woman.

"She told me all about Callie," Sloan said, suddenly not wanting the conversation to end. She wanted to sit down with this woman over a cup of coffee or glass of iced tea and hear all about Adrienne as a little girl. What were her favorite toys as a baby, when did she learn how to walk, what was her first day of school like, did she ever have a puppy? Was she an irritable hormonal teenager? How did Adrienne tell her family that she was in love? What expression was on her face when she said she was going to be a mother?

Sloan was stunned at the depth of her questions about Adrienne. She'd never thought about any of this before. They had been little more than teenagers when they met. The only thing on her mind had been the next time she could get her alone. She didn't want to know, wasn't interested, nor did they even cross her mind. Asking those questions now, wanting to know these things surprisingly didn't make her uncomfortable.

Mrs. Phillips's eyes narrowed, a frown creasing her forehead. She was looking at Sloan so intently she felt like she was being picked apart. She half expected this short, stout woman to read her mind, so Sloan quickly shut it off. They stood there so long that Sloan was beginning to feel awkward.

Mrs. Phillips held out her hand. "Thank you again."

Sloan accepted her thanks, and before she could take her hand back, Mrs. Phillips grasped it in both of hers, pulled Sloan down to her, and kissed her on the cheek.

"I hope we see you again, Ms. Merchant," she said, before turning around and walking silently down the hall.

The Uber driver dropped Sloan off at her house at a little after five, and even though she was exhausted, she couldn't possibly sleep, even for a couple of hours. Sloan hadn't wanted to leave

Adrienne, but she had no right to be there. Callie certainly wasn't her child. Hell. She wasn't even a friend of the family, let alone one close enough to sit with Adrienne.

The sight of Adrienne bent over her daughter, overwhelmed with worry, was almost more than Sloan could bear. She wanted to take Adrienne in her arms and tell her everything was going to be all right, that she would do whatever she had to, to make Callie well. Elliott had contacts and resources around the world, and Sloan would beg her to help if she had to. Anything to see Adrienne smile again.

After a quick shower and change of clothes, she drove to her office. She docked her laptop, turned on her monitor, and went into the break room for coffee. She leaned against the wall and closed her eyes as the Keurig gurgled the last few drops like it was its dying breath. She felt sluggish and her brain half a second slower than her body. But she'd powered through worse, and she would again today.

The last few days had been a whirlwind of business, pleasure, angst, confusion, excitement, and fear. Fear that she wouldn't be able to get Adrienne back in time, fear that Adrienne would again lose someone else she loved, fear that she couldn't do anything about it.

Sloan pushed the gut-wrenching image of Adrienne next to Callie in the hospital and the intense scrutiny of Mrs. Phillips out of her mind. She needed to concentrate; she needed to determine Foster McKenzie's next steps. The tour of the supplier facility had been interrupted less than halfway through. She'd talk with Elliott later today and volunteer to return to the site.

Suddenly it occurred to Sloan that her suitcase and clothes were still in Crystal River, as were Adrienne's. She grabbed her cup of coffee and went back to her office, her computer awake and ready. She looked up the hotel phone number, called, and extended her reservation a few more days. She placed a call to Adrienne's office. It was early, but she left a brief message with her assistant Ruth about what had happened and that Adrienne was at the hospital. Ruth could deal with getting Adrienne's things back to her. It wasn't Sloan's place to do that.

"How is Callie?" Sloan looked up from the screen she'd been staring at, and Elliott was standing in her doorway.

"When we got to the hospital, the nurse said there hadn't been any change."

"That's good, right? That she's not any worse?"

"That was my thought, but Adrienne wasn't so sure. But if it were my daughter I probably wouldn't think so either. Thank you for…"

Elliott took the few remaining steps into her office and sat in the chair in front of her. "Nothing to thank me for. It's what anyone would have done."

"I'm not so sure about that. Chartering an airplane to fly across the country in the middle of the night is not something anyone would have done. Adrienne thanked you, and her mother thanked you."

"Her mother?"

"She stopped me in the hall before I left this morning and made sure I knew her appreciation and to pass it on to you."

"Do they have any idea what's wrong with her?"

Sloan explained the chain of events. It all sounded so simple, yet it had been anything but. Life was complicated, relationships thorny and problematic, and Sloan didn't do any of those. Then why had she willingly spent the last six hours being mixed up in something she didn't do? And why did she want to jump right back in?

CHAPTER TWENTY-FOUR

Amen." Adrienne ended her prayer and lifted her head off the hard hospital mattress. Her back ached, her throat was scratchy, and her eyes burned with exhaustion. She'd been here, in this same spot, alternating praying to God and to Brenna to take care of their little girl and talking to Callie about everything and nothing at all. She recited every nursery rhyme she could remember, every book she had memorized from the countless times she read them to Callie, and even promised her a puppy when she got well. She told Callie everything about Brenna she could remember. The minutes ticked by like the individual grains in an hourglass, except this hour felt like an eternity.

Several hours ago, her mother had insisted she take a break, but Adrienne had refused to leave Callie's bedside. They compromised when Maria brought them each a sandwich and a bottle of water, and they ate at the small table in the corner of the room.

The doctor had come in earlier with the results of the latest battery of tests and a new set of antibiotics, and Adrienne was watching Callie closely for any sign of improvement. Her mother had finally gone home, promising she'd be back after she showered and changed her clothes. Her father stayed by her side.

"She's got to be all right, Dad. She has to. I can't lose Brenna and Callie." Adrienne turned to her father and buried her face in his shoulder.

Her next prayer was a thank you to God when Callie opened her eyes.

❖

Adrienne knew she looked like hell, but she had to thank Sloan and Elliott for everything they'd done to get her back to Callie so quickly. Callie had fallen right back to sleep after telling Adrienne she wanted a black puppy. With the tension relieved, Adrienne had finally broken down and cried. Her father had dragged her out to a waiting taxi with strict instructions to go home, shower, change her clothes. Then, and only then, could she return, he'd said. Adrienne knew when to push back and when to do as he ordered. Her father was right, as he always was. If she didn't, she would probably scare Callie when she woke up again. And she certainly didn't want to do anything to interfere with her getting well. She'd been at her bedside for over thirty hours and was exhausted.

The smooth ride of the elevator in the office building almost put Adrienne to sleep, and if not for the soft voice noting the arrival on the twelfth floor, she might have nodded off. She pushed off the back wall, her legs heavy with fatigue.

Sloan's door was open. Adrienne stood in the doorway looking at Sloan. Her head was back against her chair, her eyes closed. Her fingers were resting lightly on her keyboard like she had fallen asleep while typing.

Adrienne's heart beat a little faster, and even through her exhaustion, something tingled in her stomach. God, Sloan was striking. Her face was thin, her cheekbones prominent, and she looked exactly like what she was—a successful, attractive lesbian. Sloan had turned heads years ago and even more now. When she was young, she was hot. Now, as a woman, she was gorgeous, if not stunning.

Not wanting to disturb her but not ready to leave, Adrienne sat in one of the overstuffed chairs in the corner of Sloan's office. It was the sitting area where she and Robert had had several conversations a lifetime ago. Then it was all business, but now it was all personal. Promising herself she'd just rest her eyes for a few minutes, Adrienne leaned her head back.

Something startled Sloan and she opened her eyes. Her screen saver was scrolling through pictures of beaches, a sure sign she'd dozed off. Great, she'd fallen asleep at her desk. That had never happened to her. Pandora was playing softly from her speakers. She sat up straight, and to her amazement Adrienne was sitting in her office. No, disregard that. Adrienne was sleeping in a chair in the corner of her office. Could the last few days get any more bizarre than they already were? She'd wanted to go to the hospital to see how Callie was, but it wasn't her place.

Sloan looked at Adrienne carefully. Deep lines of worry had been on her face since her mother's call. Sloan suspected they would be there for some time until Callie was okay. But what struck her was how beautiful Adrienne was even in exhaustion. She had a natural beauty that was stunning in its simplicity. Even better, Adrienne didn't even know it.

A song on Pandora drifting from her computer speakers caught Sloan's attention. It was an older Rascal Flatts song titled "Take Me There." The lyrics told a story of someone who realizes they want to know everything about someone. It talked about how they want to go to that place in her heart, want to know about her hometown, her parents, where she learned about life and spent her summer nights, her hopes and dreams and wishes.

As Sloan listened, she realized the words expressed exactly what she wanted from Adrienne. She wanted much, much more. But who was she kidding? Adrienne didn't want anything to do with her. She was still grieving over her wife, and she had a child to consider. Her heart crashed just as Adrienne opened her eyes.

"Adrienne, how's Callie?" Sloan managed to get out, her voice shaky.

Relief flooded Adrienne's face. "She woke up a little while ago. They think she's going to be okay."

"That's good. I'm glad." Sloan didn't know what else to say. She knew what she wanted to say but had the good sense to keep her mouth shut. This was not the time. She doubted there ever would be a time. Sloan stood when Adrienne walked toward her. Adrienne put her arms around her and hugged her. It was all Sloan could do to not react like her body was telling her to.

"I can't thank you enough for what you did, Sloan. I'll forever be in your debt."

Sloan returned the hug, squeezing Adrienne a little tighter than was probably acceptable, and she buried her face in Adrienne's hair.

They stood that way for several seconds until a voice behind them asked, "How is Callie?"

At the sound of Elliott's voice, Sloan jumped away from Adrienne like she'd done something wrong.

"Oh, Elliott, I can't thank you enough for what you did for me. Callie is going to be okay," Adrienne said quickly. "I'll reimburse you for—"

Elliott's voice was soft but firm. "No need. It's the least I could do. I'm glad everything worked out."

The three of them stood looking at each other until Adrienne finally said, "I've got to get back to the hospital. I just wanted to stop by and personally thank you, both of you."

Sloan squirmed under the knowing stare from her boss.

CHAPTER TWENTY-FIVE

The bouquet of flowers felt like a lead ball in Sloan's hands as she walked up the steps to the front porch. The voices coming from the inside of the house were loud and laughing, and suddenly she was more nervous than she'd ever been. When she'd accepted Adrienne's invitation to come to dinner with her family so that they could thank her properly, Sloan didn't think it was such a big deal. Adrienne was just the messenger of her mother's insistence.

Sloan didn't do family, at least not what sounded like what was going on behind the door. Her family rarely got together unless it was for the obligatory social or philanthropic event. She couldn't remember the last time she spoke with her brother, and other than her scheduled call from her mother every other week, she couldn't remember the last time she'd talked to either one of her parents.

Sloan looked at her reflection in the window of the front door. She didn't really see the new pair of flat-front chinos, pressed to the point that a wrinkle didn't dare appear anywhere, and her long-sleeved Tommy Hilfiger button-down blue shirt with flecks of green and plum that the saleslady said brought out the color of her eyes. She had a fresh haircut, trimmed and polished nails, and a new pair of loafers. She'd convinced herself this was regular, ordinary maintenance. She shook her head. That excuse had long since expired.

What she saw instead was a *what if*. What if she'd been standing in this exact place waiting to meet the parents of Adrienne, her *girlfriend*? But Adrienne wasn't her girlfriend and probably never would be, and this dinner was far more important than she thought it should be.

She knocked loud enough to be heard over the noise inside, and the door opened just a few seconds later. Adrienne was standing there, stunning in a brightly colored dress held up by thin spaghetti straps accentuating her tan, smooth shoulders. A thin silver necklace hung from her neck. Her feet were bare, her hair was down, and her plain, simple beauty took Sloan's breath away. It had been three weeks since she left her at the hospital.

Sloan hadn't seen Adrienne in a dress often. Shorts, jeans, an occasional swimsuit, and more than occasionally naked. The bodice of the dress fit tightly with a scooped neck that, if Adrienne bent over just a little, revealed a tasteful amount of cleavage. Adrienne wasn't one for displaying her assets, so to speak. She believed that imagination was a more powerful aphrodisiac than pure nakedness. Sloan had experienced both, and she wasn't sure if she agreed with her. She recalled the times she'd sat across from Adrienne or beside her or watched her from across the room, imagining rediscovering what was beneath the cotton and denim.

"Hi," Adrienne said, her smile radiant.

"Hi."

"Any trouble finding the place?"

"No. Not at all."

"Come in." Adrienne stepped back and opened the door farther, and when Sloan crossed the threshold she inhaled Adrienne's familiar scent.

"Are those for me?" she asked, eyeing the flowers.

Sloan panicked. She'd heard somewhere you should take a gift to the hostess, and since she knew nothing about Adrienne's mother, she figured flowers were a safe decision. Now she wasn't so sure.

"Um, they're for your mother," she said awkwardly.

Adrienne smacked her on the arm teasingly and smiled. "I know that. Come on."

The room was crowded, people lounging on couches and sitting on arms of chairs; three guys were watching a football game on an enormous television set, and only a few had noticed she had arrived. A pimply-faced boy of about sixteen walked through the room carrying a stack of plates and disappeared into what Sloan saw was the dining room. Callie followed him at a run, clenching several spoons in her fists. She was adorable in her yellow dress and mismatched socks. Sloan raised her eyebrows. When had she *ever* used the word *adorable*?

"Callie."

Callie skidded to a halt and looked at her mother, chagrin all over her little face.

"Callie, this is Miss Merchant. Please come over here and say hello."

The little girl walked over and stood in front of Sloan. She looked up at her and said politely, "Hello."

Sloan held out her hand, and Callie looked at her mother for permission before she placed her tiny hand in Sloan's.

"I'm happy to meet you, Callie. Your mom has told me a lot about you."

Callie didn't say anything, just stared at Sloan. Finally, Adrienne cut her loose.

"Walk inside Grandma's house."

Before she continued into the dining room, Sloan thought she heard her say "Yes, ma'am," but she wasn't sure. Another boy, this one not much older than Callie, carried napkins and a salt and pepper shaker. It was obvious the kids had the responsibility of setting the table.

Adrienne's mother approached, wiping her hands on a green-checked dish towel.

"Ms. Merchant, I'm so glad you were able to come." Maria surprised Sloan by enveloping her in a tight hug.

When she pulled back, Sloan said, "Thank you for inviting me, Mrs. Phillips. These are for you." Sloan handed the bouquet to Adrienne's mother.

"Thank you. They're beautiful. And please call me Maria." Her voice was warm, her smile generous.

"You're welcome, and I'm Sloan. Ms. Merchant is my mother, and I'm afraid I'm nothing like her." *Thank God.*

"I need to get back into the kitchen." Maria turned her attention to her daughter. "Adrienne, introduce Sloan around but don't overwhelm her." She turned back to Sloan. "If she doesn't take care of you today or give you what you need, you come see me."

"Yes, ma'am," Sloan replied, trying to keep the smile off her face. It was clear Maria Phillips ran this household.

Adrienne took her hand, pulled her farther into the room, and stopped at each member of her family, introducing them. No way could Sloan keep track of the names of all these people. There were brothers and sisters, in-laws, grandparents, cousins, nieces, nephews, friends of the family, and even a priest. Sloan quickly lost track of who was who, though she was generally very good with details like names. All of them stopped what they were doing and welcomed her, their sincere gratitude abundant.

Frankie, Adrienne's sister, gave her more than a polite once-over. It was as if she were judging Sloan to see if she was worthy of her sister's attention. Sloan wondered if Adrienne had told her sister about their past and this was just an after-the-fact evaluation or something else. Frankie was built like her mother, short and stocky with jet-black, shoulder-length hair. She had a bump in her nose and a small silver hoop in her left eyebrow.

"Callie looks great," Sloan commented a little while later. "You never would know she was so sick." Callie had been in the hospital for four days and had been home two weeks.

"Kids bounce back fast. It's the way they get sick too. One minute they're fine, the next they throw up, and five minutes later it's like it never happened. Oh, sorry," Adrienne said sheepishly. "Mom talk."

"No problem," Sloan said. "I have a strong stomach."

Maria called that dinner was served, each family member jockeying for a place to sit. Sloan hung back, not sure where she was supposed to be until Adrienne took her hand again and led her to the table. Her father, Joe, was sitting at the head, Maria to his left, and he motioned for Sloan to sit on his right. Adrienne sat next to her mother, and Frankie was next to Adrienne. Assorted aunts and uncles and everyone else filled out the rest of the table. Anyone under what Sloan assumed to be the age of sixteen sat at the kids' table in a corner of the dining room. Once everyone was seated, Maria spoke.

"Shall we give thanks?" Everyone grabbed the hand of the person on either side of them and bowed their head. Sloan awkardly grasped Joe's hand and that of one of Adrienne's brothers.

"Dear Lord," Maria said, her voice reverent. "Thank you for this bounty we are about to receive that you have set forth for us. Thank you for bringing us together to celebrate happiness and life. Thank you for the kindness and generosity of our special guest, and keep watch over those who are not with us today. In our Lord's name, we pray." The chorus of amens around the table signaled it was time to eat.

Conversation started up as if it hadn't stopped. Dishes were passed around, serving spoons and cutlery clinking on plates.

"Sloan, Adrienne said that you two knew each other in college," Adrienne's father said.

Sloan forced herself not to look at Adrienne to see her reaction or what she was thinking.

"Yes sir, we did." That was no big deal—just a common, everyday question. What was she going to say? *Yes, we were lovers, and we fucked our brains out every chance we had*. Yeah, like that was going to come out of her mouth.

"She said you had a few classes together."

"Yes sir, we did. She was very smart. She was always the first one to raise her hand, and she made us all look stupid." Adrienne had been an excellent student, and even when she didn't seem to study, she knew all the answers.

"Daddy," Adrienne said. "I told you not to give Sloan the third degree."

"This isn't the third degree. It's just a question."

Sloan looked at Adrienne and, using her mental telepathy, urged her to say something. She didn't know what Adrienne had or hadn't said about their relationship. Unfortunately, Adrienne wasn't receiving her message.

"We had a few classes together, hung out with some of the

same people, that kind of thing." Sloan thought that sounded generic enough not to raise eyebrows.

"Are you married?" Frankie asked and was immediately met with a gasp from her mother.

"Francis, don't be rude."

"It's not rude, Mama. Lesbians can marry. Adrienne did. It's a simple question."

Sloan watched this interchange with interest. No one would think about contradicting either of her parents at their table. Well, the lesbian question is out of the bag, she thought. She'd been wondering if it would come up in conversation. "It's okay. No offense taken. No, I'm not married." Sloan saw Frankie give her mother a self-satisfied, I-told-you-so look.

"Do you have any children, Sloan?"

"Francis Anne!"

"What? It's just a question. Lesbians can have children. Look at Adrienne."

Sloan did look at Adrienne, who was rubbing her eyes and shaking her head, obviously mortified.

"No, I don't," she replied.

"Do you want one? I have one I'll give you," Frankie said, loosening the tension around them.

"Is it potty trained?"

"No, but she comes with a full set of teeth."

Sloan shook her head as if she were disappointed. "Dang. Your offer sounded good, but I don't do diapers."

They all laughed, and Sloan lifted her fork and cut into the large piece of roast on her plate.

Throughout dinner Sloan was continually amazed at the noise level and the good-natured teasing and ribbing of Adrienne's family. The only family dinners Sloan had ever attended were her own and Elliott and Lauren's, so this experience, this familiarity, this happiness was new to her. Meals at her house were quiet and subdued, with polite conversation, if any, her father preferring to have silence at the table, rationalizing that it was his time to unwind from his busy, all important, hectic day.

As a child, Sloan didn't understand, but she did know that, for the most part, conversation was controlled, if not censored, and certainly at times forbidden. As an angry, moody adolescent, she'd been thankful for the silence when her friends bitched about how their parents inquired about every minute of their day. She'd never thought anything of it. It was just the way things were at her house.

Sitting around the table with Adrienne's family was a very different experience. The atmosphere was uplifting, funny, and full of energy. She'd never laughed so much at the table in her life. These people seemed to genuinely care about each other. She felt warm and comfortable and was quite surprised when she herself joined in on some of the teasing of one of Adrienne's brothers. Several times throughout the meal she caught Frankie studying her from her seat across the table. None of the times did she look away in embarrassment. On the contrary, it seemed that Frankie wanted Sloan to know that she was keeping an eye on her, whatever that meant.

Catching snippets of conversation here and there, Sloan gleaned that they were all involved in each other's lives. One woman had talked about a birthday party she'd gone to with the woman next to her, some of the men were talking about a Little League baseball game, and some others were planning a movie outing. Everyone asked Adrienne about her life and what she was doing. Her answers always centered around Callie and things they had done together and her latest antics. Adrienne always had one eye on Callie at the other table.

One by one, people left the table, the children's table emptying first. Sloan watched in fascination how every person, including Callie, carried their plate, glass, and utensils into the kitchen. That was another thing that had never happened at her house growing up. Everything was left on the table as they found it. Bea, their housekeeper, would come in after everyone left, clean up the mess, and return the room to its pristine condition. She never thought about that either. It was just expected.

Just Adrienne, her parents, and Frankie were left at the table now. They talked about Joe's job as a letter carrier, and Maria kept

Sloan laughing with stories of the antics of the students she'd taught in high school.

Two cups of coffee and a slice of peach pie later, Sloan pushed her plate away. "Maria, that was the most delicious home-cooked meal I've had in a long time, maybe ever. I'm completely stuffed."

"Don't you cook?"

Sloan laughed. "Not hardly. I make things, but I don't cook."

"What's the difference?" Joe asked.

"This." Sloan turned her palms up, motioning to the remnants of their meal on the table. "*This* is cooking. I make things by opening a can or a packet or box. If my microwave ever went out, I'd probably starve to death."

Sloan could swear she heard Maria tsk. "Adrienne can teach you. She's a fabulous cook."

"Mama," Adrienne said, sounding shocked.

"I'm sure she is if she's your daughter. I can say she did cook a few things on the hot plate in her dorm room," Sloan added, much to Adrienne's chagrin. "But then again, ramen noodles were the staple of our existence."

"I was so broke, it's all I could afford," Adrienne said.

Sloan remembered the battles they had when she tried to take Adrienne out to dinner every night. Sloan had more money than she knew what to do with, but Adrienne had refused. She finally agreed that once a week they could go to a moderately priced restaurant; the other nights, absolutely not. They'd had a couple of serious fights about it, but they eventually resolved their differences, and the make-up sex was phenomenal. Sloan had learned to respect Adrienne and her position on that subject, and everything else for that matter.

"I need a walk," Adrienne said, pushing back from the table. "Care to join me?" she asked Sloan.

"Sure." Sloan started picking up her dishes.

"No, no, no," Maria said. "You are our guest."

Adrienne gave Sloan a look that said *don't fight her on this because you will lose*. "Thank you, Maria. Dinner was delicious. I enjoyed the conversation," she said to Joe and Frankie.

Adrienne checked on Callie, and then Sloan followed her out the back door, through the yard, out the side gate, and onto the sidewalk in front of the house. They walked for a while, neither of them speaking. Sloan breathed in deeply, noticing the spring air and the flowers that had bloomed practically overnight. This was an old, established neighborhood with tall, strong trees and mature, full bushes. They passed several people as they walked, everyone making eye contact and saying hello.

"Thank you for coming," Adrienne said, then laughed. "Like you really had any choice."

"No kidding. If I hadn't shown up I'm sure your mother would have sent the Phillips posse after me."

"You know it."

"It was fun, though not quite what I expected."

"What did you expect?"

Sloan hesitated. She needed to pull her thoughts together before she spoke. "Actually, I didn't know what to expect."

Adrienne cocked her head to one side, a frown creasing her forehead. "How so?"

"I was more than a little nervous when I got here. I don't do family things."

"Really?"

"No."

"You've never gone to a girlfriend's house?"

"No."

"Why not?"

Sloan wasn't sure how she felt about Adrienne probing her on this subject.

"Sloan?"

Adrienne never had let her get away without answering a question. "I've never had a girlfriend."

Adrienne stopped suddenly, and after a few steps Sloan realized she was walking alone. She turned around.

"You've *never* had a girlfriend?"

The question wasn't accusatory. Something more like shocked, stunned, surprised.

"I mean there's been women, obviously. But never anyone serious."

"Why not?"

Because you ruined me for anyone else, Sloan wanted to say but didn't. "I never had any time, I guess. First there was law school, then studying for the bar, then getting a job, moving up in the company, and then traveling around the world for Elliott's job." Sloan let the flimsy excuse float in the air between them. Adrienne obviously knew it was bullshit as well, but thankfully she let the subject drop as they walked on.

"Do you mind if we stop by my house for a minute? I forgot to bring something for Frankie," Adrienne asked after they turned the corner onto another street. "It's the third one on the left."

"Sure." Had Sloan missed the fact that Adrienne lived so close to her parents? Not that she would have had any idea about that.

Adrienne pushed the numbers on the keypad on the outside of her garage, the door quietly sliding up a few seconds later. Her car was inside, which explained why Sloan hadn't seen it when she arrived at her parents' house.

"Come on in. Make yourself at home," Adrienne said.

Sloan followed her into the house, through a large laundry room, and into the kitchen.

"I'll just be a minute." Adrienne continued walking through the family room and up the stairs on the right.

While she waited, Sloan looked around and saw obvious evidence that a toddler lived here. Toys were scattered about, and several Dr. Seuss books were stacked on the coffee table in front of a comfortable-looking couch with a small blanket bunched next to one armrest. She noticed a booster seat on one of the kitchen chairs, a few dishes in the sink, a coffee cup, two plastic plates with dividers in them, obviously for Callie, one Dora cup, and one Scooby-Doo cup. She could barely see the surface of the refrigerator behind Callie's artwork—pages torn out of coloring books and several pictures of Callie and Adrienne.

She walked over to a set of windows looking out into the backyard. The grass was neatly cut, and in the middle of the yard sat a large wooden swing set with a bright-yellow slide, a blue teeter-totter, and a miniature rock-climbing wall with red, blue, and purple pegs that led up to a fort complete with a telescope. A tricycle and an old-fashioned red wagon sat on the patio. Adrienne's house had more warmth and life in it than Sloan's professionally decorated place.

A page from *The Cat in the Hat* stared at Sloan when she sat down on the couch. She picked it up and perused the children's book she had heard of but never read. Frowning, she thumbed through several pages.

"I see you've expanded your reading material," Adrienne said, walking back into the room carrying a sweater.

"How do you read this?" she asked when Adrienne sat down beside her. She repeated a couple of lines from the page she was on. "It doesn't make sense."

Adrienne took the book from her and turned the page. "You have to maintain a certain rhythm," Adrienne said and started to read several pages, barely taking a breath between them.

"Wow, I'm impressed."

"Practice. Lots and lots of practice. Callie reads it to me. Actually, she has it memorized."

"That's good, isn't it?" Sloan was clueless about children and didn't know if three-year-olds could do that.

"It's just like learning a song. You hear it enough times, you memorize it. That's how I taught her our address and phone number."

"Really?"

"You'll have to ask her when we get back. I made it into a song. You know, like 'Twinkle, Twinkle Little Star' or the ABC song. She learned it pretty quick."

"I like your house," Sloan said. What a stupid thing to say. Couldn't she have come up with something more flattering?

Adrienne looked around, pride on her face. "We do too. It suits us."

"And it's right around the corner from your parents." Sloan stated the obvious.

"That's exactly why I bought it. I can't count how many times my mom or dad has come over to help out or babysit or just to give me a ten-minute break."

"It's great they're so close by and helpful."

"I don't know what we would do without them." Adrienne smiled fondly.

"I like your family," Sloan said, stupidly but true.

"They were on their best behavior today."

"What would it have been like if they weren't?" Sloan could only imagine.

"More of the same, just four times as loud." Adrienne grinned.

"Have you always gotten along?"

"Pretty much. We have our squabbles now and then, and when we were teenagers we hated each other, but for the most part we just like each other and enjoy being together. We have each other's back."

"Frankie definitely has yours."

Adrienne cocked her head again, looking at her. "How so?"

"She was giving me more than the once-over more than once," she explained, unable to think of any other way to describe it.

"Sorry about that."

"No need. Obviously, she cares about you, wants what's best for you."

"But she had no business doing that."

"Didn't she?" Sloan asked quietly.

"No, of course not." Adrienne's voice wasn't quite as strong as her objection a moment ago. "Nothing's going on between us," Adrienne said, gripping Dr. Seuss.

Sloan put the finger under Adrienne's chin and lifted it. Adrienne met her eyes. "Isn't there?" Sloan's voice was barely a whisper.

Something had been going on between them ever since they'd seen each other again. Maybe it was the experience of a loving family or the relaxed time she'd had this afternoon, but Sloan was tired of denying it. The spark that had been there in their twenties was now a smoldering flame in their thirties. She was afraid to move, almost afraid to breathe. The heat from Adrienne's skin radiated off her.

Adrienne's eyes were dark and troubled. Sloan was close enough to see the darker flecks of green on the edges.

"No," Adrienne said, her voice quivering on that one word.

Sloan saw a different answer reflected in the burning desire in Adrienne's eyes. She lowered her head and stopped less than an inch from her lips. "No?" It was a question, their mouths dangerously close.

Sloan was so close, Adrienne inhaled her breath. Her heart was hammering, her throat suddenly very dry, and she felt light-headed. What had started as a wonderful day had suddenly turned very complicated. When she had come down the stairs and seen Sloan sitting on the couch, Callie's book in her hand, she'd immediately felt warm all over. It seemed like that was where Sloan needed to be, but she'd pushed the thought from her mind when she stepped forward. Now, a few minutes later, she didn't know what was going on. All she knew was that Sloan's mouth was tantalizingly close to hers, and she didn't have the willpower to stop Sloan from kissing her.

Sloan's touch, even though it was simply the pad of her fingertip, had sent a bolt of heat through her that had settled between her legs. She thought all of this in the few seconds with Sloan so close. All Adrienne needed to do was lift her head, and their lips would meet.

Adrienne waited. *Kiss me. Please kiss me*. Then she realized Sloan was waiting for her to make the move, close the gap between them. After Adrienne had run out on her at Elliott's party, Sloan was letting her decide. For the first time in a very, very long time, Adrienne didn't think or analyze or weigh the consequences; she just felt. Then she reached up, held Sloan's face between her hands, and pulled her close. When their lips met, she knew she'd made the right decision.

Sloan's mouth was soft, her kiss gentle and undemanding, and when Sloan's tongue licked the edge of her bottom lip, the light switch of desire flicked on, and need overwhelmed her.

Sloan gasped in surprise when Adrienne pushed her onto her back and covered her body with hers. The book hit the floor at the same time she pulled Sloan's shirt from the waistband of her pants.

The feel of Sloan's warm skin was like a dam bursting inside her. Adrienne's reaction to Sloan's kiss was staggering. Want and desire exploded from her like fireworks out of their casing. She was driven to touch Sloan everywhere, feel her softness, run her fingers over curves and touch warm wetness always so responsive. She wanted to lick and taste her. She was overcome with need so intense she couldn't stop it even if she had to. Even if she wanted to, she couldn't go back now. It was too late and she was too far gone.

Adrienne pulled her dress over her head and just as easily dispensed with her bra. Sloan's gaze was like a touch, a soft caress, but Adrienne needed more, and she needed it now.

Adrienne pulled Sloan into a sitting position, and Sloan's lips closed around her nipple. Adrienne grabbed the back of her head to keep it there. God, that felt so good.

"Touch me," she whispered and raised up just enough for Sloan to slide her hand between them. Waves of ecstasy rolled over her as Sloan touched her. Every nerve ending and sensation that had been dormant came alive under Sloan's skillful fingers, her mouth on her breasts. Her body responded under Sloan's familiarity, and her first orgasm slammed into her and left her breathless but hungry for more. It had been so long since she'd been touched like this, been worshipped like this, felt alive like this. The voice in the back of her head was trying to get her attention, but she ignored it.

Sloan's fingers were soft and teasing, then hard and demanding. Her body complied with every request and made more than a few of its own. Her toes curled, and she clenched the cushions and held on as she fell into the deep abyss of pleasure again. But this place wasn't dark. Here she found light and joy, its intensity blinding her.

Adrienne's consciousness slowly floated back to the surface. Her limbs were heavy, her throat dry. She was lethargic, sated, and energized all at the same time. Sloan always did have a way of making her absolutely crazy.

She jerked her eyes open, instantly realizing what had happened. She took stock of herself and her surroundings. Sloan was under her, breathing heavily. They were both covered in sweat, her face buried in Sloan's neck. And then she remembered. Sloan had kissed her. No, that wasn't fair. She had kissed Sloan. Sloan had given her every opportunity to back away, and Adrienne had to admit and claim full responsibility for the situation she was in now.

Her dress was somewhere on the floor, her panties and bra probably on top of it. She imagined what someone would see if they walked through her front door. She lay draped on top of Sloan, who had her fingers still inside her.

What the fuck did I just do? She remembered Sloan touching her, sliding her hand between her thigh, and her own warm wetness. She'd ridden her hand, arching her back, climaxing when Sloan took her nipple into her mouth. Twice more she came that way, and on the fourth orgasm she had taken Sloan with her. Somehow she'd managed to get her fingers on Sloan's clit, and they'd fallen into a familiar rhythm until they both came again.

She inhaled sharply when Sloan withdrew her fingers and started rubbing her back. She tensed at the intimacy. A quickie on the couch was one thing, but any sort of tenderness and connection was something else altogether.

"Shh, it's all right."

Adrienne felt the vibration of Sloan's voice in her chest. *How can she say it's all right*? How could she have done this? To herself? To Brenna? *Oh my God!* She desperately wanted to jump up, put her clothes on, and rush out of here. But this was her house, and scrambling around butt-ass naked trying to find her clothes would only add to the humiliation.

"Adrienne, I know what you're thinking."

"You don't have any idea what I'm thinking." Her pride turned into anger. At that point, she lifted herself off Sloan, her skin immediately cool where just moments before it had been scalding hot.

"Hey," Sloan said, starting to get up.

"Hey, nothing. You don't have a fucking clue what I'm feeling, what I'm going through." She jabbed out the words as she snatched up her clothes. Feeling completely vulnerable, she didn't bother with her bra or panties—just jerked her dress over her head.

Sloan sat up, pulling the front of her shirt together. Adrienne bent over, picked up Sloan's pants, and practically threw them at her. "Get dressed."

"Adrienne."

"Shut up," she snapped at Sloan. "Just…" She held her hand out as if she could stop the flood of emotions coursing through her and threatening to spill out. "Please, just get dressed and go." Adrienne turned around. She knew she was being ridiculous, but if she couldn't see Sloan, then what had just happened hadn't actually happened.

"Adrienne."

Sloan was so close she could feel her warm breath on her neck. "Please, Sloan." She was begging, clenching her teeth tight. If she opened her mouth, the tension coiled inside would explode, and she wasn't sure if she'd scream and curse at Sloan or beg her to stay.

Sloan must have sensed that she was maintaining control by only a thread. Adrienne was so attuned to Sloan she knew the instant she stepped away. When she heard the door close, she risked a glance behind her. It would be just like Sloan to open and close the door, giving Adrienne the impression that she'd gone but forcing the conversation to continue. She was relieved that she had, in fact, left.

Adrienne collapsed on the couch, still warm from the heat generated by their bodies. She leaned forward, put her head in her hands, and sobbed.

CHAPTER TWENTY-SIX

Sloan stumbled down the front sidewalk and turned in the direction of where her car was parked. In their haste to come together, Adrienne hadn't bothered with the buttons on her shirt, preferring to simply pull it apart, and Sloan had been vaguely aware of the sound of buttons skittering across the floor. A return trip to Adrienne's mother's house to say her good-byes was impossible. She'd leave that to Adrienne to explain. She'd get Maria's number to thank her again for dinner and apologize for her abrupt departure.

She shook her head, trying to make sense of what had just happened. She had no idea if it had been ten minutes or two hours since Adrienne had kissed her. She rubbed her hand over her face, the scent of Adrienne still on her fingers. Her stomach clenched as she remembered the sight and sounds of Adrienne above her.

God, she was beautiful when passion filled her. Her skin was flushed and hot. Her back arched, her hands alternately on Sloan's breasts, then her own, and when Sloan had slid her fingers inside her, Adrienne had clamped around them and had her first of several orgasms. The second one came shortly after the first, the third catching them both by surprise. At some point Sloan couldn't hold back any longer. The image of Adrienne, bathed in sweat, breasts heaving as she lost control was enough to send her over the edge. Somehow in the middle of all that, Adrienne had managed to touch her, and Sloan had cried out as her second orgasm slammed into her.

What had started so quickly had ended equally abruptly, when Adrienne did little more than throw her out. And why had she said something as stupid as *I know what you're thinking*? She had no idea what Adrienne was thinking. As far as she knew, this might have been the first time she'd made love since her wife died. She groaned. "And it had to be a fast and furious fuck on the couch. Jesus, Sloan," she admonished herself.

Rounding the corner on the block back to Adrienne's parents' house, Sloan was relieved that none of her fellow dinner guests were out in the front yard. That would have been awkward, her walking up clutching her shirt closed and sneaking into her car and driving off without saying a word. But that was exactly what she did.

Instead of going straight home, Sloan simply drove around. Driving always cleared her head, except this evening she simply couldn't gather her thoughts. All she could think about was Adrienne, heat flowing through her body again, the pounding between her legs familiar and demanding.

She pulled into her garage, not having any idea what she would do tomorrow. She took a shower, knowing that if she didn't, the scent of Adrienne all over her would keep her awake the entire night. She chuckled. Who the hell was she kidding? There wasn't a snowball's chance in hell she was going to get any sleep tonight. She went into her office, trying to convince herself that she might as well try to do some work to get her mind off Adrienne. That unproductive effort lasted forty minutes.

Sloan relocated to her living room, sat on the couch, pulled her legs beneath her, and reached for the remote. Flipping through the channels she settled on one just as her favorite movie, *The African Queen*, was starting. She settled in to watch the slovenly, drunkard captain take his religious, spinster passenger down the Ulonga-Bora river in East Africa.

Sloan half paid attention to the movie, the other half fighting the urge to pick up the phone and call Adrienne. She wanted to talk with her, hear her voice. She needed to know if she was all right, because no matter what had happened between them all those years ago and all the time between, she still cared about her.

Admittedly, Sloan was more than a little rattled by the events of this afternoon, and she could only imagine what Adrienne was going through. She wasn't the one who had married someone, committed herself to one woman who had then tragically died.

Sloan had seen pictures of Brenna inside Adrienne's house. Their wedding picture sat on the mantle, Adrienne looking beautiful in white trousers and a navy, long-sleeved shirt. The cuffs of her sleeves and pants were rolled up, her feet bare. Brenna was dressed much the same, however in complementary colors. She had a flower above one ear that matched the lei around Adrienne's neck. In another frame, Brenna was pushing Callie on a swing, a large, radiant smile on her face.

On the side table in a thick silver frame was a picture of Brenna in a purple dress holding her stomach, obviously very pregnant. A few more photos were scattered around the room, and she wondered what kind of memories were in Adrienne's bedroom. Sloan had thought for a moment about picking Adrienne up and carrying her into her bedroom, where they could rediscover each other in the comfort of a large bed. But the actual event had been over almost before the thought had a chance to crystallize in her head. Then she was out the door.

Sloan went into the kitchen and poured herself more than a generous portion of Crown Royal, not even bothering with ice, and returned to her place on the couch. Maybe if she drank enough she'd be able to sleep without images of Adrienne. One could only hope, she thought, as the ending credits rolled.

Chapter Twenty-seven

Adrienne pulled herself together. She couldn't just go for a walk and not come back. She looked at her reflection in the mirror in her bathroom. "Holy mother of God." She looked like she had just been fucked, thoroughly, and more than once. No way could she go back to her mother's house looking like this. She showered quickly, taking special care not to let her hair get wet. That would be something else she would have to explain. She found her panties and bra on the floor behind the couch and forced herself not to stare at the piece of furniture she would never look at the same again. She pulled her dress over her head and at the last minute remembered what she'd come back here for. She grabbed the sweater and went out the door.

Every third step Adrienne inhaled and held her breath for three more, trying to calm her body and clear her mind. When she walked into her mother's house, she needed to put on her best lawyer face and pretend like nothing had happened. She thought up an excuse to explain Sloan's abrupt departure, though at first, she wasn't sure her mother bought it. Thankfully she let the subject drop when Callie scampered over to her.

Finally, Adrienne was able to make her excuses, picked up her daughter, and retreated to her house. Callie was wound up from the excitement of seeing her aunts, uncles, and cousins, and no way would she play quietly in her bedroom while Adrienne grappled with the ramifications of what she'd done. They went out to the backyard, and Callie was content to play on her swing set, climb the rock wall, and allow Adrienne to simply push her in the swing. She chattered nonstop like three-year-old little girls do, and Adrienne wasn't required to respond. Callie didn't mind that Adrienne was distracted, and it wasn't until the neighbor's dog barked that she realized it was almost dark. She hustled Callie inside and, after a quick dinner and an even quicker dip in the tub, put her to bed. It was only seven thirty, and Adrienne knew she faced a long night ahead.

The next morning, groggy from not nearly enough sleep, she barely said two words to her mother when she dropped Callie off before heading to her office. When she pulled into the parking lot she saw Frankie's car. She knew her attempts to dodge her sister last night had only postponed the inevitable until this morning.

Adrienne pulled into the space at the far end of the lot, and Frankie stepped out of her car. Adrienne was familiar with the determined look on her face. Frankie was content to say nothing until they were inside Adrienne's office and both had a cup of coffee in their hands.

"Do you want to tell me what's going on? And don't even try to tell me it's nothing."

Adrienne looked everywhere except at her sister while she gathered her thoughts in preparation for the third degree she knew had just begun. Frankie never danced around a topic or used clever euphemisms for what she wanted to talk about. Her bluntness was almost rude. Frankie might have been only twenty-six years old, but she was far wiser than many people much older.

"We knew each other in college."

"I know that," Frankie said, undeterred. "How well did you know each other?"

"Pretty well."

"Were you lovers?"

Adrienne hated that word—lovers. Often used to describe gay and lesbian relationships, the word was all about sex, and although sex was a primary activity in their relationship, what she and Sloan had was something more. At least she'd thought it was until that awful morning when she woke up to find Sloan gone.

She'd known their time together was ending, but Adrienne had initially considered the way Sloan had left unforgivable. Years later, after her anger had died and her hurt had healed, she'd realized Sloan had probably done them both a favor. They'd been saying good-bye for weeks. Their lovemaking had been more frequent, almost frantic. She wouldn't have had the strength to walk away and probably would have begged Sloan to stay. So, yes, they had been much more than lovers, and she told Frankie that.

"What happened?"

"We were headed in different directions. There was just too much keeping us apart."

"What's going on now?"

"I don't know," Adrienne answered honestly.

"What happened yesterday?"

Adrienne stared at Frankie. She could see Frankie knew exactly what had gone on.

"It just happened." She didn't need to go into detail. She didn't even have to put a name to it.

"And?"

"And what?" Adrienne asked, her confusion and exhaustion finally coming to a head. She got up from her chair and started pacing back and forth in front of the windows.

"And?"

"What the fuck do I know? One minute we were talking about Callie, and the next we had our hands down each other's pants." Frankie didn't even flinch at the crude description. "It happened so fast, I don't even know how or why."

"And now?"

"And now, as much as I'd like to say I didn't know what I was doing, I can't."

"Is she the first woman you've been with since Brenna died?"

Guilt ripped in Adrienne's gut, and all she could do was nod.

"You know you can talk to me, Ren."

It had been years since Frankie had used her nickname. When she was just learning how to talk, Adrienne was more than a mouthful, and she had shortened it to Ren. When Frankie had turned fifteen, she thought childhood nicknames immature and had called her Adrienne ever since. Except for that awful, awful day when Brenna had been killed.

The social worker at Brenna's school had called their mother, who in turn had called Frankie, both arriving at the command center within minutes of each other. Her mother offered comfort, and her sister took charge and asked questions that Adrienne was too upset to even consider.

"I cannot even begin to describe how I feel. I don't know whether to shout from a mountaintop, laugh hysterically, or vomit. I loved Brenna with everything I had. She was my wife. We were going to spend the rest of our lives together." She looked at their wedding picture on the corner of her desk.

Her wife—that one word conveyed the depth of her commitment. She and Brenna were partners. They had promised to be together, had pledged their faithfulness and vowed to be together forever.

"Adrienne, you knew this day would come," Frankie said perceptively. "Well, maybe not this exact day, but Brenna would want you to be happy. And that includes someone to share your life with."

"I don't know a goddamn thing!" Adrienne barked, not at her sister but herself because of the confusion boring a hole in her brain. "Obviously, I don't know what the fuck I'm doing. For God's sake, I'm a mother. I'm responsible for a three-year-old child, and I'm fucking on the couch like a horny teenager. God, what was I thinking?" Adrienne sat in the chair and grabbed her hair with both hands.

"Maybe that's exactly what you needed." Adrienne shot a look at her. "No. Think about it, Adrienne. Your first time after Brenna. Do you think it would have been any easier than what you're going through now if it had been a romantic evening complete with dinner, dancing, soft music, foreplay, and rose petals up the stairs to the bed? Warm caresses, sweet words?"

"I get the picture, Frankie."

"I'm serious, Ren. Do you think you'd feel any different the morning after than you do now? I don't know what I'm talking about. I've never been in your shoes. I know how much you loved Brenna, and this is a big deal for you. You probably would have been trying to cope with the same thing if it had happened that way. So, what difference does it make how it went down? It happened. The only thing that might have made it better was if it had been a stranger. Not somebody you have to look at across the desk."

Adrienne didn't respond, her thoughts mixing with her sister's. OMG, she would be seeing Sloan again. She had to maintain a working relationship with her after this. After they'd touched each other intimately again, touched each other's soul.

"So what are you going to do?"

"Nothing."

"Nothing?"

"Yes, nothing."

"You can't do nothing."

"I'm a grown-up, Frankie. I can do whatever I want." God, that sounded like the fights they used to have as kids.

"You can't do nothing," she repeated.

"And what do you think I should do?" As soon as the words were out of her mouth, Adrienne realized she shouldn't have said them.

"Have you talked to her?"

"No."

"Why not?"

"And just what the fuck am I supposed to say to her, Frankie? 'Was it good for you?' There's no point in asking that. It was pretty obvious."

"Don't bite my head off. You may be my older sister, and I know this is some serious shit, but you don't have to be an ass about it."

"I can be whatever I want to be about it. This is my life we're talking about. And it's not that simple."

"Don't you think I know that?"

"I know, I know, I'm sorry." Adrienne knew she shouldn't be tearing into her sister. Frankie only wanted the best for her.

"Call her," Frankie said carefully. The last time she told her that, Adrienne had bit her head off, chewed it up, and spit it back at her. "See what she's thinking. Is there any chance this could—"

"No."

"Why not?"

Adrienne looked at Frankie. That was one of the stupidest questions her sister could have asked. "Notwithstanding the fact that it's a colossal conflict of interest, I have a child."

"So? How is this a conflict of interest? You said it yourself yesterday. All this deal needs is a signature. Your job was to negotiate the deal. After that, your job is done. As for Callie, single mothers all over the world get involved with people all the time. Unless you think Sloan wouldn't want Callie," she added.

"And exactly when would I have asked her that? Before, during, or after I had my hands in her pants?" Adrienne grimaced, realizing anyone walking by her office would have heard that.

"Well, if it were before, she would have promised you anything, and after, probably the same. If during, however, if she was even capable of thinking, you were doing something wrong."

Frankie's rebuttal made it clear to Adrienne that, again, she had stepped out of line. "Well, you're right on all three counts," she said, defusing the situation even though the fire between her legs was still smoldering.

"I have no idea what Sloan thinks, and it really doesn't matter because it isn't going to happen."

"So, who's afraid of the answer to that question? You or Brenna?"

Adrienne's temper sparked again. "Don't you dare bring her name into this."

"I don't need to. Her name is all over this. Do you mean to tell me that if you had Callie by yourself, without Brenna, we'd even be having this conversation? The only thing you'd be concerned with is if Sloan would make a good parent for Callie. You wouldn't be all tied up in knots, feeling guilty for moving on."

Adrienne snapped her head around and was prepared to refute Frankie's opinion but didn't have the chance.

"That's exactly what's happening here, Adrienne. You feel guilty for moving on. You feel guilty for having feelings for someone other than Brenna, like somehow you're cheating on her, disrespecting her memory because you could want to touch someone when you had promised Brenna it would be only her. You need to get over that, Adrienne, or your life is going to be hollow and incomplete. The whole deal with this conflict of interest is bullshit. Don't make that the excuse you hang on to the rest of your life. And assuming you live to be ninety, that's over twenty thousand nights and three thousand lazy Sunday mornings that you're going to be all alone. Callie can only fill so much of that void in your life. You know as well as I do, that's one area she can't. And you'll end up being the shell of the person you were when you were with Brenna. Think about it."

Adrienne sat there, stunned at her sister's insight, the harshness of her words penetrating her fog. Frankie stood, crossed the distance between them, and kissed her on the cheek.

"Call her."

It was the last thing she said before turning and leaving Adrienne's office.

CHAPTER TWENTY-EIGHT

How was your weekend?" Elliott's voice from her doorway startled Sloan, her pen skittering across the section of the report she was taking notes on.

"Fine," she said, quickly recovering.

"Do anything special?" Elliott asked, sitting in the chair across from her desk.

Her mind immediately went to the image of her and Adrienne sprawled naked on her couch, the five or six orgasms between them. Then she thought of dinner at Joe and Maria's house. It was a fun, very enjoyable way to spend a Sunday afternoon. "Nothing much." Sloan hoped God didn't strike her dead for the second bold-faced lie she'd told her boss in the last minute. It wasn't a big deal. This wasn't about business; it was personal. It didn't matter. But holy crap, she and Adrienne mattered in business.

Elliott was looking at her, waiting, as if Sloan needed to add something. God, how did she do that? She had an instant to make her decision.

Sloan rose, walked around her desk, and closed her office door. When she returned, she sat in the chair to Elliott's left.

"Um…Adrienne and I…we…hell. I don't know what we are." Sloan turned her hands up, hoping an accurate definition would fall out of the sky and into her lap. Something tangible she could put her hands around other than her own neck to strangle herself for what happened yesterday.

"What *exactly* does that mean?" A small frown was forming between Elliott's eyebrows.

"We, um…I, um…we…" Sloan uncharacteristically stuttered. She didn't want to say they had sex on the couch, but that's exactly what it was.

"You slept with her."

Sloan hated that phrase, and in this case, they hadn't even made it to the bed. But without giving those kinds of details, all she could do was nod.

"How long has this been going on?"

"Just once, yesterday." For some reason, Sloan needed it to be perfectly clear that it was not on company time or company business.

"Are you two rekindling something?"

"No." Sloan was pretty confident that was the truth, considering Adrienne's reaction when she realized what had happened between them.

"So, it just happened?"

"There was a little bit more to it than that."

Elliott held up her hands. "I don't need the details." Elliott looked around the room for several moments. "So, this was…" It was Elliott's turn to search for the right word.

"A one-time thing that won't happen again," Sloan said.

"Isn't that what you said when I asked about this before?"

Sloan cringed, feeling her embarrassment start at the V of her collar and run up her face. God damn it, she had let Elliott down. She respected Elliott more than anyone and, after yesterday, more than she respected herself.

"What in the fuck were you thinking? This is a multimillion-dollar opportunity for Foster McKenzie, and you can't keep your hands to yourself. I trusted you, Sloan. You gave me your word nothing would happen, that there was nothing between you and Adrienne. And this is what I get?"

Elliott's voice hadn't risen, and she hadn't shifted in her chair, making her words have even more impact. Sloan, on the other hand, was having trouble sitting still while her boss was rightfully skewering her.

"I have worked my ass off rebuilding the reputation of this firm. We have been squeaky clean in everything we've done. There hasn't even been a hint of impropriety, and do you know why? Because I won't tolerate it."

Sloan couldn't remember ever being scolded like this, even as a child. It was one thing to make a mistake, an honest error based on good intent. But there was no excuse for what she'd done. None whatsoever. She wanted to slither out of her chair and down between the seams of the carpet. She was embarrassed and humiliated and had no one to blame but herself.

"You'll have my resignation on your desk by the end of the day."

Elliott looked at her, her expression hard and unforgiving. "I'll have it on my desk within the hour."

❖

"Sweetie, what's the matter?" Lauren asked. She must have been in the courthouse, because the background noise was immense.

"I just had a conversation with Sloan. She pulled the most stupid, juvenile thing that has put our reputation at risk."

"Start at the beginning," Lauren said calmly.

Elliott rehashed the conversation from the minute Sloan had closed her office door to the instant she walked out of Sloan's office.

"Oh, boy," Lauren said. "You're really going to accept her resignation?"

"Yes." Elliott didn't have to think about her answer.

"I can't talk you out of it?"

"No, Lauren, you can't," Elliott replied firmly, almost sharply.

"Of course, honey. Foster McKenzie is your thing. I don't mean to interfere. What are you going to do?"

"I don't suppose I can talk a brilliant, beautiful, sexy, family law attorney to pack up her shingle and move into the office next door?"

Lauren's laugh filled the phone, and Elliott's insides warmed. "We'd kill each other by the end of the first day."

Elliott chuckled. "Maybe, but think of the make-up sex," she said, her voice husky.

"Hmm. I'm going to pick a fight with you the minute you get home. That way we can resolve it and still get to sleep at a decent hour."

Elliott didn't know how she could laugh at a time like this, let alone engage in witty sexual banter. But Lauren had a way of putting things into perspective. That was one of the hundreds of thousands of things she loved about her.

When she dropped the handset back into the cradle, Sloan was standing in her doorway.

"Teresa isn't here. I didn't want to just leave this on her desk."

Elliott didn't say anything, her stomach clenching. All she could think about was how disappointed she was by the woman walking toward her, holding a piece of white stationery in both hands.

She glanced at the paper Sloan laid on her desk. It was official Foster McKenzie letterhead, Sloan's name and position underneath, her bold signature on the bottom. She didn't pick it up or say anything when she looked back at Sloan.

Sloan appeared to be about to say something but closed her mouth and walked out of Elliott's office.

CHAPTER TWENTY-NINE

Thank you for meeting with me, Robert." Adrienne had called first thing this morning, telling his admin she needed thirty minutes of his time.

"What is it, Adrienne? You look upset? Is it Callie?" He motioned for her to sit in a chair across from his desk.

"No. Callie is fine. I need to recuse myself from this deal with Foster McKenzie. In fact, I probably need to resign from being your lawyer altogether."

"What?" The old man lost all color in his face.

"Something happened that I'm deeply ashamed of. Something that can't be fixed."

"Was it illegal?"

"No," Adrienne said firmly. She wrung her hands. "But it was unethical."

"What is it?"

Adrienne could barely get a word out. Not only was this her client, but Robert was a deacon in his church, deeply religious, ultra-conservative, and had been married to the same woman for fifty-three years. For her to admit to an affair with opposing counsel was one thing, but when it was with a woman, that was something completely different. However, he knew she was a lesbian and about Brenna.

"Adrienne?" Robert's voice had a harsh edge to it now.

"I had an inappropriate encounter with an employee at Foster

McKenzie." Adrienne hoped that would be enough. Robert was old but he wasn't stupid.

"Who?"

Adrienne swallowed hard and took a deep breath. "Sloan Merchant."

Robert frowned, his confusion apparent. For several moments, he simply stared at her as if there might be more. But she didn't have anything else to say. Adrienne saw the exact moment he understood the exact nature of inappropriate.

"I see."

"There is no excuse for my behavior. I will, of course, return my fees for this deal to you in a cashier's check by the end of the day. I've prepared a list of attorneys I recommend to—"

"No."

Adrienne stopped speaking, Robert's interruption surprising her. "Excuse me?"

"No. I don't want another lawyer."

"But…" Adrienne was completely confused.

"But nothing. You are my lawyer and you will remain my lawyer. You've been with me from the very beginning, Adrienne. You have been as instrumental in making Auburn a success as anyone else on this team. Do you love this woman?"

His statement and quick change of subject stunned Adrienne. It was the last thing she'd expected when she had practiced her resignation in the car on the way over here.

"I did at one time," she answered honestly.

"And now?"

"It's complicated."

"Of course it's complicated," Robert said quickly. "Love is complicated, relationships are complicated, and people are complicated. What's not complicated is that if you want something, you work at it. You work hard at it. You work hard *for* it."

"But…"

Robert held his hand up.

"This inappropriateness…" He used air quotes to make his point. "Is it inappropriate because Sloan works for Foster McKenzie?"

Adrienne nodded.

"That's just phooey."

"Phooey?" Adrienne knew her mind was muddled from lack of sleep, but she wasn't following him.

"That's an old-guy technical term, *phooey*. I think today they say 'to hell with it.' My grandson would probably say 'fuck it.'"

Adrienne tried to stifle a chuckle.

"Rarely do you have a chance to find someone who makes you happy. Don't pass it up just because society or some archaic notion says it's not right."

"This isn't a societal or archaic notion. It's a conflict of interest. They drilled that into our head in Ethics 101 in law school."

"Well, I don't have a problem with it, and if that makes me unethical in this situation, then so be it."

"Robert, you are the most ethical man I know."

"And that's why we're having this conversation now. But not only am I ethical, I also surround myself with smart people. I saw that in you right after I met you. Now," he said, rising and coming around from behind his desk. "I don't want to hear any more of this nonsense. Throw that list away. I don't need it or want it. If, however, some other firm were to offer you a ten-million-dollar retainer, I'd have to let you go, but I'd let you in on a great little company you can invest it in."

Adrienne mirrored his smile, relief just on the edges of her comfort. She was still uncomfortable with this entire situation.

She drove back to her office on autopilot, her mind racing over the events of the last twenty-four hours. Sloan sitting at her parents' table, like she was meant to be there, and then they'd had sex, and then she'd thrown her out. While she'd lain awake last night, she'd remembered the dozens of times she and Sloan had made love. Their first time was tentative and clunky and awkward, and they'd laughed together until their orgasm took their breath away. They'd learned each other's wants and desires, and discovered those secret places that caused a shudder, a quiver, or a moan of desire. They'd made love indoors, outdoors, in private, and more than once where they could be found by anyone walking by. They'd reached for each other in the dark, with the lights on, and in the middle of the day. At times they hadn't been able to keep their hands off each other, and other times they were content to sit next to each other and simply read a book. They'd debated politics, the pros and cons of abortion, whether NASA should spend trillions of dollars to colonize Mars, and who was the better captain of the starship *Enterprise.* Sloan had taught Adrienne how to speak French, and Adrienne had taught Sloan more than the nasty words in Spanish. They had fought fairly but fiercely and made love so tenderly that the memory brought Adrienne to tears. No wonder she hadn't slept last night.

She pulled into the parking lot, put her car into park, laid her head back on her seat, and closed her eyes. A few minutes later, light tapping on her window startled her. Ruth was looking at her, concern on her face.

Adrienne opened the door, grabbed her bag, and got out.

"Are you okay? I saw you pull up a while ago and thought you were finishing a call. Then when you hadn't moved, I thought something might be wrong."

"I'm fine," she replied. She wasn't really fine, but she would be. She followed Ruth into the office and set her mind to get back to work. Work had been her savior, her salvation, and her lifeline at one time, and it would be again.

CHAPTER THIRTY

"Do you think Sloan will ever find what we have?" Lauren asked.

The light on the bedside table cast a soft glow over the bed. A light breeze blew in from the open window. They'd gone to bed an hour ago, but Elliott had had other ideas, and they were just now catching their breath.

"We just finished making love, and you want to talk about Sloan?" Elliott tried to clear the residual orgasmic thundering from her brain.

"I like her. I want to see her happy."

"I like her too, but she was the last thing on my mind." Actually, when Elliott made love with Lauren she wasn't capable of thinking.

"Do you remember the first time we made love?" Lauren asked.

"Is that a trick question? Of course I do. I'll never forget it." Lauren's back was against her front, Elliott's arms wrapped against her. She loved to fall asleep this way, but Lauren obviously wanted to talk.

"Tell me what you remember."

"Why? Did you forget?" Elliott asked, tickling Lauren lightly.

"A girl never forgets her first time," she said, rubbing her ass into Elliott's crotch.

God, that was sexy, Elliott thought.

"I just want to hear it from your perspective."

"It was good for me."

"Stop, you crude Neanderthal. Be serious."

"Well," Elliott said, "I'd invited you to my house for dinner. You were wearing a pair of navy pants and a white shirt. I don't think I ate much because I was a nervous wreck. After dinner we were on the deck having a glass of wine, and I wanted to touch you so bad I felt like I might explode. I'd planned to give you all the time you needed, but God, I wanted to put my hands on you. Actually, I wanted to put more than my hands on you. I was almost at the end of my rope. Then you looked at me so calmly and told me to go ahead." Elliott sighed, remembering that moment. "I thought I'd come out of my skin with joy.

"I touched your face and traced your lips that drove me out of my mind wanting to kiss them, and the look you gave me took my breath away. I took the clip out of your hair, which felt like bands of soft gold. Then I finally kissed you. I tried to stay in control, but my body kept telling me something else. Then you put your arms around my neck and pinned me against the railing. That's when I completely lost it. I remember thinking that you were the most beautiful woman I'd ever met."

"You told me that," Lauren said wistfully. "And I believed you. But it took forever for you to get my clothes off."

"No way was I going to rush it or you. However, I remember thinking I needed to send a thank-you note to whoever invented the front clasp on your bra."

"I thought I was going to come when you took my nipple into your mouth."

Elliott chuckled. "I seem to remember you yanked my shirt off after that."

"I needed to touch you too."

"I slid my fingers inside your pants and lightly pressed right here." Elliott pressed the sensitive spot between her legs, and Lauren responded like she had that first time.

"I remember thinking that if we didn't lie down, I might fall down."

"Damn, I'm good," Elliott said teasingly.

"Yes, you were. When you pulled my pants off I knew there was no going back. And I didn't want to."

"You felt so good." Elliott remembered how it felt to be skin to skin.

"No. What felt good was when you finally touched me."

"Like I had any choice? You grabbed my hand and put it there."

"You weren't going fast enough." Lauren's voice was husky with desire again.

Elliott shifted them both until they were in the same position they'd been in that special night. She still lost her breath when she felt Lauren's warm, moist center. She remembered everything about that night and treated Lauren and herself to a repeat.

Elliott slowly explored with her fingers while gently kissing Lauren, their tongues expressing their mutual desire. Lauren began to move rhythmically beneath her, and her hips began to thrust. Elliott responded in tempo to Lauren's increasing wave of desire.

Lauren buried her face in Elliott's neck, her body arching off the bed as she climaxed into Elliott's hand. Elliott continued to stroke her as the spasms peaked a second time, holding her close and whispering that she loved her. She eased her caresses and gathered Lauren to her. Lauren's hands were still in her hair, and as they loosened their hold, Elliott raised her head and looked at the woman she had just made love to. Lauren's eyes were closed, and sheer pleasure was imprinted on her face; she was the most beautiful woman Elliott had ever seen. A sheen of sweat covered her neck and drew Elliott's lips once again. As she kissed and licked the sensitive skin, she began to stroke her again. Lauren immediately raised her hips in response.

Elliott quickly shifted her position and replaced her hand with the first tentative touch of her lips. Lauren was breathless, and her head began to swim as Elliott slowly used her tongue to explore every inch of her.

"Oh, God, Elliott."

Elliott cupped the firm ass of the woman she was fully enjoying. She lifted Lauren slightly to allow greater access and opened her eyes; this time, she wanted to watch as Lauren climaxed. The clitoris beneath her tongue became hard, and Lauren gripped the sheets with both hands, writhing on the bed. She came with a greater intensity than before, and Elliott almost climaxed herself while watching her beautiful wife shudder in release.

As Lauren came down from her orgasm, Elliott slowed her tongue, tasting the juices that flowed freely. Breathing heavily, Lauren gasped each time Elliott's tongue lightly slipped over her clitoris. Eventually Elliott left the warm, fragrant place and rolled over onto her back, taking Lauren in her arms and cradling her as the aftershocks of her orgasm left her. Lauren settled in as if she had always been there. Elliott pulled the sheet up to cover them both. She gently stroked Lauren's back and moved strands of wet hair from her face.

"You're right. You are *very* good at that." Lauren sighed contentedly.

They lay spent then, their breathing more even as the minutes passed. As her body settled, warm and sated, Elliott realized Lauren had fallen asleep. She reached over, turned off the light, and pulled the rest of the covers over them both.

Elliott lay in the dark for quite some time, considering Lauren's original question. She had never thought of Sloan as the settling-down type. Elliott knew she dated, or at least had a never-ending supply of women in her life. Elliott had been very much the same before she met Lauren. She'd been driven by her career and never considered life with just one woman. One at a time, yes. Just not one—period. But all it took was one woman, one tiny woman to shift her world, and she had never been the same. And, most importantly, Elliott never wanted to be.

Lauren sighed and, if possible, snuggled closer, shifting Elliott's attention away from Sloan to her wife. It sounded trite and corny and a major cliché, but Lauren was the best thing that had ever happened to her. She wrapped her arms tighter and breathed in the clean scent of Lauren's hair. She was happy, more content than she ever thought she would be. Her life was perfect. What else could she ask for?

CHAPTER THIRTY-ONE

Sloan poured the dark liquid into her glass, her hand a bit unsteady due to the three other times she'd refilled it. She probably needed to stop, or at least slow down. But WTF? She was in her own house, she wasn't driving, she wasn't going anywhere, and she had nothing to do. If she wanted to sit on her patio and get shit-faced drunk, she could.

Sloan had stopped by the liquor store after leaving Foster McKenzie. She picked up a bottle of Crown, a six-pack of Coke, and a pack of Marlboros. The first was well on its way to being empty, the second sitting on her counter unopened, the third on the table beside her, one of the cigarettes missing. She had no idea why she'd bought them; she hadn't smoked since she was a teenager. It just seemed like the thing to do. But the first two or three puffs had made her cough her lungs out, so she'd dropped it into her water bottle.

She needed to figure out what she was going to do, but she'd think about that tomorrow. Today she was just going to escape. She needed to stop thinking, stop analyzing, stop reliving every moment since the day Adrienne had walked into Elliott's conference room. That would get her nowhere but miserable. Spending her afternoon like this was completely unproductive, but she didn't care. She deserved this. She'd worked her ass off for years. She deserved an afternoon for herself, even if the reason was gut-wrenching.

Wallowing in self-pity wasn't helpful, but right now a little bit of selfishness bullied its way in. She didn't have to worry about money. She'd invested the money her grandmother left her when she died, and that account was growing handsomely. Elliott paid very well so she had quite a bit in her savings. She could take her time and figure out what she wanted to do. However, she was sure she wouldn't get a glowing recommendation, or any recommendation for that matter, from Foster McKenzie.

Sloan looked around the room. It reflected her life. She had the finest furniture, but no one came over to sit on it. She had a chef's kitchen, but rarely did it have a plate in the sink. Her dining-room table had never been used, and her refrigerator was spotless inside and out. She couldn't remember the last time anyone had visited her.

Was her life really that empty? She had all the exterior symbols of a successful woman but absolutely no one to share her time with. She didn't have a dog, a cat, or even a fish. Her life was nothing but a shell, and it wasn't surprising that she had cracked so easily. And she had never seen it coming.

CHAPTER THIRTY-TWO

Adrienne had three days to prepare herself for the next meeting with Sloan and Elliott. They were due to sign the final paperwork and would probably open a bottle of champagne and toast their deal. She dressed carefully, putting on another of her don't-fuck-with-me suits. She needed all the external armor she could get to fortify herself from the onslaught of emotions when she saw Sloan.

Adrienne caught Robert's look when Elliott said that Sloan would not be joining them. Nothing more was said about her, and Elliott proceeded to talk through the final revisions to their agreement. As she and Robert talked, Adrienne worried if Sloan was seriously ill. She wouldn't have missed this meeting.

Seventy minutes later, Adrienne held her breath when Robert said, "Give Sloan our best, and we hope to see her next week."

Elliott was gathering up the paperwork and hesitated before she said, "Sloan is no longer with Foster McKenzie."

The papers in Adrienne's hand slid to the floor, the silence in the room overwhelming. Had Sloan quit? Had she been fired because of what happened? Had Sloan told Elliott? Those and many other questions flew through her brain in an instant.

"I'm sorry to hear that," Robert said. "I enjoyed working with her. We both enjoyed working with her." He pointed to Adrienne. "She was always very personable and very professional."

Elliott frowned like she'd tasted something sour, and at that moment Adrienne knew she was aware of what had happened between them. The only question was how she found out.

"What do you think happened," Robert asked when they were in the elevator.

"I don't know."

"Have you talked to Sloan?"

"No." Adrienne had given Frankie the same answer yesterday, and the day before, and the day before that.

"Are you going to? I know it's none of my business, but maybe you should." Robert's response was less volatile than her sister's had been.

"Yes. I'll call her when I get back to the office."

"Please give her my best. If there's anything I can do, anything at all, like talk to Elliott, anything, please let me know." The bell rang, signaling they had arrived in the lobby.

❖

Adrienne had stalled long enough. Callie was in bed, and her hands shook as she dialed the number she had memorized. The phone rang several times before Sloan's voice mail picked up, her voice friendly and familiar.

"This is Sloan Merchant. I'm unavailable at the moment, so please leave your name and your number and a brief message, and I'll get back with you as soon as I can."

Adrienne didn't leave her name or her number. Caller ID would disclose that information as soon as Sloan checked. When the phone rang several minutes later, she grabbed it. It wasn't Sloan's number, but her heart raced anyway.

"Adrienne Stewart."

"Hi, Adrienne. It's Lauren Collier."

"Yes, Lauren. How are you?" Adrienne answered politely, her mind racing to try to figure out why Elliott's wife was calling.

"I hope this isn't a bad time."

Even if it were a bad time, Lauren was, after all, the wife of their primary investor, even though Lauren would never play that card.

"No, this is fine."

"I apologize. I've been remiss in following up with you. I enjoyed our conversation at the party and have been meaning to call you. Can we have lunch? Maybe the day after tomorrow?"

"Sure. Let me check my calendar." Adrienne opened her laptop, input the password, and clicked on the calendar. She scrolled ahead to Friday. She was scheduled to have lunch with Frankie, but she could easily, and gratefully, cancel.

"Sure. That'll be fine. Where did you have in mind?"

"There's a little place downtown, not far from Elliott's office, called the Stillwater Café."

"Yes. I know where that is." She didn't, but she'd find it.

"Okay. Does eleven thirty work for you?"

"Eleven thirty is perfect."

"I'm looking forward to it. I'll see you then."

"Thank you, Lauren. I look forward to it too." Adrienne's curiosity was piqued even more. What did Lauren want? Was it as simple as friendship? Maybe she could get some information on Sloan.

If Adrienne had a dollar for every time she checked her phone after Lauren's call and the time she put Callie to bed, she'd probably be able to pay her daughter's outrageous preschool tuition for next year. Her phone was working, the ringer turned up to its loudest setting, and by the time she'd talked herself in and out of calling Sloan a dozen times, it was after ten. She put it on her first-thing-to-do-tomorrow list and went to bed knowing she would spend another night tossing and turning.

Adrienne called Sloan the next morning, that afternoon, and the two days after that. After the third day, she stopped trying. Sloan obviously didn't want to talk to her. Apparently, she blamed Adrienne for losing her job. Adrienne was, after all, the initiator of their little tryst on the couch. What a fucking mess.

❖

Adrienne couldn't decide what to wear to lunch with Lauren. She didn't have any appointments, and typically on days like today, she'd dress in either khakis or jeans, and occasionally, in the summer, shorts. However, she didn't think the last two were appropriate for lunch with Lauren Collier. After changing her outfit three times, she settled on a pair of navy trousers and a checkered shirt topped with a pale-blue vest. She pulled out matching socks, tied her shoes, put her hair up in a clip, gathered up Callie, and headed out the door.

The Stillwater Café was on a corner, the storefront facing Stevens Boulevard. It had a large outdoor garden seating area in a space between the main restaurant and the building beside it. A few minutes early, she tried not to fidget and look at her watch too many times. Lauren had said this was just a casual get-to-know-each-other-better lunch, but something told her it might be more than that.

As Lauren walked through the front door, Adrienne was, again, struck by how simply beautiful she was. She had shoulder-length, strawberry-blond hair that looked thick and wavy. Her blue eyes were clear and appeared not to miss a thing. Lauren held her hand out in greeting, and Adrienne took it. Adrienne hoped her own hand wasn't clammy with nervous perspiration.

Lauren had made reservations, and the hostess quickly escorted them through the restaurant and out onto the patio. Slightly uneven bricking added to the rustic décor, and Adrienne watched her footing. The last thing she needed was to stumble and sprawl in front of Lauren. She was relieved when they were seated at a table under a large oak tree. The waitress arrived quickly, took the drink orders, then disappeared, leaving Adrienne and Lauren to scan the menu.

"Thank you again for inviting me," Adrienne said, opening the conversation.

"Thank you for coming." Lauren placed her menu on the table, seeming more interested in their conversation than what was for lunch. "I know you're busy, and I'm glad you were able to squeeze me in."

"You just happened to pick the perfect day. Yesterday or next week would be completely out of the question," Adrienne commented, not worried about the little white lie.

The waitress returned with their drinks, and after they had the opportunity to look at the menu, they ordered. Adrienne chose something light, her stomach in knots.

They exchanged small talk, focusing on the weather and the recent presidential race, and Lauren inquired quite extensively about Callie.

"You and Elliott don't have children?"

"No." Did Lauren have a wistful look in her eyes, or was Adrienne just a typical sappy mother who thought everyone wanted the child?

"The timing hasn't been right."

"There's rarely a good time, and often not the right time, but you just go with what comes. Once you have a child your time is never your own anyway."

"It's important to carve time out for yourself, isn't it?" Lauren asked, sipping her iced tea.

"Yes, but it's hard. I can't speak for all mothers, but I'd rather spend time with my daughter. She's only little once, and soon enough she won't want anything to do with me. Until then, I'm content being with her."

As their coffee was served, Lauren asked, "Did you know Sloan is no longer with Foster McKenzie?"

Adrienne stopped stirring the sugar cube she'd just put in her cup. "Yes. I did. I had a meeting with Elliott earlier this week."

"Do you know why?"

Adrienne studied Lauren, trying to determine a hidden meaning behind her question. Would she go home and tell her wife every word of this conversation?

"I don't plan to tell Elliott the contents of our conversation. This is just between you and me."

Adrienne felt comfortable with Lauren and trusted her. She shook her head.

Lauren seemed surprised. "Have you spoken with her?"

"No. I've tried to call her several times, but she doesn't pick up. What did Elliott say about why she left?" Adrienne was tired of answering questions. As a lawyer, she was supposed to ask them, and answering made her uncomfortable.

Lauren looked her squarely in the eye. "It had something to do with you."

"Me?" Adrienne asked automatically, then realized she didn't need to pretend. Obviously, Lauren knew everything. "Of course it did." She sighed and slumped back into her chair. "How did Elliott find out?"

"Sloan told her."

Adrienne suspected that was the case, just as she had told Robert. "And Elliott fired her."

"Sloan offered her resignation, and Elliott accepted," Lauren said sadly.

"Robert wouldn't accept mine."

"I wish Elliott had done the same. Sloan is a fabulous attorney with far more insight into the operation of Foster McKenzie than anyone other than Elliott. She's a great woman and, admittedly, might have had a slight lapse in judgment."

Adrienne wouldn't have characterized it like that. "It was my fault," she interjected. It was important that Sloan wasn't the bad guy here. "I made the first move," Adrienne added, heat creeping up her neck at the memory.

"I appreciate that, Adrienne, but Sloan is a grown woman capable of making her own decisions."

"But—"

"But nothing." Lauren's voice was firm, then softened. "You two have history?"

Adrienne chuckled. "Boy, do we ever." This time the heat was between her legs.

"May I ask why it ended?"

"I was headed to art school in Italy and she was going to Stanford."

"Art school? That's a long way from law school."

"Yeah, well, life happens sometimes, as they say. I don't regret it. I love what I do, and I paint in my spare time. But, of course, with a three-year-old I have no spare time."

Lauren laughed, then asked, "Did your relationship with Sloan influence your work on the deal you all are working on?"

"Absolutely not." Adrienne sat up straight to make her point. "I admit I knew who Sloan was before the first meeting, and by the look on her face, she had no idea it was me. I'd gotten married and changed my name. I had the impression that after she was done with whoever did her research, they would have a new…uh, you know what I mean."

Lauren smiled, and her entire face lit up. No wonder Elliott had put a ring on her finger. A very large, sparkling one.

"I would have bought tickets to that."

Both women laughed, envisioning what that scene must have been like. "So where are you now? With Sloan, if I may ask."

Adrienne should have been offended. This was none of Lauren's business, but she needed an objective view of things. Frankie was too close and too opinionated. Adrienne could never think when her sister was carrying on.

"Nowhere." That one simple word suddenly felt like the loneliest place on earth. "Like I said, I've tried to call, but she won't pick up. Other than going over to her house, which, by the way I don't know where she lives, I'm…nowhere."

"I know where she lives," Lauren said quietly, fighting a grin threatening to spread over her face.

Excitement ran through Adrienne, then dimmed. "I don't know," Adrienne said. "If she doesn't want to talk to me, I'm not going to force the issue."

"How do you feel about her?"

For the second time, Adrienne should have told Lauren to mind her own business, but instead she said, "I don't know. What we had was a long time ago. I have a child to think of."

"And you're a widow."

Anger rushed to the surface, and Adrienne barely controlled her temper. She glared at Lauren.

"I'm sorry. That was completely out of line. My best friend lost her husband several years ago. When she even thought of dating again, she'd tell me everything she was going through. We read several books on the subject, and I went with her to a support group for several months. When she ultimately did start dating, we'd talk for hours. After she finally took the plunge, so to speak, she said she came home and threw up. I know her life and yours aren't the same, Adrienne, but the concept and the issues are similar."

Adrienne took several deep breaths. Lauren was only trying to help and offer insight. Adrienne jumped at the opportunity like a lifeline.

"I cried for what felt like forever."

"And how do you feel now?"

"My father asked me the same question a few nights ago," Adrienne said remembering their conversation. It had taken a full box of tissue, but she got the entire story out. Her father didn't judge or give her advice. He just offered complete emotional support.

"He said, 'Adrienne, don't think if you become involved with someone else that you have to forget about Brenna. You never will.' He said that Brenna had died, but that my love for her hasn't, and it never will. He said that I'll never replace her and should never try. He warned me not to compare anyone to her because they will always come up lacking. Brenna was unique, just as we all are. My love for Brenna was as distinct as she was, and I can't expect to find the same thing with someone else. That love, if I find it, will also be as distinct as she is."

"Your father sounds like a wonderful man."

Adrienne warmed inside. Her father was always there for her. "He said I needed to open my heart for the chance to fall in love again. He also said, 'You need to honor your past, but you don't need to live in it.'"

CHAPTER THIRTY-THREE

The insistent pounding on her front door was irritating and obviously not going to stop anytime soon. Sloan rolled to her feet and on her way to the front door mumbled, "Go the fuck away."

"Sloan, I know you're in there. Open the door."

Fuck, just what she needed. The wife of her ex-boss…no, that was a low blow. Lauren was her friend. In the last few days, Sloan had realized she didn't have many friends. She had dozens of business associates and an address book full of women she could call, but other than Lauren, no real friends—the kind she could hang out with, eat pizza and ice cream and commiserate on how she'd fucked up her life.

"Sloan." The pounding was louder. She checked to make sure her clothes were decent and opened the front door.

"It's about time. Your neighbors down the hall were about to call the police."

"Very funny," Sloan replied. "I don't have any neighbors. I have the entire floor." She didn't invite Lauren in, simply left the door open and went back to her cushion on the couch where she'd spent most of the morning. At least she'd been productive for a change. She'd worked on her CV, made a few phone calls, updated her LinkedIn page, and avoided a call from her mother.

Lauren helped herself to two bottles of water from the refrigerator, placing them on the table between Sloan and the chair where she sat down. "So tell me what happened."

"Do you want the juicy details or the highlights?"

"Don't get smart with me, Sloan," Lauren said, almost before Sloan finished her question. "I'm not here to take your shit. I'm here to help you."

"Help? Are you offering me a job in your firm? You know my family, Lauren. I have no experience in healthy familial relationships."

"You know, Sloan, I'm your friend. And as your friend I owe this to you. You need to pull your head out of your ass or wherever it is you're wallowing. It is not flattering."

Sloan rose and walked to the windows overlooking Mission Bay, her anger and self-pity almost overwhelming her. "I am the stereotypical fall from grace. I'm a cliché. Sleep with the other side's attorney. Ruin my career because I can't keep my hands to myself. I don't know who I'm angrier at—me for not being stronger and saying no or me for telling Elliott. I could have gone on having the best job of my life working for someone I admired and respected. But no, I had to fuck it all up by not keeping my hands off Adrienne, and then I couldn't keep my mouth shut."

Sloan continued looking out the window, her back to Lauren. Several minutes went by, and Lauren didn't say anything. She didn't refute her comments or agree with them. She didn't even acknowledge them. It had been so quiet for so long, she half expected Lauren to either be gone or asleep. She was neither.

"Are you finished?" When Sloan didn't answer, she said, "I asked you a question, Sloan. Are you finished with your pity-party? Your speech to whom? Yourself? Adrienne? It certainly isn't me. I'm not going to listen to this bullshit."

Sloan was stunned. She'd never seen Lauren like this. She was a hard-ass bitch. The times they'd been together, they'd been having fun at dinner, parties, in relaxed friendly situations. Rarely anything serious.

"Do you want to do it again?"

"What? Fuck up my life?"

"No, see Adrienne. I'd ask if you're already seeing each other, but I can't detect any traces of a fully satisfied woman. Have you talked to her?"

"No."

"Have you called her?"

"No."

"Has she called you?"

"A few times."

"And why haven't you picked up?"

"Because I don't want her pity."

"What makes you think that's what she's going to give you?"

"Come on, Lauren. I'm the one that made her lose her job."

"What makes you think she lost her job?"

That comment hit Sloan in the gut. Had Adrienne been fired over this? Had she told Robert? Of course she would have, for the same reason she'd told Elliott. "Did she?" Sloan asked, not sure if she wanted to know the answer to the question.

"No, she didn't. Robert wouldn't even accept her resignation."

"Maybe I should go work for Robert." Either that or Elliott should take a lesson from him, she thought, then immediately felt sick to her stomach. That was a petty, knee-jerk thought that Elliott did not deserve. Sloan knew Elliott would do the right thing when she told her.

"So why are you here? Except to, I don't know, give me shit?"

"What are you going to do?" Lauren repeated her question.

"About Adrienne?"

Lauren nodded.

"Nothing."

"What did you do the last time you broke up?"

"What?"

"What did you do when you and Adrienne broke up?"

"I got in my car, drove across the country, and three days later attended my first class at Stanford. What are you getting at?"

"You just walked away?"

"We had no choice."

Lauren looked at her skeptically.

"We were going in different directions."

"What's your excuse now?"

Chapter Thirty-four

Sloan Merchant is here to see you," Ruth informed Adrienne late one afternoon. She dropped her pen, the papers on her desk muffling the sound. Her stomach clenched, her heart raced, and her throat was suddenly so dry she could barely swallow. She'd spent the last week convincing herself that she'd never see Sloan again.

"Adrienne?" Ruth asked.

Adrienne quickly looked around her office. A stack of mail was in her in-box, her briefcase still perched on the chair where she'd put it at six this morning, and a half-empty coffee cup sat on the corner of her desk. A pair of walking shoes lay in the corner where she'd tossed them last week.

"Sure. Have her come in." Adrienne stood up, her legs almost not cooperating, and made sure her shirt was tucked neatly into her skirt and her hair still secured at the nape of her neck. She tried to swallow a few times, but the fist in her throat made that difficult.

She thought she was prepared for Sloan, but seeing her took her breath away. In addition to looking tired, a bit drawn, and like she'd lost a few pounds in the weeks since she'd seen her, she was still striking. She was dressed casually in a pair of Dockers and a light-brown shirt that matched the color of her eyes.

Ruth hesitated in the doorway, her expression asking Adrienne if she needed anything, including for her to stay.

"Thank you, Ruth," Adrienne said, and Ruth closed the door behind her.

"I wasn't sure if you'd see me."

Sloan's voice was husky and sent shivers down Adrienne's spine. "Why do you say that?" Adrienne's voice was surprisingly strong, in direct contrast to the shaking of her legs and the tingling in her fingertips.

"Because I pretty much ignored you for the last two weeks."

Two weeks and four days, Adrienne thought but didn't say. "Sit down." She indicated the chair across from her desk and not in the casual seating area across the room. She needed the barrier of her desk between them. As it was, if she wasn't careful she might just crawl over it and into Sloan's lap. She was finally able to sit down, relief flooding her that she'd made it this long without her knees buckling.

"How are you?" Adrienne didn't need to bother with any preface to her question. Sloan had to have known that she was aware that she was no longer at Foster Mackenzie.

"I'm all right."

Adrienne knew her well enough to realize that wasn't the entire truth.

"I heard you closed the deal." Sloan sounded sad.

"Yes, we did." It had felt surreal that Sloan hadn't been there in the room, placing her bold signature on the last page of the contract. As it was, Elliott's new attorney was a stuffed shirt with a Windsor knot in his tie so tight she thought his head would pop off like a cork on a champagne bottle.

Adrienne had a thousand questions, but she didn't ask any of them.

"How's Callie?"

"She's…she's fine. Thank you for asking."

"Frankie called me."

Adrienne didn't think she could be more shocked than when Ruth had told her Sloan was here. "What?" she managed to choke out.

"I said Frankie—"

"I heard what you said. Why in the hell did she do that?" She was furious with her sister. What happened between her and Sloan was just that, between her and Sloan. "Frankie had no business doing that."

"That's what I told her."

Adrienne could only imagine her sister's reaction. "What did she want?"

"I don't know what she *wanted* to tell me, but what she told me was that I needed to pull my head out of the sand, and you needed to pull yours out as well, and that we needed to talk."

"Is that why you're here?" Adrienne asked hopefully but at the same time afraid the answer might be yes.

"No, well…some." Sloan fidgeted in her seat. "Then Lauren came to my house and basically told me the same thing."

"Lauren?"

"Yes." Sloan quirked her mouth and nodded.

Adrienne let out a sigh and leaned back in her chair. "Does everyone think they belong in our business?"

"I haven't heard from your mother," Sloan commented, doing that nervous thing with her fingers.

"I have, and my father. Trust me, it was enough for both of us. So why are you here, Sloan?"

"Because, at the risk of you throwing me out again, I think we do need to talk. And I came here hoping that if people are around, you won't."

Adrienne owed Sloan at least an apology, and at most an explanation.

"Why did you call me?" Sloan asked before she had a chance to do either.

"I wanted to see if I could do anything. Talk to Elliott or…"

Sloan looked around her office. "So, it was a business call?"

"I think you know the answer to that," Adrienne replied, her eyes instinctively roaming over Sloan's body.

"I don't know the answer to anything, Adrienne," Sloan said, getting to her feet and walking around the room. "Nothing. I don't know why you came back into my life, why you drive me to distraction, why I can't stop thinking about you. I don't know why…why it happened, and I don't know why you threw me out. I don't know why I didn't return your calls, and I'm not sure why I'm even here."

"I do."

Sloan was looking out her window but turned to look at Adrienne when she spoke. "Why did it happen? Because we wanted it to. Why did I throw you out? Because I couldn't deal with the fact that you were the first woman I'd been with since my wife died. You didn't return my calls because I was the reason you lost your job, and I have no idea why you're here. I'm just glad you are."

Sloan's heart raced at Adrienne's last five words. "So, where do we go from here?" Sloan asked tentatively.

"What are you going to do?" Adrienne asked, offering Sloan a way out. "Any firm would snatch you up like that." She snapped her fingers.

Sloan hesitated before answering, as if weighing her answer. "A few firms have contacted me. I told the out-of-towners I wasn't interested."

"Why not?"

"Because there are things here that make me want to stay."

"Like?"

"I've met someone new," Sloan replied, looking right into Adrienne's eyes.

Adrienne's heart crashed, and she clenched her teeth on the sob of despair threatening to escape. A blanket of complete anguish like none she'd ever experienced washed over her. Since Sloan had walked into her office, Adrienne's emotions were on a roller coaster, and she was now on the downhill run. At that moment, she knew she was hopelessly in love with Sloan. It was different from years ago, and, as her father said it would be, much different than what she had with Brenna.

"I see." She tried to keep her voice steady.

"I'd like to date her."

"Date?" Adrienne asked, her heart starting to sink.

"Yes, date. I've never been interested in dating until now."

Adrienne swallowed and shored up her emotions. "And what's different about now?" she asked hopefully.

"I'm ready. I mean, I wasn't before, but I am now."

"So, what's changed?"

"I have. She has."

"She? I thought you said you met someone new?" *Oh, God, I don't want to hear this.*

"I did. I knew her years ago, and I thought I knew her pretty well. But now I want to know a lot more."

I can do this. "Well, you don't need to worry about having some other activity going on around you to fill in the void in conversation."

"So we wouldn't have to go to the movies?"

"Right. Movies are good because there is limited talk time before, and you can always talk about the movie after." *I can do this.*

"Dinner?"

I can do this. "Meals are always good. But only if you feel comfortable eating in front of her. But don't order pizza or spaghetti. Too messy."

Sloan nodded, seeming to accede to Adrienne's comment. "A walk would be okay?"

"Yes, walks are good. In a nice park or on the boardwalk." *I don't want to think about this.*

"Do I hold her hand?"

What felt like a gut punch hit Adrienne as she remembered how Sloan used to hold her hand walking to class. "That's not as formulaic."

"Hmm. So, when the date's over, do I kiss her?"

I definitely don't want to think about this. "Again, that's not formulaic." Adrienne looked at Sloan's lips and remembered their taste. She swallowed, hard.

"So I need to figure it out myself?"

"Yes. I think you can figure that one out."

Sloan focused on her hands in her lap. "So, what if the woman has…a…child?" It was after the question that she looked at Adrienne.

"A child?"

"Yes. We knew each other years ago when we were in college. You know how it is when you're young, dumb, and stupid. You don't know what you have, and you let things slip through your fingers without even knowing it. So, a lot of years have passed and she has a child. A beautiful, towheaded daughter with inquisitive eyes and an infectious laugh. She scares me to death because I don't know a thing about children. But I'm willing to learn, if she'll give me the chance."

Adrienne sat there dumbfounded and speechless. Sloan was talking about her. Sloan was talking about *her, and Callie*.

"This dating thing is confusing and hard, and I haven't been able to find the fucking rule book." Sloan crossed the room and sat back in the chair she'd recently vacated. "Adrienne, I can't begin to know what you're going through. You loved Brenna, and you always will. Callie is Brenna's daughter, and she always will be. But I love you. Not like before when we didn't know a damn thing about life or what we wanted, but I truly do love you. I know that you may not be ready to think about me in that way, so that's why I'd like to date you."

Sloan's expression turned serious. "I know you can't love me like you loved Brenna. I don't expect you to, and I don't want you to. I want you to love me for me, with all my quirks and devilish charm."

Sloan smiled, and Adrienne's heart melted a little more. She got up and started pacing again, her fingers doing that nervous-gesture thing again.

"I don't have a job yet, but my car is paid for, and I do own my own home and have money in the bank. I don't know anything about dating, especially about dating a woman with a child, but I will be patient. I'll give you space, and I will completely understand when you cancel at the last minute because the babysitter hasn't shown up or if you have to leave because Callie doesn't feel well. I won't be upset if you're late because Callie insisted on wearing something in the hamper or she couldn't find her shoes. I'll be the best," Sloan waved her hands in front of her, "whatever it would be called, to Callie. I'll take my lead from you on that one. What I can promise you is that I will never, ever make you choose between me and Callie because I know I will lose. Now, I know you may not be ready to date, and you may not even want to date me. But when you do, and I hope it's me, I'll be here. Waiting for you."

Sloan's words staggered her. Never in her lifetime did she expect to hear anything like them from her, and certainly not directed to her. Adrienne's heart was beating fast, her breathing so shallow she was light-headed. Across from her sat an amazing woman who was once the girl she fell in love with. But today, right now, right here, she was hers again.

Not certain her legs would hold her but certain of one of the most important things she'd ever done, Adrienne got up and walked around her desk. She stopped in front of Sloan and cupped Sloan's face in both hands. Sloan's eyes were the expression of her soul and always had been, at least to her. What she saw inside was acceptance, determination, hope, uncertainty, promise, courage, commitment, trust, conviction, and a little bit of fear. She inhaled her scent and felt her heat, her nervousness palpable.

"I don't know how to do this. But what I do know is that I want *you* to help me figure it out. I want *you* in my life. I want *you* in Callie's life. We've been through a lot, Callie and I, and I'm ready to move on. It won't be easy. A very wise man once told me that love is complicated, relationships are complicated, and people are complicated. What's not complicated is, if you want something you work at it. You work hard at it. You work hard *for* it."

Adrienne kissed Sloan, softly, but pulled back before it turned into something else. Something much more than was appropriate for her office, however private. "Now, take me home. I need you to take me to the place where I lose my mind. I need you to take me to that magical, mystical, earth-shattering place where I don't care about anything but your mouth on me and your talented touch. Take me to where the sun burns bright and the stars explode. Take me higher than you've ever taken me before. I love you, Sloan, and want *you* to take me there."

Sloan gathered her up in her arms. "I thought you'd never ask."

EPILOGUE

"Elliott called me today."

The sun had just touched the water on the horizon. Adrienne could almost hear the sizzle as it dipped farther under the horizon. She lay in Sloan's arms, watching Callie play in the sand near the water's edge. She shifted so she could see into Sloan's eyes.

"What did she want?"

"She didn't say, other than she wants to have lunch when we get back from Jamaica." Their suitcases were packed, their passports ready, and their flight was in three days, the day after their wedding.

"What do you think it's about?"

Sloan gathered her closer and kissed her. "I don't know, but I have more interesting, important things to think about."

"What's more important than talking to the most successful venture capitalist in the country?"

At that moment, Callie doused them both with a bucket of water and a giggle. Adrienne had her answer.

About the Author

Julie Cannon (JulieCannon.com) divides her time by being a corporate suit, a wife, mom, sister, friend, and writer. Julie and her wife have lived in at least a half a dozen states, traveled around the world, and have an unending supply of dedicated friends. And of course, the most important people in their lives are their three kids, #1, Dude, and the Devine Miss Em.

With the release of *Take Me There*, Julie will have sixteen books published by Bold Strokes Books. Her first novel, *Come and Get Me*, was a finalist for the Golden Crown Literary Society's Best Lesbian Romance and Debut Author Awards, *Rescue Me* was a finalist as Best Lesbian Romance from the prestigious Lambda Literary Society, and *I Remember* won the Golden Crown Literary Society's Best Lesbian Romance. Julie has also published five short stories in Bold Strokes anthologies.

Books Available From Bold Strokes Books

Beauty and the Boss by Ali Vali. Ellis Renois is at the top of the fashion world, but she never expects her summer assistant Charlotte Hamner to tear her heart and her business apart like sharp scissors through cheap material. (978-162639-919-8)

Fury's Choice by Brey Willows. When gods walk amongst humans, can two women find a balance between love and faith? (978-162639-869-6)

Lessons in Desire by MJ Williamz. Can a summer love stand a four-month hiatus and still burn hot? (978-163555-019-1)

Lightning Chasers by Cass Sellars. For Sydney and Parker, being a couple was never what they had planned. Now they have to fight corruption, murder, and enemies hiding in plain sight just to hold on to each other. Lightning Series, Book Two. (978-162639-965-5)

Summer Fling by Jean Copeland. Still jaded from a breakup years earlier, Kate struggles to trust falling in love again when a summer fling with sexy young singer Jordan rocks her off her feet. (978-162639-981-5)

Take Me There by Julie Cannon. Adrienne and Sloan know it would be career suicide to mix business with pleasure, however tempting it is. But what's the harm? They're both consenting adults. Who would know? (978-162639-917-4)

Unchained Memories by Dena Blake. Can a woman give herself completely when she's left a piece of herself behind? (978-162639-993-8)

Walking Through Shadows by Sheri Lewis Wohl. All Molly wanted to do was go backpacking…in her own century. (978-162639-968-6)

A Lamentation of Swans by Valerie Bronwen. Ariel Montgomery returns to Sea Oats to try to save her broken marriage but soon finds herself also fighting to save her own life and catch a murderer. (978-1-62639-828-3)

Freedom to Love by Ronica Black. What happens when the woman who spent her life worrying about caring for her family finally finds the freedom to love without borders? (978-1-63555-001-6)

House of Fate by Barbara Ann Wright. Two women must throw off the lives they've known as a guardian and an assassin and save two rival houses before their secrets tear the galaxy apart. (978-1-62639-780-4)

Planning for Love by Erin Dutton. Could true love be the one thing that wedding coordinator Faith McKenna didn't plan for? (978-1-62639-954-9)

Sidebar by Carsen Taite. Judge Camille Avery and her clerk, attorney West Fallon, agree on little except their mutual attraction, but can their relationship and their careers survive a headline-grabbing case? (978-1-62639-752-1)

Sweet Boy and Wild One by T. L. Hayes. When Rachel Cole meets soulful singer Bobby Layton at an open mic, she is immediately in thrall. What she soon discovers will rock her world in ways she never imagined. (978-1-62639-963-1)

To Be Determined by Mardi Alexander and Laurie Eichler. Charlie Dickerson escapes her life in the US to rescue Australian wildlife with Pip Atkins, but can they save each other? (978-1-62639-946-4)

True Colors by Yolanda Wallace. Blogger Robby Rawlins plans to use First Daughter Taylor Crenshaw to get ahead, but she never planned on falling in love with her in the process. (978-1-62639-927-3)

Heart Stop by Radclyffe. Two women, one with a damaged body, the other a damaged spirit, challenge each other to dare to live again. (978-1-62639-899-3)

Undercover Affairs by Julie Blair. Searching for stolen documents crucial to U.S. security, CIA agent Rett Spenser confronts lies, deceit, and unexpected romance as she investigates art gallery owner Shannon Kent. (978-1-62639-905-1)

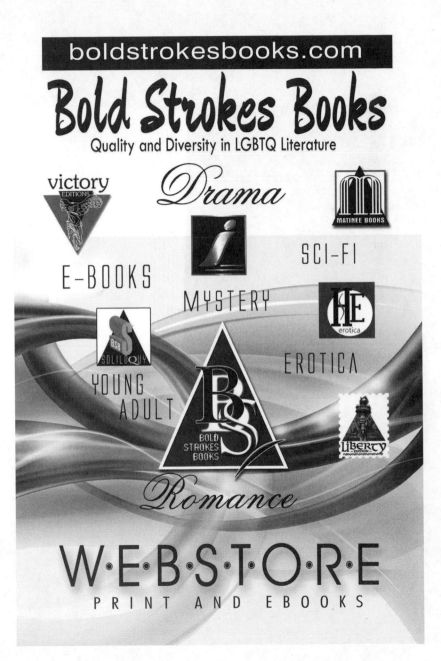